i

ANGIE'S SOULMATE

Bitsey Gagne

ANGIE'S SOULMATE

BITSEY GAGNE

Bitsey Gagne

This book is a work of fiction. The characters, incidents, and dialogue are drawn from the author's imagination. They are not real. Any resemblance to actual events or persons, living or dead, is entirely coincidental.

Angie's Soulmate is lovingly dedicated to my Uncle Con, Harry Knott, who encouraged me to follow my dreams and complete the sequel to my first novel, *Evangeline Shores of Forever*. Were it not for his gentle prompting and belief in my ability, this second book in The Pirate Series may never have been completed.

I hope you enjoy the continuing story of Angie and her friends. Thank you so much for your support in making my dream come true.

Bitsey Gagne

We fell into a chasm,
a spiraling abyss.
All that we believed,
somehow became a reality.
Our love fell through the curtains of time.
before our souls
everything aligned,
so True Love could be found.

In that once glance, our spirits entwined
and become one,
our souls forever in adulation,
a love that was never ending
even in death.
In life our love was lost
but was found in eternal rest.

—Bitsey Gagne

Descendants of Jacob Harriot

Paul Albright ——— ♡ ——— Mary Albright
(~Greenville)

Isabella Harriot
(Albright)

Allen Albright
♡

Masie Lane
(Albright)

~George Harriot Jr

Sandy Albright
(White)

Jones Lane

Sally Brown┐ Angela Harriot   Anna Jones Healy Albright   Isabella Lane ┬ James Lane
(Harriot) └Matthew Harriot (Albright)   Brittany Williams ─ Robert Lane
                                                          (Lane)   Abigail Lane
                              Harry Jones   Arthur Williams   (Smith)

        Frank Jones ─ Linda Jones   Frederick Williams   Cynthia Lane

Descendants of Evangeline Alexander

Joseph Alexander ——— ♡ ——— Elizabeth Alexander
(White)

Thomas Alexander   ~George Alexander

Descendants of Emily Alexander (White)

James White ——— ♡ ——— Sally White
(Albright)

Sarah White   Emily White

Descendants of Roger Brown

David Brown ——— ♡ ——— Samantha Brown
(Hill)

Joseph Brown ─────────── Robert Brown
Rebecca Brown   ♡
(Smith)   Sally Brown
                         (Harriot)

Tony Brown ─── Mary Brown

William Jacob Brown ┐
~Georgia Evangeline Brown ┘

Present Family Tree

Alexander Family

Robert Alexander ——— ♡ ——— Sarah Alexander
(Albright)

Anna Alexander   Evangeline Alexander   Stephen Alexander
(died at 6)

Robert Alexander   Elizabeth Alexander   Matthew Alexander
♡
Emily White

Harriot Family

Thomas Harriot ——— ♡ ——— Frances Harriot
(Dane)

Jacob Harriot   Walter Harriot   Thomas Harriot   Mary Harriot

White Family

Johnathan White ——— ♡ ——— Elizabeth White
(Greenville)

Emily White   Isabella White   David White

Brown Family

George Brown ——— ♡ ——— Mary Brown

Benjamin Brown   Charlotte Brown   Eleanor Brown
James Brown   Richard Brown   Samuel Brown
Roger Brown
adopted
grandson of Blackheard

Bitsey Gagne

TABLE OF CONTENTS

Prologue

My family, friends, and I are all settled around the parlor table at Shepard Inn, reviewing the latest clues to the whereabouts of Blackbeard's treasure and making plans for our trip to Cat Island. My brother Matt and his fiancée Sarah are anxiously planning their upcoming wedding in the Bahamas, which is our official reason for traveling to Cat Island. But we'll also be on a treasure hunt.

We are thrilled that we have found the last clue we hope will lead us to the pirate treasure. We are also worried about the dangers if others learn that we have Blackbeard's treasure map. Paul Albright, my grandfather and a local historian, has been enjoying himself doing research for this trip. My sister Sally's husband, Robert Brown, has been helping him.

Sally and Robert Brown have been teaching at the cozy little school on Ocracoke Island on North Carolina's Outer Banks since the beginning of the semester. The island has been an anchor for my family for two generations— or maybe I should say three generations, since Sally and Robert's twins, three-month-old Evie and Jacob, were born on the island on the Fourth of July. The babies have developed their own separate personalities. Evie is high-spirited and keeps her parents and Georgia, their nanny, busy. Little Jacob is a happy, content, and docile little boy.

The weeks leading up to their births were amazing. I traveled to Ocracoke for the summer, like my family had for many years, and decided to stay permanently. My brother rekindled his long-ago love for Sarah and proposed. My sister and brother-in-law, who also came to the island just for the summer, were surprised when Sally went into labor earlier than expected, and even more surprised when their baby turned out to be twins! It was serendipity that they were both offered jobs at the island school. So, they both decided to stay permanently and put their Maryland home up for sale. It helped that Robert's father gave them his family home on the island as a gift.

Even my mother has moved permanently to the island. And I am so glad of that. I worried what would happen at the end of the summer when she returned to the house where she and my father had lived for so many years before his unexpected death last fall. It is wonderful that we are all together again living in a place that has so many happy memories for my family. My father is even buried here, in the little cemetery that is walking distance from the historic cottage I rent.

Like the rest of us, Sally and Robert's babies are linked to the spirits of Evangeline and Jacob, star-crossed lovers whose tragic story two centuries ago led us to the pirate map. Sally believes Evangeline and Jacob are watching out for her twins, and that gives her peace of mind.

Sometimes Evangeline and Jacob appear to us; Sally can sense whenever they are near, and Evangeline's spirit has appeared before Sally quite often since the babies' birth. Her husband, Robert, can't get used to the idea of having ghosts as protectors to their twins.

Amid all that has happened, I have also managed to fall head over heels in love with Thomas, an amazing islander who renovates historic homes. I didn't think I was ready to let my guard down and open my heart to anyone, but I have—and it is wonderful. Thomas and I are still living in the cottage that once belonged to Evangeline and her son, young William. Sometimes we see Evangeline and Jacob's spirits on the dunes when we walk our golden retriever, Max. Max remains ever protective of me since I was kidnapped earlier in the year.

My lifelong friend Emily continues to manage the Oxford Pub with her devoted friend, George, by her side most nights. I still pull out my guitar and sing for the crowds at night and help at the pub if we are busy. George and Emily have been inseparable since my kidnapping.

George worries that something might happen to Emily. He even stayed in her home for a short time when we were in direct danger from my kidnappers. He's back in his own place now, but I know he misses staying with Emily. Their bond strengthened over the summer, but they still haven't taken the final leap toward a love relationship. The girls and I are always teasing Emily about this.

Isabella, my mother, continues to spend most of her time with David Brown. David, Robert's father, has been staying in our family home while he renovates his mansion on the island before he relocates to let my sister and brother-in-law have the house to themselves. For now, Sally, Robert, Georgia, and the twins are also staying in the old family mansion.

Jim and Sally White, Emily and Sarah's parents, are so glad that they moved back to their home on the island to be with their children and friends. Sally

White has been enjoying helping Sarah with her wedding plans. Jim has been helping Sarah and Emily manage the inn and in the pub. The Whites once ran the properties until they retired. They hadn't realized how much they missed the quaint little island until they came back this past summer—and decided to stay.

Today our group is reexamining the clues and the landmarks on the completed treasure map of Cat Island. Sarah and Matt have picked out the location for their December wedding ceremony, but none of us have traveled to Cat Island yet. Now our plans are starting to come together for the upcoming journey to search for Blackbeard's treasure.

There is so much still to do before the trip. I have a meeting planned with my agent in Maryland to give him my latest songs and recordings. He feels certain that several of my songs will hit Number One by the end of the year. Two songs that I recorded—one about the twins and the other about my father— have already climbed into the Top Ten on the country music charts.

I'm not the only one seeing professional success. Things could not be going any better for the guys and their renovation company. Matt has been working with Thomas and George to renovate old homes on the island. The folks on Ocracoke love their work. The islanders have jobs lined up for the company until the end of next year, and more requests pour in daily.

Chapter 1

Saying Good-Bye

My brother, our mother, and I are taking the long journey back to my childhood home in Ripley, Maryland. We need to pack up all our belongings from our past and move them to our new homes on Ocracoke Island.

Mom was emotional the other night when we talked about the house in Ripley, wiping tears from her eyes. "I dread this trip," she said. "I have procrastinated as long as possible. I can't put it off any longer. My home goes to settlement at the end of October.

"I'm still amazed that our whole family has made the island our permanent homes," she added. "We have so many memories to pack up from our old lives in Maryland."

Matt hugged her. "I know Mom. Angie and I were talking the other day about how much we were dreading this trip and that we wished it was over." I reached over and wrapped my arms around both of them. "We'll get through this together. We are here for you Mom."

Now, this morning, my mother, Matt, and I will drive to Maryland. Thomas kisses me gently before he gets up and heads off to a renovation job for a couple of neighbors down our lane, Bob and Sue. "I'm going to miss you while you are away," he says, as he wraps his arms around me. "Angie, I am so in love with you."

I smile at him. "I can't imagine my life without you." We linger in each other's arms, then I laugh. "I really need to get up and get ready for my trip home." We both shower and start to prepare for our day.

When Matt bangs on our door, Thomas greets him with a towel wrapped around his waist. Matt teases Thomas. "Okay man, stop molesting my sister." Thomas just laughs. "Hey, Matt, come on in for some coffee. Angie is still getting ready to go."

The smell of coffee brings me into the kitchen. I breathe in its rich aroma. Thomas hands me a mug and I sip of the creamy coffee. "Oh, this is heavenly.

Yummy," I say. "Is this new coffee? It has such an earthy flavor. Hazelnut? That's one of my favorites, along with my two favorite guys."

I head to our screened in porch, to lounge for a minute with the guys. "Thanks for waiting for me, Matt," I tell my brother.

Just before I head out the door toward Matt's blue Ford 4x4 truck, I grab to-go cups for Matt, myself, and one for our mom. I kiss Thomas. "Bye, honey. I'll see you when I get back. I'll call you once we get there."

He kisses me back, and waves at Matt. "Bye, Angie, Matt. You guys have a safe trip. Matt, I'll let you know how things go at Bob and Sue's." When Matt, Thomas, and Thomas's brother George decided to work together restoring old homes on the island, they never imagined how in-demand they would be.

I throw my bright green duffle bag into the backseat then I jump into Matt's truck. It smells like vanilla or sugar cookies from the air freshener that hangs from the rearview mirror. I turn to my brother. "It's going to be a really long day. It's so warm and cozy in here. I feel like I could go back to sleep."

I turn on the heated seat and lean back as we drive over to Mom's house to pick her up. The orange-and-white U-Haul trails behind us as Matt pulls into the circular oyster-shell driveway. I sigh. "Oh, Matt, I am not looking forward to this trip. I hope Mom does alright. This will be so hard for her."

Matt grimaces. "I know. It's going to be hard for all of us, like losing dad all over again."

David and Mom come out the ornate white front door onto the front porch. David hugs my mother and squeezes her shoulder. "Be safe. Remember, it will be over soon. Isabella, call me if you need to. I am here for you."

I think to myself, how sweet my brother-in-law's father has been to Mom. I open the truck door and climb into the back seat after I wave to David and greet Mom with a hug.

"Mom, I warmed the seat for you—and here's some coffee," I say. "Bye, David. See you later. Hold down the fort."

David laughs. "Will do. Take care of yourselves and have a safe trip."

Mom waves to David, and I see her wink at him. "Bye, David," she calls to him. "Send me pictures of the twins, my little angels. I'll call you and let you know how things go."

The air is crisp, but the sun shines brightly through our windshield. It makes me squint my sleepy eyes when we drive aboard the ferry to make the faraway journey to our old home in Maryland. Standing outside the car, as the ferry sets off, the fresh sea air invigorates me. I breathe in deeply and take in the gorgeous seascape. There are only a few other people making their way back to the mainland this morning. Most of them are headed to their jobs on Hatteras Island or further inland.

I see Sheila from Conner's Grocery. She greets me with a smile and a hug. "Angie, I've been meaning to tell you that I just love your new song about the twins," she says. "It really speaks to my heart."

I grin. "I'm so glad that you like it. Thanks, Shelia," I respond. "I am working on another one about Ocracoke Island. I've finally started on my first novel, too."

She brushes highlighted blonde hair out of her pretty hazel eyes. "I'm so happy for you. I can't wait to hear your new song or to read your book."

"I'm supposed to meet my agent from Washington, D.C., when we get back to our old hometown in Ripley," I tell her. "I am going to give him my latest recordings. My last songs—including the one about the twins—are getting a lot of attention."

Shelia gives me a high five. "That's cool. I'm so happy for you."

I shake my head. "Only problem is that he keeps asking me when I will be doing a tour," I say. "I told him that I'm not sure if I will ever do a tour. I really enjoy my life on the island with Thomas and all my family and friends. I can't imagine being away on the road."

Matt and Mom hear what we're saying as they come up to join our conversation. Matt gives Shelia a hug. "Hey, Shelia. How have you been? Can you believe it? We are so proud of her. I always knew she would make it big one day." Mom beams with pride at his side.

I punch Matt on the shoulder. "Well, what about you, Thomas, and George? Sheila, you should stop by and see some of the work they're doing. They are really recapturing the beauty of these old island home when they rehab them.

"Stop by my cottage one day—they did a wonderful job on it," I continue. "Better yet, Thomas and I would love to have you and Bill over sometime for dinner."

Shelia laughs in happy agreement. Then she turns to my mother. "I spoke to Sarah the other day. She tells me that the B&B is rented through the end of this year and most of the next summer. The island is busy!

"And how are you?" she continues. "How are you, Sally, and Robert—and your grandbabies—doing?"

Mom grins. "Sally and Robert just love their new teaching jobs at Ocracoke Island School. And I am totally enjoying my new grandchildren. They are just so cute," she says. "It's also great to be on the island with my dad. He is happily researching Blackbeard's life and deepening what he knows about the history of Ocracoke Island. He plans to write a new book on Blackbeard and the Lost Colonists.

"My mother and I are having a great time with our children, grandchildren, and friends," she adds. "Plus, it's always lovely to spend time with the Whites."

After a pause, my mother points to Shelia. "By the way, your mother tells me you have some news to share, too."

Shelia blushes and places her hand over her tummy. "We just found out six weeks ago," she says. "Bill and I have been trying to have a baby for over a year now. I can't believe my mother told you."

I squeal with delight. "Why didn't you say anything? I'm thrilled for you. You've wanted to be a mom for as long as I can remember. You'll have to connect with Sally."

"Where is Sally?" Sheila asks. "I thought she would be taking the trip back with you." Shelia raises her eyebrows.

I shrug. "Sally and Robert couldn't come with us because of their jobs—and Evie and little Jacob are keeping them busy. They'll go back to Clements,

Maryland, on their next school break to pack up their old home. Their renters are going to buy it in the spring. Looks like we've all got good new to share."

Shelia points to the fast-approaching shoreline. "Wow. Looks like we made it to Hatteras already. Amazing how time flies when you are catching up on things. I guess we better get back into our cars." We move toward our vehicles as the ferry gets ready to pull into the port. Sheila turns back and waves to us. "It's been great catching up with you guys. And Angie, I'll have to get with you one day and plan a get together."

I nod. "Sounds good and congratulations on your new bundle of joy!"

We get into Matt's truck and continue the journey back to our family home in Ripley. The time flies by on the road and, before we know it, we're at our old childhood home. Matt pulls into the gravel driveway. The country blue shutters and oak-stained front door welcome us. I sigh. "It's sad to think this will be the last time we come back to the house we grew up in."

The autumn sun reflects off the maple and oak trees, igniting glorious shades that range from crimson to copper to yellow to bright orange. Mom points to the trees. "I can't believe how big those trees have grown since your dad planted them over twenty years ago."

A sadness creeps over me as I think about my father. "I remember being a little six-year-old kid when he planted those trees. He had me help put the dirt in the hole."

I dread the task ahead: packing up our belongings. I breathe in the fresh country air when we climb out of Matt's truck and stretch our legs after the long drive. My mom, Isabella, opens the front door of the house for the last time. I see her hand tremble slightly when she turns the worn, brass key in the lock. She exhales deeply. "Well, here goes. Time to pack up our past lives. Are you kids ready for this?"

Matt hugs her and we both say together, "We are here for you." The house welcomes us, as it always has, with an aroma of cinnamon and vanilla. It is the smell of home.

Chapter 2

Memories

Mom throws open the curtains and windows to let in the fresh autumn breeze. Dust motes float up through the sunshine that streams through the windows. She laughs. "I'm going to need to dust a little bit before we leave. Luckily, the new owners know we haven't been living here for several months. You know, they even wanted some of the old furniture. And thank goodness, they said that they wanted to do all the painting themselves."

We wander inside and look around at the pictures that stare back at us. These walls have watched us grow up over the years. I smile, "Look at these photos of us. Matt, Sally, and me, through elementary, middle, and high school," I say. "I know we will be making new memories, but I can't help but feel sad for the life we're leaving behind now."

Suddenly I start to laugh. "Check out that toothless grin in this picture of me from second grade! It cracks me up every time I look at it."

We bring in all the empty cardboard boxes for packing. I reminisce about my childhood as I wrap our treasured pictures in newspaper. The dust tickles my nose and makes my eyes water.

Mom's tears flow freely while she packs up her life spent with our dad, George Harriot. Matt and I try to ease our mother's pain, but we are having a hard time dealing with our own feelings. With every memento, a new memory emerges. It is like gazing into a looking glass from the past.

I hold up a picture of us from a whitewater rafting trip in West Virginia. "Oh my goodness, do you remember this trip? Our rafting guide's name was Possum. Matt, you almost fell out of the raft. The water was so rough and frigid. What fun we had."

Matt busts out in laughter. "I remember that trip. I think I was only about twelve or thirteen. I thought I was going to die. It was so scary."

Mom looks at us with teary eyes and grins, lost in her own thoughts and memories of that day. My heart feels fragile, like it will shatter at any time. I can only imagine how my mom must feel as she pores over treasures from the past.

Our plan is take back to Ocracoke only the things that hold special memories for us. The rest will go to several of the different charities in Charles County, Maryland. One charity is the Arnold House, which helps homeless people find housing and prevents hunger. Another is the Charles County Children's Aid Society. It assists families struggling to survive.

Each of us is having a hard time saying good-bye to our family home. For Matt and me, it is the house we grew up in. We are deep in thought as we go through our belongings from our past. Each item we pick up triggers a memory.

Before she left for Ocracoke Island last spring, Mom had packed up a box for each of us to help us remember our dad. Matt opens his box and pulls out a child's baseball mitt. "Mom, you kept this. Awe, I remember the hours that Dad spent trying to teach me how to catch. I was terrible and he was so patient," my brother says. A tear slips out of Matt's eye and drips down his nose.

Mom hugs Matt and tousles his hair. "Of course, honey. I knew it meant a lot to you, those times that you spent with your father."

"Thanks, Mom. It does mean a lot." Matt hugs the old, tired mitt and smells the earthy scent of the leather.

Mom had packed up and given away all of Dad's clothing earlier in the year. I touch the little pendant—half of a heart—from my father. I can still remember the day he gave it to me. It was after our last visit to the island before his unexpected death. It had been a glorious summer that year. When we arrived home, my father asked me to come into his office. I recall the look on his face when he opened the tiny box. He reached into a small wooden coffer and pulled out the necklace. "This necklace once belonged to our ancestor, Evangeline," he told me.

As my hand touches the necklace, I get goosebumps up and down my arms. Suddenly a misty vision of Evangeline appears before us. She whispers, "The time is right." Both of us stare at a ghostly figure and, just as quickly as it came, it disappears. I remember my father's words when he turned to me that day. "Evangeline came to me in a dream when I was on Ocracoke Island before we left to come home. Angie, she wanted me to give you the necklace. Evangeline has been appearing in my dreams over the last few years. She told me that we will be given clues to a map that would lead to Blackbeard's treasure."

I sigh to myself as I remember that day. It seems like such a long time ago. My heart aches for my dad. I miss him so much.

My mother comes out of my dad's office. She is holding a tiny cedar box, the same one that once held the necklace my father gave me. "Look what I found in your father's office. It looks just like the boxes we found that belonged to Evangeline."

My brother and I are amazed to realize that the box she is carrying is just like the ones we found on the island over the summer, the little boxes that held clues from Evangeline. I reach out to take the box from my mom. "I remember the vision that we had on the day dad gave me the necklace that belonged to Evangeline."

As I grasp the small coffer in my hand, a vision of Evangeline appears before us.

"The treasure is close to being found. You must be very careful on your adventure as there could be peril. Beware of the caverns and tunnels. They could be dangerous. Keep the clues a secret. There are threats around every corner." Then she vanishes before our eyes.

I search through the box. "Look there are other jewels. Here's a gorgeous garnet hair comb. There's an emerald broach, a pearl necklace, and a diamond ring in here. Hey, these gold coins look just like the ones we found under the floorboard at Evangeline's cottage! When Dad gave me the heart pendant, he told me it was among other keepsakes passed down through the generations for the last two hundred and fifty years."

Matt rifles through the box and, unbelievably, holds up a small notebook with Evangeline's name on the cover.

"Do you think this was Evangeline's diary?" I ask him and my mother.

Matt smiles and hands me the journal. "This should help you write your novel about Evangeline. I can't understand why Dad never shared these things with us?"

"Evangeline told him that the time was right to give me the necklace. My guess was that we needed to find the other clues we stumbled across during the summer before we found this box," I say.

We can't wait to get back to Ocracoke and show these new treasures to the others.
We share one final heartfelt night in our old home. We are saddened to say good-bye to a place that hold so many memories. We put logs in the brick fireplace, settle in around it, and recall long-forgotten stories about the special times we have shared here.

Matt chuckles out loud. "Mom, do you remember the time that you caught me sneaking back in to the house one night after I had gone out to meet some of my friends?" Mom laughs and wipes the tears from her eyes. "How could I ever forget that? I was so mad at you but also so relieved when I pulled you through the window. You looked like you didn't know whether to come in or jump back outside."

Laughter mingles with tears later when we hug and kiss each other good night. I look at my brother and mother. "Here it is, the last night we'll spend in this house. I will always cherish our family home and the memories that we made here. We are so lucky."

Our hearts are heavy. Mom put her arms around us. "Leaving here feels like losing your dad all over again. I feel like I am saying good-bye to him by moving away, but I know in my heart that he would want us to move on with our lives," she quietly says.

I enter my childhood bedroom for a final night in this familiar space. It still smells like lavender and roses from all the candles and incense I lit when I was growing up. I fondly touch the half-heart pendant around my neck. My father, George, appears before me and I gasp in disbelief. He reaches out his hands to me. "I know it's a shock, but I wanted to tell you how much I love and miss all of you. I am at peace. You do not need to worry about me."

He reaches out to touch my face. I feel a gentle breeze caress my freckled cheek. Gentle tears roll down my face and my heart aches to feel his arms around me. He warns me, "Listen to what Evangeline has told you so that you will all stay safe."

I wipe my tears. "Do you think it's possible for us to find the treasure?"

He smiles. "The real treasure awaits you. Anything is possible if you trust your heart," he says. "You have truly discovered your soulmate in Thomas. Tell your grandfather that he will find our ancestors that have been lost in history."

I start to open my bedroom door. "Let me call Mom and Matt to come to see you."

He shakes his head. "No, my dear Angie, they will see me tonight in their dreams. I will come to you in your dreams tonight, too—and many other nights to come. You will never be alone. I will always be there to help and to protect you all."

His hand brushes the tears from my face. He kisses my forehead and I feel a whisper of a touch. Then he disappears in a mist. I am left standing in the middle of my room with my heart shredded but, somehow, I feel like I have finally been able to say good-bye to him.

I crawl into my childhood bed, and I tightly hug my soft downy pillow. I only wish that I could have felt my father's arms around me one last time. Suddenly, I am so tired that I fall asleep instantly. I dream of moments shared with my dad.

I see him running and chasing behind me when I learn to ride my first two-wheeled bicycle. I feel him pick me up in his arms. He brushes away my tears when I fall off the bike and scrape my knees. I see him lift me over his shoulders and then wrap me tightly in his arms when I lose my first Tee-ball game. I see us celebrate by eating ice cream when my team wins the championship. Our life together unfolds gently in my dreams.

Next I see him standing beside me, looking down at me and grinning from ear to ear when I leave for my first prom. "You're so beautiful, my baby girl. You have turned into a raven-haired beauty. I can't believe you have grown up so fast. I love you sweetie." The look on his face when he tells me that he loves me brings me unbridled joy.

I see my father anxiously sitting in the audience when I receive a song-writing award after I submit the country song I had written to a competition. He looks so proud of me. Tears of joy glisten in his eyes. I feel as if I can reach out to touch him. The dreams feel so real.

I next see my father walking Sally down the aisle when my sister marries Robert. His sweet smile is like a kiss of sunshine on her cheek as he gives her away to the love of her life. Sally hands me her white rose-and-lily bouquet as she takes Robert's hand. I can even smell the sweet floral scent in my dream. I see myself lift the bouquet up to my face to breathe in its heavenly scent.

My heart aches as I watch my father giving me the pendant that once belonged to Evangeline. My dreams always feel like I am there at that very moment. In this dream, I see Evangeline tell my father that the time is right for him to give me the necklace.

And then I see myself answering the phone on that dreary, foggy day when I found out that my father had died. My broken heart feels as if it is being ripped from my chest. But the mood is lighter with the next image, a pearly vision. My father in the room when Sally is delivering her twins. I hear his voice quietly telling me: "Yes, I am always with you. Never fear. I will protect you all. And I will see you again. Tell your mother to move on with her life. I only want her happiness."

When I wake up, my face is dripping wet with tears. My heart hurts, but I feel that I have made peace with my father's passing. I decide to wait until our drive back to the island to tell the others about my visit with Dad.

We finish loading the orange and white U-Haul with our beloved possessions. We leave our family home for the last time. We all have tears in eyes when our mom says, "Good-bye, old home. You have held so many special memories." She closes the door and turns the lock for a final time.

Matt tries to be brave, but tears fall from his sad blue eyes. He wraps his strong arms around both of us. "We leave behind us all that was precious. We had a childhood that most people will never experience. We have been so lucky to have lived here with our wonderful family and dear friends."

With my hand over my heart and tears in my eyes, I whisper, "Bye, Dad, I love you." As we drive away, Mom tries not to cry but fails. Tears rush down her cheeks as countless happy memories race through her mind.

Mom turns around from the front seat and I reach to take my mom's hand in mine. "Dad came to visit me last night in my room just like Evangeline does. He is still with us in spirit and he says he will always protect us. Dad wants you to move on with your life, Mom. He told me he only wants your happiness.

He visited me as a spirit and then appeared to me in my dreams later in the night."

Mom tells us that my father visited her dream last night, too. She moves her hand over her grieving heart. "He let me relive all the special moments of our life together. I finally feel that I have started to heal from losing your dad. I will always miss him, but I will be okay."

We are relieved to hear her say this. We have been worried about her ever since our father died last year.

Matt whispers, "Dad came to see me last night, too. I was so surprised how much better I feel since he helped me to relive our life together. I miss him so much. He won't be able to see me marry Sarah."

"Believe me, he will be there in spirit," I reply. "He was there when the twins were born, but he didn't show his spirit because he didn't want to take away from the moment. And he was worried his presence might make everyone sad. He will always be here to protect us."

We continue our long drive, each of us lost in our own thoughts and memories of my father. Later in the journey I tell them what my father said about Thomas. "Dad told me that I have found my soulmate in Thomas. He said Thomas really does love me and that I should let him into my heart. He said Thomas will always love and protect me."

We had stopped at the Wawa in Chesapeake, Virginia, the last exit before the toll. We always stop there to gas and get their fabulous coffee. Then it's back on the road. I text Thomas to let him know when we reach Kill Devil Hill, where the Wright Brothers Memorial is located. It is off season, so the traffic is not too heavy, and we manage to catch all the traffic lights just right.

My vanilla flavored coffee from Wawa has turned cold, but I take one more sip, savoring the last drop of its sweet caramel taste. I stick my face out the window in the back seat and inhale the salty air as we near the ocean. "Awe, I love it. A little slice of heaven," I say.

Matt takes the beach road. Some of the dunes have been washed away near Milepost 1. I see Goombay's Grille and Raw Bar, one of my favorite restaurants. My mouth waters whenever I think about the spicy steamed shrimp the chef cooks up. The staff always offers up welcoming smiles when they serve their great local seafood. We talk about whether we should stop, but we decide to keep driving. We're all anxious to be home.

I love to see the sparkling ocean waves when I peek over the eroding dunes. Passing by the shops reminds me that the girls and I—and our mothers—will need to get busy planning Sarah and Matt's wedding. I look at Matt and grin. "I can't believe that you and Sarah will be married in December. My best friend will be my sister-in-law. It makes me so happy."

We finally reach the light where the road veers to the left onto Highway 12. Another leg of our journey is behind us. I see the Bodie Lighthouse rising above the mossy green cedars that line the roadway. The golden seagrass billows in the gusty Carolina breeze and the ospreys feed in the marshy sound. My heart flutters when I see the Bonner Bridge ahead of us. "I can never remember the bridge's new name," I say aloud. "Oh well, it will always be the Bonner Bridge to me."

We whirl past the Oregon Inlet Fishing Center. Most of the boats have ended their fishing charters for the day. It can be complicated to maneuver through the deadly channel, but the water is calm today, with barely a wave crashing on the shoreline. Matts points at the beach. "Look at all those trucks on the point. The fish must really be biting today," he says. "Maybe we can get a day to fish and relax on the beach before it gets too cold."

Smiling, Mom agrees. "That sounds nice. I haven't been out in the surf to fish at all this season. I don't know where the time has gone this year. It's already the end of October."

After a minute, she continues. "I'm so glad I didn't have to stay in Maryland to sign all the contracts on my home sale. It amazes me how everything can be done electronically nowadays."

The sun shines brightly over the sound as the kiteboarders, pelicans, and snow geese fly over the shimmering water and salt marshes. Semipalmated Plovers and sandpipers are feeding in the mudflats, searching for crustaceans. A few brightly colored windsurfers and paddleboarders are enjoying the Indian summer weather. The sun has started to dip into the surf, igniting the light to make ribbons of brilliant yellow and tangerine.

I gaze out and then point to the horizon. "We are going to have another magnificent sunset tonight. Look at those beautiful coral, lavender, and golden colors already forming on the shoreline."

Matt smiles. "You'll definitely need to take some pictures of the sunset tonight. It's almost as if the Outer Banks is welcoming us home."

Mom sighs tiredly. "Not much further now. We are on the home stretch—and thank goodness," she says. "I don't know about y'all but I'm so ready to get out of this truck. What a long day."

Chapter 3

Our New Life

We finally reach the ferry at Cape Hatteras that will take us to our new lives on Ocracoke Island. It has been a grueling six-hour drive. I always get a sudden burst of energy when we reach the ferry and today that is also fueled by my impatience to see everyone back on the island, especially Thomas. We have with us all our meaningful belongings from our life in Maryland. I still can't believe I have moved to the island on a permanent basis. It has always been my dream.

Matt drives his truck onto the Hatteras-Ocracoke Island ferry. "I'm so glad that we didn't have a long wait to get onto the ferry," he says. "This breeze feels awesome."

The sky has turned a glorious golden orange. Puffy white clouds above us glow a spectacular yellow in the late light of the day. They look like cotton balls lined in gold. Seagulls squawk overhead, searching for handouts. As we stand together on the ferry, watching the water, Matt hugs me and my mother. "I don't know about you guys, but I'm glad to be out of my truck and able to stretch my legs. I can't wait to be home."

We all nod in agreement. Mom points to the shoreline. "We are almost there. Guess we'll need to get back in the truck."

The ferry chugs up to the arrival dock on the shore of Ocracoke Island. The ferry crew directs us off the vessel. Matt's truck clinks over the metal ramps and its tires bounce over the serrated grates. We are surprised to see Sarah, Emily, George, Thomas, and David waiting for us on the docks. They wave wildly, excited to have us back.

Relief fills Isabella's face when she sees David among them. "I hadn't realized how much I have missed him," she tells me. "I've come to depend on him so much for his support and friendship over the last year."

Next week it will be a year since my father suddenly passed away. There are tears in my mother's eyes as she falls into David's arms. He holds her gently and wipes away her tears. He kisses her on the forehead and strokes her silky brown hair. I smile, happy that my mom has such a wonderful man to support her.

Our group is caught up in hugs and kisses galore. Matt rushes into Sarah's loving arms and kisses her passionately on her soft pink lips. I hear him whisper that he loves her and has missed her. Thomas has me in his arms. "I missed you so much. I don't want to let you go." He kisses me gently and our passion erupts. I can't wait to get him home so we can be alone.

Emily and George watch the happy reunions and wonder if they will ever find true love. And then we notice the spirits of Evangeline and Jacob watching us from the shoreline. Emily hears Evangeline's voice in her ear. "You already have a true love. You only need to reach out and take it for your own." Emily giggles and looks at George, wondering if anything will ever happen between the two of them.

It is late in the day and the sun is starting to melt into the Pamlico Sound. The light changes as colors of orange, periwinkle purple, and crimson red emerge and float down into the ebbing tide to the west. To the east, ominous storm clouds are forming as a cold front approaches. We see ebony-colored clouds start to appear over the white-capped shoreline. A strong end-of-day gale force wind starts blowing, sending the ferry flags fluttering upright.

Members of our welcoming posse rush to their cars. We all ride back to my mom's home to help her unload the things in the U-Haul. With luck, we will get everything into her home before the storm arrives. I am riding in the back of George's truck with Thomas. Emily and George are up front. I rest my head on Thomas's shoulder and shudder as my mind travels back in time to the terrifying day when I was kidnapped by those thugs Rusty and Ricky. I shiver and a chill runs down my spine. Thomas rubs my shoulders and kisses my cheek. "How was your trip?"

I am so glad that I am here in his arms. I smile. "It was a good trip. I need to show you guys something." I open my backpack and pull out the tiny coffer we found in my father's office.

Emily turns around in her seat. "Where did you find that box?"

I explain, "This was the box that held the necklace my father gave to me last summer." I hand her the box. "I didn't remember the box until my mom brought it out of my father's office." Then I add, "There is a journal that we found, too, that had once belonged to Evangeline! I will have to read it to everyone later."

I hold up the journal. "Evangeline appeared at my family home in Ripley. She warned us again about the dangers that we could be facing in our search for Blackbeard's treasure.

The three of them are astonished to hear how Evangeline appeared to us in a vision at my old childhood home. I touch my necklace. "I am sure I am linked to her by this necklace."

My eyes well up with tears up. "It was crazy. My father also visited me while I was at home. He came to say good-bye to me, and later that night he reappeared in a dream. He helped me relive our life together and some of the memories that we had shared."

I try not to cry as I tell them about the dream, but it is hard. I wipe the tears from my eyes with the back of my hand. "I finally feel like I was able to say good-bye to him."

No sooner have I spoken than the storm rolls in.

Chapter 4

The Storm

We pull into the circular oyster shell driveway in front of the white-pillared beach house my family has called home every summer for as long as I can remember. The rocking chairs are bouncing wildly in the salty, gusty air. Sally, Robert, and the Whites rush out to greet us. Everyone helps carry boxes into the large parlor and living room.

The robust Carolina winds gain even more strength, and the outdoor chimes are jangling fiercely. We manage to get all the boxes in before the tremendous storm unleashes torrential rain. The squall encircles the old home and pelts huge raindrops on the ancient windowpanes. The house groans as the wind howls around the old plantation home.

The lights begin to flicker, and a lightning bolt strikes somewhere nearby our house, followed by a crashing roll of thunder. The tornado siren blares, frightening the twins who both begin to wail. The ominous warning fills the air. Greetings are forgotten as we all hurry downstairs into the storm cellar. Georgia hands one of the babies' car carriers to my brother. "Matt, can you take this down with you? I will take the other down with me."

Isabella opens the basement door that leads down to the tornado shelter. The dusty stairway holds numerous labyrinths of cobwebs, and it smells musty. David and Robert grab the candles and lanterns that are at the top of the stairs.

I carry Evie and Sally has Jacob in her arms. Isabella warns everyone, "Be careful. These old wooden stairs are a little rickety." She adds: "We rarely use the storm cellar, but we can wait out the tornado warning in here."

She leads us down into an old forgotten room. As she gets ready to open the door, she turns to Jim and Sally White. "Thank heavens you guys brought dinners with you for everyone and hadn't unpacked them yet. Matt, Angie, and I didn't stop to have lunch. I don't know about them but I'm starving."

My mother opens the creaky door to the little room. "Your father prepared this room many years ago," she says to me. "He was such a planner. He was always prepared."

The dark chamber holds a fold-up table and fold-up chairs, ten of them to be exact. Mom points to the tables, chairs, and cots. "He even thought to add several army cots in the room with a storage chest full of old quilts."

It is cool and musky in the old room. My father had even equipped it with old propane lanterns and an ancient hand-cranked battery-operated radio in case there was ever a power outage.

The twins, cradled in my arms and Sally's arms, whimper. They are both scared by the loud thunder crashes. The dogs—Max, Ace, and Skippy—are whining and trembling next to Thomas and George. Matt cranks the ancient shortwave CB radio. "Dad thought of everything. Let's see if I can get the local radio station tuned in and get an update on the weather," he says. "I haven't seen this thing in years. Remember how we used to play war games with it?"

I reflect on that memory from of years gone by. The old AM-FM radio crackles when Matt finally finds WOVV, the Ocracoke community radio station. OBX—Outer Banks—Voice is giving a weather report: "A tornado warning is in effect until 8 p.m. There was a tornado sighting in Salvo. The funnel cloud was seen heading down Highway 12 toward Avon. There are numerous downed trees and several structures have sustained damage. Luckily, there are no injuries reported. Everyone in the community is doing well."

Isabella trembles. "I remember the night the F5 tornado passed through my backyard. Do you know that it has been fifteen years since that tornado devastated parts of our hometown in La Plata, Maryland? The wind was said to have reached 260 miles an hour. The tornado flattened parts of downtown La Plata. We were so lucky that it happened on a Sunday. The tornado passed right over Archbishop Neale School. So many people could've been killed that day."

David squeezes her shoulder. "I remember that like it was yesterday. It looked like a war zone in La Plata. Helicopters were flying all over the town."

He shakes his head and starts to set up the tables and chairs with the help of the other guys. "Thank goodness George thought to add these old olive-green army cots with wool blankets. You never know. We could be here all night. We have four more hours to wait until the tornado warning is over."

Jim and Sally unload the meals from their cardboard cartons. "We went to the local church dinner and bought the dinners. They are normally really good," Sally says.

My stomach growls. "They smell heavenly. We haven't eaten anything since breakfast."

David says grace, blesses the food we are about to eat, and adds an extra prayer, "Please keep everyone safe from the storm. I feel so blessed to be surrounded by all of you."

David takes his granddaughter into his arms and splatters kisses on little Evie's belly. She coos in delight. Her brother, Jacob watches the exchange and coos in response. The twins are exceptionally alert for being just three months old.

We all sit down to enjoy the special seafood dinner. There is an array of succulent steamed shrimp seasoned with Old Bay. The zucchini and squash have been roasted on a grill, which helps to add to their flavor. The meal is a huge success and appreciated by all of us.

My sister Sally and I start to clear away the clutter. I place some of our garbage in a big trash bag. "Dad even thought to stash away some trash bags in this little den," I point out.

The babies fall asleep in their car carriers with Georgia nearby to help keep an eye on them. To kill time, George, Thomas, Robert, and Matt explore the little storm cellar. Matt laughs. "When we were little kids, we would play hide and seek down here. We used to tell tales about how the pirates roamed the island and hid their treasures. I loved scaring the girls by telling them ghost stories and island folklore. It was so much fun. They would scream and run back upstairs with their pigtails flying."

Mom grins. "You used to make me crazy scaring them like that. The four of them would come racing up the stairs and tattle on you. It's so hard to believe that was twenty years ago."

Thomas is playing with the old built-in shelf in the room, trying to figure out how it was made. He reaches his hand under the shelf and finds an old latch. He pulls on the rusty latch and the bookshelf screeches open to reveal a hidden passageway.

My grandfather exclaims, "Ooh, this should be fun! Before your family, this home was owned by another pirate. His name was Jack Rackham, otherwise known as Calico Jack. He was a well-known pirate in the early 1700s. Back in the day, he visited this area so much that he secured this property here on Ocracoke Island, but his permanent dwelling was said to be in the Bahamas where he navigated along the shoreline and raided merchants' vessels."

The guys decide to explore the passageway while I join the girls to catch them up on our trip to Maryland. They guys step into the untouched tunnel. It is dark, dusty, and lined with antiquated torches. Matt lights one. "Wow, look at those dust mites floating in the air," he says. "Ooh and look at that huge spider web glowing in the flame light."

Matt, George, Robert, and Thomas move into a long-forgotten vestibule that leads to another small wooden doorway. Thomas pushes on the door. It creaks open to expose a tiny room. "It looks like something out of an old waterman's cabin, a portal lost in time," Thomas says. "I bet this room could tell some stories."

Robert raises his eyebrows and gestures towards the room. "I bet Calico Jack used this room to hide away from his captors way back when."

Inside the petite room is a large cedar captain's chest, a rickety wooden nightstand, and a decaying burlap cot with a rough-slatted frame. On top of the crooked timber nightstand sits an old frame containing an antique sepia picture. The timeworn image shows a woman dressed in pirate attire. She is holding out her hands and draped over her fingers are jewels, gold chains, rubies, emeralds, and sapphires.

Matt picks up the old, relic-framed picture. "Wow, do you think this is Anne Bonny? Look at that fiery red hair. She was said to have a hot, blooded personality to match her flaming hair."

Thomas takes the bygone picture from him and examines it. "I think you might be right."

Robert inspects the picture. "If this is her, it's one of the very few pictures there are of her, as most were said to be lost at sea. Matt, your grandfather Paul, and I were looking into them as part of the research we were doing on Blackbeard. Anne Bonny was one of the few well-known female pirates. It was said that she was in love with old Calico Jack."

George points. "Look at this ancient cedar chest. I wonder if it belonged to Calico Jack and Anne Bonny?" He opens the stout wooden chest. "There must be a whole wardrobe of old pirate clothes in here," he exclaims. "They look like they are over two hundred years old. And look! Here's a map of Nassau, Bahamas. It is dated 1712."

Thomas finds an antique gold watch in the chest. "There is an engraving inside. It is inscribed, 'To Jack, Love, Anne.' Can you believe it?" They stare in amazement at the watch, wondering if it and these other things could actually have belonged to Calico Jack.

They take a closer look at the map of the Bahamas. It has several areas marked with an X. Matt points to the spots. "Do you think we have found another map, this time leading to Calico Jack's treasures? Wouldn't that be cool?"

The guys start laughing, patting themselves on the back. Robert said, "Let's go back and show the others what we've found. They are not going to believe this."

The guys retrace their steps through the dust-ridden tunnel and back into the storm cellar. They carry their latest finds from the chest. Matt emerges into the storm cellar first and excitedly takes the photo over to his grandfather. "Look, Grandad! Look at this picture we found. We think it may be Anne Bonny."

George holds out the old map of the Bahamas. "And look at this old map of the Bahamas. It has spots marked on it. Do you think it could be Calico Jack's treasure map?"

Thomas, Robert, and George show us all their other discoveries from the cedar chest. Paul laughs. "Do you know what this means? This stuff is historic. And now we have a chance to find Calico Jack's treasure, too. Who would have thought that these things have stayed hidden in this storm cellar for all these years only to be discovered because of a tornado warning? This is so exciting."

Matt sits down on one of the old weary army cots and yawns. "We will need to do some more exploring in the passageway, but I'm whipped. What a long day."

We are so thrilled with all the new findings but, like Matt, Mom and I are exhausted after our long day.

The radio squawks. "We have an all clear. You are free to come out of your storm shelters. The tornado warning has come to an end. Please be safe out there everyone. There are several trees down and a lot of debris on the roads."

Chapter 5

The Last Encounter

After a long, tiring day, everyone decides to head home to their beds. As we exit the storm cellar, I say, "I feel like I have been in a time capsule."

I walk up the stairs of our old family bungalow. As soon as we open the basement door, the familiar smell of cinnamon hits me from the spicy candles that my mother loves to burn. I sigh because it reminds me of home. We step out onto her windblown porch, and it looks like a bomb has gone off outside. Branches and leaves cover the yard. Sand has blown over the stone walkway.

Sarah, Matt, and the Whites leave in their trucks and head home to see what has happened there. Emily, George, Thomas, and I follow them in George's truck. The roads are littered with tree branches and leaves. Gritty tan sand has blown over the oyster shell road; parts of the road are flooded.

We listen to the radio as the announcer gives an update on the storm damage on Roanoke Island. "Luckily, there have been no fatalities from the tornado," he says. "The tornado went straight down Highway 12. Some homes have sustained minor roof and shutter damage, but all buildings remain standing. The funnel cloud followed the highway and did not affect many residences."

George teases me. "Did you bring that storm with you guys all the way from Maryland? It sure did get here right after you arrived."

I grin and explain, "Sometimes, I think tornados do follow me. When I lived in Ripley at my mom's home, I saw one pass right through our backyard. Hopefully this was the last one we have to experience for a long time."

George stops his truck and Thomas and I say goodnight and head to my cottage. George drops Emily off a little farther down the road at her front door and walks her up to her steps. Thomas says to me, "George told me he really misses living with Emily. He misses the closeness that they shared when they were in her house together for that short period when we were worried about you girls and your safety." Thomas and I walk hand-in-hand toward our cottage. I sigh. "If only the two of them would open their eyes. Maybe, one day."

Max is not to be forgotten. He is jumping up and down between us. He does not want to be left out. We take him on his nightly walk on the beach.

The air has gotten chilly from the cold front that moved in with the storm. There is a cool breeze blowing through the seagrass tonight, making a whishing sound. Max runs up and down the shoreline, excited to be outside after the long time we spent in the storm shelter at my mom's beach house. I am so relieved to be back on the island—back home! —and I am bone tired. I can't wait to rest my head on my soft cool pillow. I am also happy to be with Thomas. I bring his hand up to my lips. "I really missed you last night when we were in Maryland. I can't believe how much I've come to rely on you."

Max has found a stick and brings it over, wanting to play with Thomas. Thomas ruffles his ears and tells him, "Not now, buddy. It's time to get Angie home."

I yawn. All I want is to stretch out and go to sleep. I am exhausted. Thomas wraps his arms around me and takes Max's leash into his other hand. The two of us are deep in thought, thinking about the events of tonight.

Thomas breaks the silence and asks, "Do you think it's possible to find Blackbeard's treasure and Calico Jack's treasure?"

I laugh and tell him, "I never dreamed that we would find Blackbeard's treasure maps, much less Calico Jack's. We need to be cautious. Evangeline keeps giving us warnings about impending danger if we aren't careful in the caves."

Goosebumps are appearing on my arms as I remember the earlier warning, she gave us. "Remember that Evangeline warned us again to keep our clues a secret."

I take my long raven-colored hair out of its ponytail and shake it before running my fingers through it. I shiver, remembering the last time we were warned by Evangeline. It could have turned deadly. "I keep thinking about the night Rusty and Ricky kidnapped me," I tell Thomas. "It seems like a lifetime ago, almost like a dream or nightmare."

We finally arrive home. It feels great to walk into our little cottage together. Thomas kisses my neck and telling me how much he has missed me. I wrap my arms around his neck, kissing him gently on the lips. My body tingles at his touch. "I'm home but I'm so tired I can barely see straight." I can't help but stifle a yawn.

Thomas lifts me in his arms and places me on our bed. He kisses me on the forehead. "I want to feel your body under me, but I know it has been a hard couple of days for you. Sleep. I'll just lay down beside you."

I curl my body up against his and fall soundly asleep. Max is tucked up in his bed. Before I fall asleep, I hear Thomas's gentle breath and see his chest rise and fall. The stress melts away, and I know that I have found my heart.

I fall into a peaceful slumber and dream again of Evangeline. I see her friend Roger running up to her little cottage. He has a young boy with him, who is frantically asking Evangeline to come with him to the mainland. The wee boy explains, "My mother is heavy with child, and we need you to come help."

Evangeline lifts her child, William, up in her arms. "Roger, can you take him over to Emily and Robert's home at the inn?" Roger rushes the babe over to her dear friend's home.

I see Evangeline readying herself to go to the Roanoke Island. She gathers up her midwife bag so that she can help with the delivery of the little one that is soon due to arrive in this world. I hear her tell herself, "Please let all be well."

The sun is rising over the horizon. Beautiful shades of lemon, gold, coral, and tangerine fill the morning sky. Evangeline is on a boat. Roger and Evangeline's father navigate it across the treacherous bay and then inland. It takes them several hours to cross the channel. The boy was sent to get Evangeline paces back and forth on the deck. She tries to reassure him that all will be fine. He cries. "My mother nearly passed the last time she had a baby. Her belly is twice the size that it was the last time she had a babe," he says, distraught.

I feel the stress level rise in Evangeline, but she tries to hide the concern in her voice. "You will see. All will be well," she tells the boy. She takes his young frame in her arms and rocks him gently to comfort him.

I see them arrive on the coast of Roanoke Island. There is a carriage waiting on the docks for them. I see the horse and carriage race down the sandy, dirt road. The driver exclaims, "My lady's time is near. We must hurry."

I feel the carriage rumbling as it rushes over the sand and pebble road. The morning breeze is gentle. The seagrass is willowing and waving in the air. It looks like golden slivers in the rising sun. They arrive at the humble home of Alice and Joe Chapman. There are several other anxious children in the tiny cabin. Their ages range from two years old to ten years old. Joe is one of the local watermen. He makes a fairly good living. They get by and he catches most of their food.

Alice has a small vegetable garden behind their quaint cottage. In my dream, I see her lying on the feather bed in her little cottage. She is drenched in sweat as the contractions rack her abdomen. She is whimpering in pain. "I think the babe is too big," she whispers to Evangeline.

Evangeline feels her belly, realizing that there are two babies. One is breech. "It is going to be a long day. The lady is carrying twins," Evangeline thinks to herself. "Two babes, fear not. I'm here for you all."

I watch as Evangeline helps the lady deliver the first child. "You have a wee sandy-haired girl." The infant arrives in the world wailing, much to Evangeline's relief. The second child is not so lucky. She is the breech birth. I watch as Evangeline turns the second child so that it can be delivered. Alice screams in pain as Evangeline maneuvers the child. Her tiny legs and arms are flailing in the air. Finally, the baby girl emerges, and her sharp cry pierces the air.

Evangeline sighs and takes a deep breath. "Another wee girl we have. Not quite done yet we must deliver the afterbirth so as not to get childbirth fever." She wipes the sweat from her brow with the back of her hand and mops the mother's brow. She worries about childbirth fever as many a mother has lost her life to it.

Evangeline examines both infants to make sure that they are healthy. Alice's sister, Megan, helps to clean the babes and wraps them in swaddling clothes. Joe has built a little crib and that's where the twins will rest their tiny heads. Luckily, Joe made a big crib—the babies easily fit in it together. He built the crib from the cedars that grow in the neighborhood. Alice has sewn a little mattress and a tiny bedspread to match.

Evangeline thinks back to when she was on the ship that brought her family over from England. She smiles to herself as she remembers Roger, Jacob, and her brother, Robert, building cribs for the babies born on their boat. She and her friend Emily had sewn blankets for the babies on the ship with the help of Emily's mother. Those were such happy memories.

She wonders to herself how Jacob is doing. She has heard from one of the local fishermen that he has married a young heiress in Williamsburg. All her dreams of them being reunited with him were blown away with that news. She brushes a tear from her cheek and shakes out her long raven colored hair. She knows Jacob will never leave the lady that he has married. She heard that Jacob and his wife already have two children and third on the way.

Jacob will never know that he and Evangeline have a child together. She and Roger decided it will be best for everyone to think her child, William, belonged to Daniel, the pirate who kidnapped her.

Evangeline wraps her arms around herself and longs for Jacob's embrace but knows that she will never feel it again. She should find someone and get on with her life, but her heart will never love another.

Evangeline has her faithful companion, Roger, by her side on most days. Her father has tried to encourage her to commit her life to Roger, but she tells him that she will never be able to give him her full heart and he deserves better.

It has been a long day. With the babies and their mother safe, Evangeline walks out of the small cabin. The pine needles and sand feel soft under her tired feet. She stretches her legs, arms, neck, and back. She never realizes how stressed she is at a birth until it is over.

The day is dwindling, and it has started getting dark outside. Fireflies twinkle in the distance. The gentle breeze from the morning had turned into a sweltering heat. She will have no choice but to spend the night on Roanoke Island. The channels are too dangerous and treacherous to cross at night.

The shoals have buried many a ship that tried to maneuver through the channels. Evangeline misses her sweet little William, but she shall see him on the morrow. She knows he is safe with his auntie, uncle, and his cousins. Her friend, Emily, was married to her brother while Evangeline was held captive on Cat Island. When she finally was able to escape and return to her family, she was delighted to find that Emily was now her sister-in-law.

Roger and her father had left her to her midwife duties and, earlier in the day, sailed further inland to obtain much-needed lumber for a new barn and baking supplies for the pub. Alice's sister offers Evangeline a fish porridge and cornbread, and Evangeline realizes she hasn't eaten since breakfast and her stomach is growling. Her mouth begins watering when she takes the first spoonful of the stew. "Thanks, Megan, for the soup," she says as she tries to stifle a yawn.

The little ones gather around her when she starts singing one of her lonesome songs. Her voice sounds angelic and entrancing. All the Islanders love to hear her sing. The lonesome sky melts into glorious shades of orange, tangerine, and cantaloupe, filling the sky as the sun dips into the tranquil sound.

Evangeline finishes her stew and looks up at the starry sky. She wishes that she could be home but knows that tomorrow will be here soon. She can no longer hold back her yawns and asks the family if there is anywhere, she can lay her head.

I watch in my dream as the family takes her to a little cot to rest her weary body. She feels the tension drain from her and she falls into a fitful dream. In Evangeline's dream, she watches as another birth is occurring. Evangeline asks the woman, "Who are you and what is your name?"

The woman answers, "My name is Eleanor Dare. My colony came over on a ship many years ago, in the year of 1587. This is my daughter, Virginia. She was the first baby born here on this island." Evangeline's dream ends at the same time my dream ends.

I roll over and I rub my eyes in disbelief. I realize that I have just had a dream about Evangeline dreaming about one of the Lost Colonists. I think to myself, "Somehow, we must all be linked."

I remember my previous dream in which I saw Evangeline speaking to a ghost of a woman on Cat Island. The woman tells her that her name is Virginia. The woman is a spirit and comes to Evangeline as Evangeline appears to me, in a mist. I wonder if this is the same Virginia.

I stretch and get up from the warm bed to face a new day. I rise to the rich caramel aroma of fresh coffee brewing in the other room. I can't wait to drink in its honey-colored flavor.

The brilliant sun has already risen and morning daylight streams into the cottage. Thomas has somehow managed to get up and take Max with him without waking me. I must really have been exhausted. I pick up my tablet and write down my latest dream. I need to tell my grandfather about this dream.

My grandparents are supposed to come over to the inn this morning to look at the items that we found last night.

I walk over to the old-fashioned resort and bring the little box with me which was the one that held my precious necklace that my father had given me from Evangeline. When I see my grandparents, I open the box to show them the journal that had once belonged to Evangeline. The journal tells of her capture and years on Cat Island, so many years ago.

I share the journal. "We found this diary in Evangeline's trunk. It was when she was living on Cat Island. I wonder if it holds any secrets that might lead us to the treasure."

Chapter 6

Evangeline's Capture

We step back in time, sitting in the private parlor, as I read the first pages of Evangeline's diary to the others. "Okay, so I remember my dream about Evangeline being captured by Daniel Teach's men?" Listen to what she wrote in her diary," I say.

Roger came to visit me today. I have been here on the island for about a month. He gave me this journal so I can write down my thoughts and feelings while I am here. My name is Evangeline Alexander. I was captured by a pirate. His name is Daniel Teach. He is said to be Blackbeard's grandson. I can remember the fateful day when my life was changed forever. I was sitting on the shores of Ocracoke Island. My heart was breaking as I waited for my love, Jacob, to return and make me his wife. It had been months since he had left to help his family set up their homestead. I was reading a letter from Jacob.

My dear Evangeline,

I'm writing to tell you that I will be delayed a bit longer than I feared. My love, Papa has passed. He succumbed to malaria. My dearest, I will not be able to come for you for several more months. I am now the man of the family, and I must earn money for my family. I have found work with a local woodworker and furniture maker. I will come for you as soon as I can.

My Everlasting Love,

Your Jacob

Tears are streaming down my face and my teardrops land on the letter. I am so sad that I can barely stand it. I pat my belly. I speak into the whirling Carolina breeze and tell my unborn child that all would be well. I am wrapping my arms around my legs when I hear drunken raving men come up behind me. I am in fear for my life. The men grab me by my arms. They drag me down the sandy dunes. I fight against the wicked men to no avail.

All my screams are lost in the strong Ocracoke gale. I battle for my life, trying to tear out of their grasp, but it is in vain. I recognize the brutal unshaven men who capture me as part of the rough, murderous crew that belongs to Daniel Teach's ship. They drag me up onto a narrow wooden gangplank. The wretched reek of the men, the foul smell of rum, and the vile smell from poor toileting is overpowering. I vomit on the dirty men's filthy feet.

They throw me into a small, windowless room. It is ghastly. I land on a tiny dirty cot that smells musty and acrid. The more I fight, the more they beat me, until I finally stop struggling. I curl up into a tiny little ball, bruised and bloody. I am violently trembling in fear for my life and the life of my unborn child.

One of the men has long braided dark hair with a scraggly beard. Another man has brown skin with a rugged beard. They are both trusted men to Daniel. Their stench, pungent with spirits, and their body odor make my belly lurch and flip. Finally, they leave me alone.

I search the small room for ways to escape. There is a shabby armoire with a looking glass on it. I peer at my battered face and barely recognize myself. My tears mingle with my blood and dirt from my capture. I pray to God for someone to help me. My agonizing fear is that my tender life is certainly over. My cries are answered by a small meow as a tiny black kitten winds his way up around my scratched-up ankles. I picked up the small kitten and my tears fall on the poor little creature. I find comfort in its presence.

My anxiety is escalating when I hear loud footsteps outside my door. It slams open. "My name is Jeffrey. I am taking you to see the captain."

I try to fight him. I am screaming, "No, I will not go!"

The hallway is pungent and stinking. The sickening smell makes me want to puke as he pushes me through an open doorway. I fall at the feet of the captain of the ship. He is the well-known and treacherous pirate. He grabs me up from the floor. "Remember me? Daniel Teach. I remember your glorious body from the docks in Florida."

I am terrified as he lifts me to my feet. He threw a wench's dress at me. "Put this dress on. I want to see your lovely body. I want to see you undress in front of me."

I scream in his face, "I will never be yours! You cannot make me!"

He slaps me so hard across my already bruised face that I fall limply in a heap to the wooden floor. Blood drips from my mouth and nose. Tears stream down my face and mingle with my own blood. I taste the metallic flavor of my blood.

He rips the whorish dress with his large burly hands. I shake violently as he watches me. My body is grotesquely purple and my bruised skin sore as my torn gown is ripped from my abused body.

I try to keep my face away from his face by lowering my chin. I to try to avoid his gaze. He grabs my face with his large brawny hands. He wipes the tears and blood from my face. His large muscular hand lowers his trousers to reveal his massive manhood.

I can barely look at him as his mouth covers mine. He pushes me down onto the dirty ragged covered bed. His bulky form lays over me and he forces himself into me. He rips through me. He covers my mouth to quiet my screams. He takes my nipples into his mouth. His body is rapidly moving up and down until he shudders, burying his seeds deep inside me.

I fall into blackness as I pass out under his grasp. I wake up to Daniel wiping my tears and stroking my hair. "I am sorry I hurt you, my little bird. You just need to surrender your body to me. Surrender yourself so you will not feel the pain of my beatings if you do not give yourself to me. You now belong to me."

He covers me with the worn coverlets and leaves me to lay there. My head is turned away from him as he pulls up his pantaloons. His large bulky frame fills the doorway. "You will always be mine from this day forward."

My life on his ship is the same every day. He has me brought to him so that he can have his way with me. My only comfort is the little black kitten who saves me from insanity. My body betrays me daily when my sickness in the mornings makes me grasp my basin and vomit until nothing remains. The crew think it is the just the sea that makes me sick, but I know better. I have not had my monthly for over two months. I think of Jacob as I run my hands over my belly. I am still in fear for my life and for the life of my unborn child. My breasts are sore and tingly.

I have been on the sloop for over two weeks. The crew makes me anxious when I am led topside for fresh air. The pirates make lewd comments when I pass by them although not in the presence of the captain, Daniel. Jeffrey, the first mate is my captor. He brings me my meals and a bowl of food for my kitty. He has kind eyes and I believe he is fond of me. He no longer drags me but coaxes me gently when he is bringing me to Daniel for the daily violation of my body.

Daniel is becoming more tender with me. He often strokes my hair and nips at my breasts when takes me and my nipples into his mouth. I no longer fight him as I realize it is futile. He wraps his arms around me. "You are mine now forever. I am going to cover you in jewels."

Daniel keeps me with him now at night, most nights anyway. I wake up at times to find his arms draped over me. Most mornings he has his way with me. I am no longer modest around him. When I am with Daniel, I rarely wear clothes.

When I am topside some days, I see Roger and he sees me. He loves to stop by to visit me. He pretends not to know me and shushes me when I recognize him from our ship's crossing together from England. One day when I am in my room, he knocks on my door. I throw my arms around him and beg him to help me escape. My tears of despair fall on him.

He wraps his arms around me. "I promise you that I will find a way to get you home. You must be patient as Daniel is a very dangerous man. I will come to visit you when I can. We need to be careful so Daniel does not become jealous. I have not been able to come to see you often because they are guarding your room."

After I've been on board the sloop for over a month, Daniel starts letting me go topside alone. There are three other women on our ship. Most were captured by the crew to be their wenches.

One of the girl's is Sally; she is the wench of Jeffrey, Daniel Teach's first mate. One day when I am with her, she wipes a tear from her eye. "I have been on board—when we are not on the island—for over two years," she confides. "I am from South Carolina. I was captured a couple years before you. I miss my family so much. My father is a fisherman. I swear one day he will come for me."

Daniel allows me to read some of his books. I've started teaching some of the others how to read. Sally has been instructing me on how to make pottery. Jeffrey collects clay for her so that she can make her pots. It feels so good to work with my hands. It eases my tension. I have started to settle in on this ship. It has been three months since I have seen my monthly. I have a small bump of a belly. I have not told Daniel yet that I fear I am with child.

Roger comes to see me when he can, and he is my saving grace. I think Roger suspects that I am with child, but he can't bring himself to ask me. Sometimes I can feel his eyes on my belly. I feel so ashamed that Roger will realize that the baby is Jacob's.

If I could only tell him that the babe belongs to Jacob, but I can never tell him as I fear we would perish if Daniel ever suspected it is the child of my love, Jacob, that is growing inside me. I will hold this secret close to my heart and protect it at all costs.

There are two other girls on board this vessel that I also befriend. Their names are Katrina and Eleanor. Katrina is very heavy with child. "I was captured over a year ago when my family was docked in Port Royal, on the island they call Jamaica. I am from England, too. My papa thought that we could have a good future in the New World."

She is often tearful when she speaks about her family. "We were headed for Virginia when I was captured," she says. She is the same age as me. She has mousy brown hair and is very fair. She has the most beautiful green eyes. She belongs to Joseph Jones, the quartermaster.

Eleanor was captured at the same time as Katrina. She has wavy blond hair. She has been given to the ship's doctor, James Payne. James is a gentle soul and dotes on her. The girls have helped me to stay sane. We spend most of our days doing chores around the sloop.

You could imagine my surprise when I walked into the galley to help make our supper meal when I see our old cook, Robert Williams. We call him Cook. He sailed with my family and others who left England to start new lives in the colonies. We spent so many months together on the ship and he was always good and kind to us. He envelopes me in a big bear hug. His toothless grin warms my heart as my tears fall on his well-worn apron. I think of how emotional I have been since I have been with child.

Cook teased me. "You are even more beautiful than I remembered," he said. "I was captured at the same time as you were. But I have not had an opportunity to seek you out on this ship." Then he added, in a whisper, "Roger and I will find a way to get us home."

Cook had become like an uncle to me on our voyage across the sea to the New World. So now my life with the pirates has become filled with old and new friends, but it is still so hard being away from my family. I have been on board this ship for four months now. My belly has become round with my child. I finally told Daniel that I am going to have his baby. He surprised me and was ecstatic. He has moved me into his cabin permanently. He kisses me gently on my cheek, pats my belly, and he talks to our child when we lay in his bunk.

I have given up trying to get away from him, but he will never know that this child is not his. He treats me quite well and genuinely seems to care for me. His lovemaking has become gentler. I guess I should consider myself lucky, but I long for my family and Jacob.

One night, Daniel tells me, "We should reach the island in another moon." He is speaking of the Caribbean Island that he and his men use as their homes. We arrive a couple weeks later.

I am standing topside with the other girls when the island comes into view. It takes my breath away to see how the coral-colored sand reflects off the aqua sea. The palm trees wave, welcoming us to this paradise. I have become so close to my new friends. They will be the key to my survival.

The women are left on the island now when the pirates head off to plunder and pillage. Soon we are anxiously awaiting the arrival of Katrina's baby. She has been having pains often over the last week. Her back aches. I am sure her time is near. Eleanor and I promise her that we will be there to help her when the baby is born. I am so glad that I helped Sandra deliver babes on our way to the New World. I will know what to do.

The time is flying by, and I am turning 19 years old today. It is now September 7, 1757. Robert, the cook, has made me a delicious, sweet cake. It is made from the fresh fruits on the island. He also has prepared us a wonderful feast. I daydream daily about Jacob, and I think about the day when we will be reunited.

Roger and Jeffrey made rocking chairs for the porch of the house where I live with Daniel. The house is a little bungalow with a wide porch. Daniel and Roger made a cradle for my new baby—or "our" new baby, as Daniel calls it. The baby will be here in a few more months.

Daniel has given me a beautiful emerald brooch for my birthday. It is quite lovely. Roger surprises me with a gift of one of his charcoal drawings that he framed himself. When Daniel is away, Roger shows me a hidden compartment in the frame where I can hide my journal. It is just perfect as I have been hiding it under a rock in the fireplace hearth.

Today Joseph came running to find me. "Katrina lost her water and the babe's birth is eminent!"

Excited as I am, I fear the birth as it is the first time, I've brought a new life into this world alone. Thankfully, we have the ship's doctor to help us.

I race with Joseph to the home he shares with Katrina. Eleanor is already there. Katrina is crying out in pain, rocking back and forth on her hands and knees. "It hurts me less when I sit this way," she says between contraction spasms.

I quickly wash my hands and ask Joseph's servant to bring me some boiled water. I remember how Sandra had used boiled water to clean all the items we used when I helped her to deliver a child on our journey to America. Katrina's pains are minutes apart. I check the baby's position just as Sandra had shown me last year. I cringe. The baby is upside down. I pray to God that I can do this. A vision of a woman appears before me. I rub my eyes in disbelief. She is in a mist. "Fear not, my name is Virginia," she tells me. "I will guide you as you deliver the babe."

I blink my eyes, not sure if I am truly seeing this vision. The spirit is a young woman dressed in clothes from years gone by. She is in her early 20s. I recognize her garment from drawings I have seen from the late 1500s.

I check Katrina again and see a foot emerging. Virginia whispers, "You must find the other foot and pull the baby into the world."

I breathe in deeply. "Follow what I tell you to do, Katrina. You must push with all your might. With the next pain, I will find the other foot and gently, but steadily, pull your child into the safety of the world."

She pushes and I am able to bring the baby into the light. Eleanor helps me tie twine around the birthing cord. "We will use the cutlass to cut the cord," I tell Elizabeth. "We must wash it first in the boiling water. Place the babe on Katrina's chest to milk the child."

I fall to my knees praising God and the spirit of Virginia vanishes from my sight. I tell no one ever about her presence as I fear they will think me crazed.

"It is a boy!" rings through the cottage. Eleanor rushes to tell the news to Joseph, who is pacing outside. I finish cleaning up the babe and help deliver the afterbirth with the assistance of Amelia, Katrina's servant.

Joseph rushes in to see young Katrina and his baby boy. He is beaming with pride as he kisses his precious Katrina on her cheek. Her eyes fill with tears. "Joseph, I want to name the child Joseph Evan Jones." Then she looks at me. "I want to make his middle name Evan, which is short for your name, Evangeline."

I place my hand up to my heart. "I am flattered beyond belief." The baby has curly black hair and is as fair as Katrina. It is such a joyous occasion.

I am overjoyed that what could have been a treacherous birth has gone well. I walk back to my home, tired from the long birth. I enter my cottage and the vision of a woman appears before me. "I was brought to this island after being captured when I was but a babe. My name is Virginia Dare. I am a long ago relative of your family."

I blink then rub my eyes as I listen in astonishment. "Virginia, are you one who vanished with a whole colony from Roanoke Island so many years ago?" I ask her.

Virginia laughs, "'Tis true. I was born on the Roanoke Island. I am here and will be here to help you to stay safe. My family has had visions of their ancestors. This has passed on to you."

I massage my ever-growing big belly. A tiredness overtakes me. Virginia vanishes, but before she leaves, she adds, "I will always be here for you."

I am in disbelief. I have never believed in spirits, though I have always felt a presence from my past.

The days pass into weeks, which turn into months. My time is coming near. My belly is large with child. I walk daily with my friends to my secret hiding place, a small blue lagoon behind a beautiful waterfall. Eleanor, Katrina, her new babe, and I seek out the solitude of this sanctuary. The warm water is a clear crystal blue and is wonderful for swimming. Swimming eases my aching bones. My ankles are quite puffy. The water as I float makes me feel less enormous. I know that my time is near and wish my mama and Jacob were here."

Eleanor and Katrina have become like sisters to me. I touch my belly and tell them, "I am so afraid of giving birth and taking care of this wee one." My friends have sworn to be by my side when my baby arrives. In another vision, Virginia, too, promises to protect me. She has a calming effect on me despite her being a spirit. She exclaims, "I swear I will keep you safe."

Roger also helps me and is forever doting. He makes me feel more secure.

Daniel anxiously awaits the birth. My fears are that I will not be able to protect my child. I think to myself—but do not tell my friends—that Daniel is unaware the baby is not his. I do not know what he would do if he ever found out. The baby hangs low in my womb. I think the birth will be any day now.

My baby, William, arrived on February 7, 1758. I was terrified that I would die in childbirth. Oh, how I miss my mama and papa. Eleanor and Katrina were there to help me deliver my babe, who came into the world screaming. It was such a welcome cry. The pain of the birth was unbearable at times. I thought I would surely perish. A vision of

Virginia came to me and helped to bring a calm over me. I dared not tell the others I saw her, for fear they would think me insane.

I whispered to my babe, "William, I think you have Jacob's eyes. They have the same beautiful golden flecks, just like your father's. I will spoil you, my little son."

I sit and stare at his little face. I love holding him, his tiny body in my arms. I love the rocking chair that Roger and Jeffrey made for us, and I rock the day away.

Daniel is quite a proud papa and dotes on little William. He barely lays the child down when he is in the room. I guess I should consider myself lucky. My life on the island has become very ordinary. Little William is a happy child. He rarely cries and sleeps through the night. I can barely believe he is almost three months old. He coos and smiles when you talk to him.

Roger came to visit me the other day. He cannot come over very often. "I do not want to make Daniel jealous of me," he explains. "Yet, I feel like I'm home when I visit you."

He tells Daniel that he is there to see him, but I know better. Roger always brings me little treats that Cook has made for me. It has become one of the highlights of my days.

"Angie, why don't you take a pause," my grandfather says. I set the journal down and tell the others that I had a dream about Evangeline's story the other night. "In my dream, I watched as Evangeline settled into her new life on the island, although she still longed for her home and her family. In the dream, it had been over a year ago since she had been kidnapped from the shores of Ocracoke Island. She told me she still thought of Jacob daily but knew that he had probably gotten on with his life."

There is silence as we all digest what we have heard. Then I resume reading.

"I wonder to myself if I will ever make it back home. I spend most of my days taking care of my darling William.

The rest of the hours, I teach the others on the island how to read and write. Roger has made me a board to write my lessons on. Eleanor and Katrina help me with my classes. I am now the local midwife and have delivered three bairns since I came to the island. My visions of Virginia continue, especially whenever I feel lost, scared, or lonely. She also appears before me whenever I bring a new baby into the world. My visions of Virginia are like a ray of light in a dark room.

I found out yesterday that Eleanor and James are having a child. Eleanor has been very helpful taking care of Katrina's babe and my own, but she has long yearned for the time when she can have her own. She is very much in love with James. He dotes on her and pampers her daily. He has become even more dedicated to her since they found out she was with child. She gleams with excitement at the thought of being a mother.

The girls and I like to take walks with our children to the lagoon behind the waterfall. It is so secluded that we can swim in our shifts without fear of being seen. The water is glorious and so refreshing from the summer's heat. Young William and Katrina's child, Evan, splash in the crystal blue shallows. Behind the waterfall, there is a cavern where we shelter if there is a violent storm. Daniel told me that he has hidden some of his treasures in the caves on the islands. He said there are hidden tunnels in the caverns. Roger says we will take some of those treasures with us when we escape this island. I sigh. I cannot wait for that day to arrive.

Time passes and one day I see myself in the looking glass. I am turning 20 this year. I cannot believe this is my second birthday here on this island.

I rub my hands over my face. "I guess my family and Jacob think that I am dead," I think. "Jacob has surely moved on with his life. Oh, how I miss my family, especially on days like today, holidays, and birthdays."

I pick up my son, hugging him to me. "I fear you and I will never make it back home," I whisper to him. "I want my family to meet and love you, William. They are missing seeing you grow up. I cannot believe you are already seven months old."

I am quite spoiled this year for my birthday. Cook has prepared another special cake. This year it is made with pineapples. The juice from the pineapples is so sweet. It drips down my chin. It is a delectable cake.

Daniel gives me a beautiful strand of pearls, but my most precious gift is from Roger. He has started doing paintings in addition to his sketches. He presents me with a lovely watercolor that shows me rocking little William on our porch, and it is quite spectacular. It is very special to me. It has a hidden compartment for me to hide my private letters and my precious papers.

Daniel writes me many love letters. In them, he gives me clues to where his grandfather, Blackbeard, has hidden his treasures. It seems likely this booty may be buried right here on this island. According to Daniel, his grandfather was a good comrade to a man named Arthur Cat. Daniel says that is the origin of the island's name. There are so many hidden tunnels in caves that would be perfect for hiding buried treasure.

It is the year 1758 and Christmas is here already. The time has flown by. My son is now ten months old. A memory passes by me as I recall Christmas on the sloop that brought my family to the New World. Roger and Cook have tried to re-create that special day. We had a wonderful feast of roasted pig and all the wonderful fruits and vegetables from the island. The girls and I have made ornaments out of seashells. We put them on the palm trees. We made each other special gifts. Daniel bought me some soft silk materials and beautiful linens. I told him as I held up the special cloth, "I will make new clothes for us."

Roger and Jeffrey have made Eleanor and James a cradle for their new baby. It reminded me of the cradle that my Jacob, Robert, my brother, and Roger had made aboard our ship to America for Lucy and Jim's baby. That cradle had been quite lovely, with Lucy and Jim's initials carved on the inside of a large heart. We had all guessed when their child would be born. They carved the babe's initials onto it once the little one arrived.

On Cat Island, Eleanor is now very large with child. I rub her belly and tell her, "The babe may be born any day now. I promise to be there for you to help you deliver your child."

I take little William to our special place to swim in the lagoon. My son is floating in my arms. I love watching him splash in the water. I look up to find that Roger is watching us. I gesture for him to step nearer. "Come in and join us. The water is heavenly."

He takes off his shirt showing his tanned, muscular body. His manhood is bulging in his pantaloons as he slides into the water. He takes William from me and, as he does so, he accidentally brushes his hand against my breasts. My nipples point out of my shift. He reaches out to me. "Oh heavens, my Evangeline. I am unable to help myself. I need you close to me."

I feel his hardness between us. My groin tingles, and he kisses me passionately on my lips and grasps my bottom. Then he suddenly stops himself. "I am so sorry. I apologize profusely."

I feel the heat rise in my face. "No need. I was also caught up in the moment."

He takes my hands in his. "We can never let this happen again," he insists. "Daniel would surely kill both of us."

We play in the water and enjoy the day. We talk about our plans to escape. We explore the cavern behind the waterfall. "I helped Daniel hide some of his treasure in the cavern further in the cave," Roger confides. "We hid it behind a large rock. When we go back to my hut, I will draw a map to help us find it later. I plan to steal some of the treasure before our escape back home. We will bring Cook with us when we escape, too. We must wait for the perfect time."

I think of the others brought to this island by force. "Katrina and Eleanor might want to escape," I tell Roger, "But I am not sure. It is complicated because I believe they are both in love with the fathers of their children. I think their minds have been changed since our capture."

Then I add, excitedly, "Do you think it is possible that we might one day leave this place?"

Roger sighs. "Do not worry. I will get you and your baby home to your family if it is the last thing I do. You need to sew the jewels that Daniel has given you into the hem of your gowns. Hide the clues, map and love letters Daniel has given you in the hidden compartment of the picture frames that I made for you. You must never tell anyone of our plans as it could be fatal for both of us."

I turn to Roger and say, "We must meet again soon to plan our escape. I can talk with Cook while I am helping him with dinner. We must be careful that no one ever hears of our plans to escape. We must wait until the time is right."

Our plan moves forward. I sew all my jewels Daniel has given me into the hems and secret pockets of my gowns. The two pictures Roger has drawn for me—with frames containing hidden compartments—will come with us, too. Cook is stashing away dried fruits and meats to take on our journey home.

Sally, who lives with the first mate, Jeffrey, has become one of my friends. She and her husband visit my home with Daniel frequently. Once, when we are away from the men, Sally starts crying. "I still miss my home and family. Jeffrey says he will take me home one day. He is tired of pirating. He would like to go to North America and make a living one day. I am so thrilled at the idea." She has a two-year-old girl named Catherine. I speak to Roger and tell him of her plans to escape. "Sally and Jeffrey plan to escape one day. Maybe they can come with us," I say.

"I will try to help them, too, but say nothing to them until the actual escape as it could be dangerous," he warns. "The more people who know, the more the chances we will be found out."

Ours plans evolve. Joseph, Katrina, Eleanor, and James have all become a part of my life. I will miss them when we are gone. Their children, Evan, and Amelia, play with my young William. They all love to play together on the seashore.

Roger and Jeffrey enjoy working together to make furniture for the others on the island. They have become skilled at woodworking. Oh, how I hope Jeffrey and Sally can come with us on our grand escape, but I dare not breathe a word.

I watch as we celebrate our third Christmas on the island. All the women have made gifts for the others. We decorate the palm tree with seashell ornaments and popcorn strings we have made. At one point, I cannot stop my tears. I tell Eleanor and Katrina, "It does not feel like Christmas. It is so warm here, and I miss my family.

But I am blessed to have you to share this special time with."

Roger has made William little wooden blocks to play with and carved him a small wooden boat. Daniel gives our son toys he brought back his latest trip to Jamaica.

Daniel has also brought me back gifts: two beautiful ruby hair combs and a dazzling sapphire bracelet with a key hidden in it. "This key will unlock my treasure chest," he tells me. "I found these sapphires. They are the color of your eyes." He shows me how to remove the key from my bracelet.

He brings me jewelry after each of his journeys. I act pleased as I take the treasures he offers me, but I tell Roger how I really feel. "I know that these once belonged to another and were stolen. I act excited but really it makes me quite sad thinking of the people who have lost their precious possessions and, quite possibly, their lives. He tells me he plans to cover me in jewels."

William turns two today. Roger and Daniel are away on a trip to the Bahamas. We celebrate my son's birthday with my friends, Sally, Eleanor, Katrina, and our children. Robert has taught me how to bake a cake with fresh fruits and frostings. You should have seen the frosting on my William's precious face. He enjoys his sweet treats. I am so glad that I learned how to cook over the last few years.

Later that evening Roger comes running into my bungalow. "Hurry, you must pack your things! We are leaving now!" he shouts. "There was a vicious storm while we were on our way home, and Daniel has been lost at sea. I am now the captain of his ship as I am his only relative.

"We must hurry and make our escape before other pirates in the area become aware of Daniel's death."

Roger hurriedly helps me pack my gowns into the cedar chest he made me. The jewelry is hidden in the garments. We grab the charcoal picture and watercolor painting Roger gave me. The hidden compartments of their frames hold all my love letters, clues, and Daniel's maps to Blackbeard's treasure.

Roger hugs me, "Sally, Jeffrey, and the others are coming with us. Sally and Jeffrey will make port in South Carolina. They plan to find her family there and make a life together. Joseph and Katrina will make their home on Ocracoke Island. He will make a loyal quartermaster. He is very much like me and has never liked being a pirate. James and Eleanor Payne also plan to come with us to Ocracoke Island. So, your dream has come true."

My head is spinning. I gather up my belongings and all of little William's things that I can load in my chest. My babe is whimpering in my arms, unsure of what all the commotion means. We run to the ship—Roger and Jeffrey help get my chest on board. As Jeffrey lifts one of my bags, he calls to me, "Hurry, ma'am, we must get sailing before the other pirates find out Daniel is dead. Once they know, they will surely try to take his ship and crew."

With a full crew and Cook—our friend Robert—we set sail.

"Some of the men on board are only here to help us on our journey. Once they leave us on shore, they will return to their life of pirating," Roger explains. "We are lucky they respect us. They vow to get you back to your home."

I am both sad and overwhelmed with joy. I shed many tears of joy. "I am truly sad that Daniel has perished, but I cannot wait to be back with my family. I feared this day would never come," I say. I think back on that fateful day when I was captured by Jeffrey and his mates and dragged aboard this very same sloop, kicking and screaming. I tremble remembering that day.

I stand on the bow of the ship with a steady breeze blowing through my dark hair as I watch the tiny coral-colored beach disappear into the horizon. My friends Eleanor, Sally, and Katrina stand with me as the island grows smaller and smaller until we can no longer see it.

I pat little William on his back to soothe him, then I turn to my friends. "I have longed for this day when we could escape. I am so happy to have you here with me, my friends. Our crew is loyal to Joseph and will see us safely to our destinations. Some of them plan *to stay on with Roger and use this vessel as a cargo ship. Roger says others will join as mates on other pirate ships. For now, they will keep us all safe."*

I think of my family and wonder what changes have occurred in my absence. I was but a girl when I was taken. I now return as a woman. I tell my friends on the ship, "I worry if William will be accepted by my family. I am afraid of what Papa will say about me having a child out of wedlock. I hope I will not be such a disgrace to my family."

To myself, I wonder what my love Jacob is doing and if he has moved on with his life. I wonder what he would think of our little William. I cannot believe it has been three years since I was gone. I was 17 when I left in him and now, I am 20 years old. No one will ever know that William is Jacob's child. The shame would be too much.

It takes four long weeks for us complete our journey. We made port in South Carolina so Jeffrey and Sally could go on to find her family. When they were married aboard our ship, Sally explained, "I do not plan to tell my family that Jeffrey was my captor. I fear for his life if it were found out that he was a pirate. He would surely be hung in the gallows. I will tell them that he rescued me from the pirates."

One day I hear a crew member yell, "Land ho," and I feel my heart beating wildly in my chest. I am home and anxious to be reunited with my family.

We arrive at my family home. I knock on the heavy wooden door, calling out, "Papa, I am home." I believe I that I almost gave my papa heart failure. I stand in the doorway with Roger and William.

My father grabs me and hugs me so tightly. Tears pour down his cheeks. "My dear child, I thought you had perished in the sea. Roger, you have brought my girl home to me. But how… what happened? Where have you been all these years and who is this young child with you?" Our tears are flowing freely, and we are shaking in joy.

Elizabeth, my sister, hears the commotion and comes rushing out. David White, Emily's brother, is now my sister's husband. He also rushes out. They carry a toddler. My sister hugs all of us. "We thought you had drowned at sea, except Emily. She always thought you were still alive. We searched for days for you. Papa was heartbroken, as we all were." Roger takes little William from me so that I can tell everyone the story of my capture.

I tearfully explain. "I was abducted by Daniel Teach's crew and taken to a place called Cat Island. As you will remember, Roger took a job with Daniel—and Roger was able to rescue me. Daniel was a dangerous villain. He kept me as his possession. My son was born on the island. He is Daniel's child."

I continued. "Daniel drowned at sea, so Roger was able to help us escape. Because he was Daniel's only relative, he now has control of the ship."

Elizabeth cries and hugs me. "We thought you had drowned in the surf. We found your heart pendant necklace, the letter from Jacob, and the letter you had written to him. We did not know what had happened to you."

Chapter 7

The Attic

There is silence in the room as I stop reading and close the journal. Evangeline's homecoming is the last entry.

The story ends there, and I can feel Evangeline's pain. There isn't a dry eye in our group. We are all thinking about Evangeline and Jacob, the young couple who were never able to meet again. My friend Emily wipes a tear from her eye. "Wow, that was amazing. To think Jacob and Evangeline were never reunited. It's just so tragic. He went on with his life because he thought she was dead. He never even knew William was his son."

Sarah asks, "Do you think there is another journal hidden somewhere on the island about the rest of Evangeline's life? Can you imagine how it was back then having to rely on letters to communicate with everyone?"

Emily shrugs. "The rest of her journals are probably on Cat Island or in one of her chests upstairs. We will have to keep looking to see if we can find any more journals. We are so spoiled nowadays, just being able to call, text, or email the ones we love. When Evangeline lived, there were times when family members didn't know for weeks, maybe months or even years if one of their loved ones had died. Just think about the Lost Colonists and their fates. To this day, no one knows what happened to them."

I grimace. "Well, maybe we will find out more when we visit Cat Island. I'm curious to see if this Virginia woman who showed up in my dreams and visited Evangeline will make an appearance when we visit the island. In the meantime, I guess we should get busy with our research and plans."

Paul holds the journal in his hands. "There is so much history and information in this journal. I think that maybe we might just be able to find Blackbeard's treasure."

Sarah picks up the diamond ring and emerald brooch we found in the coffer in my father's office, and they spread them out on the table beside the pearl necklace and garnet hair comb. I still can't believe my father had all this stashed away without telling us.

"All those letters and other pieces of jewelry that we found during the summer in other hidden boxes and secret compartments make so much more sense now," Sarah says. "I thought maybe those jewels were part of Blackbeard's treasure, but now I think they were the gifts Daniel had given to Evangeline, gems that he had pirated. If this isn't from Blackbeard's hidden treasure, it means those riches are still to be found."

Paul smiles. "We should start trying to put the clues on the map to so we know the best places to search on Cat Island. There are so many areas that we can look. For certain we will have to locate the lagoon where Evangeline and William used to swim. I think that will be a good place to start."

My grandfather points to the pieces of map that we found during the summer. We have spread out on the table. "Look at this map of Cat Island. There is one area on the map that has a triangle pointing down with a circle in the center."

He explains. "The triangle pointing down stands for water and in the center is a circle. The circle inside the triangle means that there is a cave inside the water. Beside the symbol, there is a picture of a dagger. That is a symbol for danger—and it goes along with the story of the booby traps Daniel set up to guard his treasures against thieves. There are some other symbols on the map."

Matt is looking at one of the letters. "Roger and Evangeline were really quite smart separating the different sections of the treasure map. I still can't believe we have been able to find all the pieces.

I sigh. "I feel like we are still missing clues we need to find the treasures."

Sally points to the attic stairs. "Maybe we need to explore the rest of the chests in the attic here and at David's home." George nods in agreement. "Remember that we're going to renovate my home next," he says. "Who knows what we will find there?"

Thomas laughs. "Yeah, for sure. You never know what we might find. Maybe even another pirate's treasure map."

We all laugh at that, even as we excitedly wonder if it is truly possible to find Blackbeard's treasure.

Robert smiles and says to Sally, "I think we need to hit the sack. Our twins await us, and we have a big week ahead of us with working on our new house tomorrow."

Robert hugs his dad. "I can't thank you enough for such a wonderful gift—the house! I feel like I have already hit the jackpot. I have a beautiful family and a spectacular home."

Matt pats Robert on the back. "Thomas, George, and I will be working to help you guys. What time do you want to start in the morning?"

Sally yawns. "Not too early. I need to get the twins fed before I can come over to help."

We all decide to call it a night. As Thomas and I walk back to my cottage, I put my arm around him and grin.

Chapter 8

The Planning Continues

We all begin looking for as much information as we can find on Cat Island. The next time we're all together, Paul tells us about a place called Mount Alvernia that he says we need to visit.

"It used to be called Cosmo Hill and it has the highest peak on the island with an elevation reaching 206 feet," he says. "There are thought to be numerous underground caverns and caves on the mountain. It would be a great place to hide treasure.

"It's a little farther away from where Daniel and Evangeline were living. But we definitely can keep it on our radar," he adds. "Oh, and remember that Arthur Cat, the man that the island was named after, was a good friend of Blackbeard. The island was originally known as San Salvador, but later was renamed after Arthur Cat."

As he explains that the island has a lot of history and so many places that we can visit, we start taking note of where he thinks we should look. He mentions Mermaid Hole, also known for a folklore of mermaids capturing young children. It was thought to be a legend invented to prevent children from drowning if they ventured too closed to the water.

"According to the books I've been reading, there are four blue holes that have several underground caverns and passageways," he says, excitedly. "Did you know that they used these underground caverns to hide during storms and hurricanes? Can you imagine? It must have really been scary."

I remind them that in some of my dreams I have seen Evangeline go to a place with a waterfall and a lagoon, and there is a cave behind the waterfall. "I wonder if this would be a good place for us to start," I say. "In my dream, I saw Evangeline take young William to the lagoon to swim. Evangeline told me that this was their special place, a place where she would go to hide away from Daniel, to be alone and dream about Jacob."

My mind wanders back to that dream. "I can feel everything that Evangeline felt. All her love and sadness at missing Jacob and her family. And I can also feel the love that she feels for William."

Paul points to a waterfall on the map. "That does sound like a good place to start. We just must figure out where it is," he says. "Hopefully, once we get to the island, we can identify the different landmarks from your dreams, and we'll be able to find her special place.

"When Robert and I were researching the island, we also read about a place called Orange Creek," Paul continues. "Apparently, there is a plant on the floor of the creek that makes the water look orange. Our research indicated that you can only get there by kayak. Luckily, the place we're going to stay has a lot of kayaks and diving equipment we can use to explore the island.

"We will still need to be careful that none of the locals figure out one of our true reasons for going to Cat Island," he warns.

Thomas speaks up. "There is another good location that we will need to check out. It's called the Big Blue Hole. It is a freshwater lake that flows into the sea through the caverns. The freshwater mixes with the saltwater. If nothing else, it looks like a great place to go snorkeling."

He gets a look on his face like he is remembering something, then he continues. "Once when we were in Mexico, we went to an eco-park that had a cavern where you could actually see the mixture of the salt and the freshwater when you snorkeled. It formed what looked like a veil in the water. It was really cool. You girls are really going to love it when you scuba. It is unbelievable the sights you can see."

Emily has a big grin on her face. "I am so glad that we signed up for scuba diving classes. It's something that I'd always wanted to do. It's gonna' make for quite an adventure," she says. "I hear that the tropical fish around the Bahamas are beautiful. I can't believe we're going to get to do this experience together. "

Sarah laughs and kisses Matt on the cheek. "And I get to marry the love of my life on a beautiful tropical Island. Who could ask for more than that? Unless …," she pauses, "we find the buried treasure that once belonged to Blackbeard!

"I can't wait to get to our resort, Shannon Cove. It really looks beautiful. It's right near Orange Creek, which you guys were talking about. The website said it's very close to Bain Town," she continues. "I've been in contact with the owners, Maria, and Gregor. They offer many different dive sites, including the ones that you guys were just talking about. They have all the snorkeling and dive gear that we will need right there on site.

"I was looking at pictures on the website the other day. Oh, my heavens, you should see the beautiful sunsets. And the dive sites look absolutely gorgeous. The water is a crystal blue, and you can see to the bottom of the sea."

Paul picks up one of the ancient maps. "Well, with all these clues, we shouldn't have any problem finding the treasure—that is, if it's actually still there. The wedding is definitely a great cover up for our plans to find the buried treasure. I'm sure there are still pirates down there on the island who would love to get their hands on Blackbeard's loot.

"Sarah, by the way, how are your wedding plans going? Have you girls already picked out dresses and all?" he asks.

Blushing, Sarah replies, "That's one of the reasons why the girls and I are having a planning party tonight. We are going to pick out our dresses."

Sarah has always been a dreamer. Ever since we were little girls wandering the island together, with our pigtails blowing in the breeze, and swimming in the cool Carolina surf, she has dreamed of becoming Matt's wife. Sarah has asked Emily to be her maid of honor. My sister Sally and I will be her bridesmaids. As Sarah talks about the wedding, I spot tears in the eyes of her mother, Sally. They are tears of joy as she watches her girls.

My mother, Isabella, hugs Sarah's mom and says, "I know how you feel. It's so hard watching our girls grow up. Emily and Sarah are just like my girls, too. The years just keep flying by and it's hard to not think of them as children. But just wait until you have grandchildren!"

My mother adds, with a touch of sadness in her voice, "We're so lucky to have all our memories."

David wraps his arms around Mom and kisses her lightly on the cheek. He knows she is thinking of my father, George. And I suspect he is thinking of his dearly departed wife, Samantha.

"I know it is crazy watching them grow up so fast," David says. "George and Samantha would be so proud of all our kids."

David has been so good for my mom. I can't even imagine how much it hurts not having my father by her side. David is a godsend. He has become like a second father to me and my siblings. We are so happy he is with us.

After we finish going over our plans and research, we leave to go to the mainland. The girls and I, as well as Sally, Sarah's mom, my mom, and my grandmother, Mary, are heading to a bridal shop called Weddings by the Sea to look for Sarah's wedding dress. Sarah is absolutely ecstatic.

"I have dreamt of this day for as long as I can remember," she says. "Years ago, when we used to go up in the attic and play dress up, I can remember that the wedding dress that belonged to mom was up there. We used to play dress up with it all the time.

"I can't wait to see what dresses we decide on," she says. "Weddings by the Sea is supposed to have a great selection. The owner told me there are a lot of tourists that like to come to the Outer Banks to get married."

Emily taps her phone. "I called ahead to schedule an appointment to try on dresses. The shop has everything a bridal party will need—even for a bridal beach wedding."

By the time we reach the bridal store, Sarah's face is flushed with excitement. Sally hugs her daughter. "Sarah, you are going to make such a beautiful bride, darling."

Sarah's beautiful blonde hair flows gently down her back. Her green eyes glow brightly when she stands in front of the full-length mirror. She has chosen an ivory-colored gown with a V neck. It has beading and sequins around the neckline and the bodice. Sarah knew she wanted the dress the moment she saw it. The front of the gown is shorter in the front than in the back.

Emily gasps when she sees her sister in the gown. "It's going to be a perfect dress for a beach wedding. You look so pretty," she says.

Their mom chooses a coral-colored skirt and a matching jacket. She has the same beautiful bright green eyes as Sarah. Tears prickle her eyelashes as she looks at her gorgeous daughters.

We are able to find bridesmaids dresses for my sister and me. Sally hasn't gotten dressed up since she had the twins. "I'm so excited," she says. "This style is perfect for a beach wedding. I just love it." She dances and prances around us in the dress Sarah has chosen for us, knee-length dusty-rose dresses with V-necks and chiffon lace.

When it comes time for my mom to pick out her dress, she goes with a misty, sky-blue gown that matches perfectly her pale blue eyes. A hint of sadness flashes briefly in those eyes. "I can remember back to the day when your father and I were married on Ocracoke Island. We were married on the sandy shores in front of the Shepard's Head Inn."

My grandmother hugs my mom and kisses her on the cheek. "You look as beautiful now as you did back then. I know how much you must miss George."

Emily is having trouble finding a gown. She has always been such a tomboy. "I never wear dresses. This is all totally foreign to me," she says. Sarah picks out a pale wisteria-colored dress for her sister. "Here, try this one, Emily. It will look great with that strawberry blonde hair of yours. Your hair is darker than mine."

She tries on the dress. When Emily walks out of the dressing room, we are in awe at the transformation. The fabric flows gently over her thin frame. Her bright green eyes sparkle, and the color of the gown accentuates them. Sarah cries out to her sister, "It's perfect. Emily, you look so beautiful. Just wait until George sees you."

Emily blushes furiously. "Oh, be quiet. You know we're just friends. He doesn't feel that way about me."

I laugh. "You're so wrong Emily. George is crazy about you."

Now it's time for my grandmother, Mary, to find her dress. She finds an aqua colored dress that reaches just below her knees. Her gray hair in combination with the color of the gown makes her hazel eyes shine. Today they're green with flecks of gold that sparkle as she watches her daughter, granddaughters, and her friends. "You girls make me so happy. I have never been happier than I am today," she says. "I am so glad we decided to stay on the island with the rest of the family."

Our blessed group leaves the little boutique after we find just what we need for Sarah and Matt's wedding. We drive over to one of our favorite spots on the Outer Banks for lunch. Mom pulls into the parking lot of Goombay's Grille and Raw Bar. "This is the perfect place for our special lunch. They always have some of the best local seafood and fresh summer veggies," I say. "I love their steamed shrimp and vegetables. Everything here is always tasty."

After lunch, we head back to Ocracoke. The sun is sparkling like diamonds over the water as we drive over the Bonner Bridge down Highway 12. Sarah says, "They may have changed the name, but this bridge will always be the Bonner Bridge to me."

Whitecaps are splashing over the sand bars in the channel. Pelicans and seagulls glide over Pamlico Sound. Above them, puffy white clouds float across the crystal blue sky—the color of sky you see after a hurricane. The ferry chugs through the aqua-blue water, and our little group stands at the bow of the ship. We watch the dolphins frolic in the breakers.

Sarah smiles at us. "It has been such a wonderful day. Thank you all for making it so special."

Sally hugs Sarah. "I wouldn't have missed it for the world, but now I miss my babies. You know, I haven't been away from them since they were born, other than the half days that I go to work. I thank God every day that Georgia is able to help us with the twins. This is the first time in a long time that I've had a girls' day out. I love my new teaching job at the little island school—and a half-day teaching is just perfect."

My mind drifts and I smile thinking about Thomas. I haven't had a minute alone with him since we came back from Maryland. I was so exhausted the last couple nights after the drive and the storm and that I literally fell asleep when my head hit the pillow. How I long to feel his strong muscular body up against mine.

Emily teases me. "Are you daydreaming about Thomas? You have that love-glazed look in your eyes."

I laugh and say, "How did you know?"

The ferry pulls into the dock as it always does, with the familiar sound of the gears shifting—chugga, chugga, chugga, chugg. It's not long before we're back home from our fun-filled day. Sarah must go check on the inn. She left her father, Jim, in charge of the B&B. Emily and I are both scheduled to be at the pub at 4 p.m. The hours this time of year are shorter. There is a crisp breeze blowing across the Bay. Fall is coming quickly, and the evenings are getting cooler.

Isabella, Sally, and Mary are going to David's house to see the latest renovation work. My sister looks at her watch,

"I need to check on the twins first, but I'll see you all later," Sally says. She hugs us all good-bye. We all head off in different directions.

Chapter 9

More Secrets Found

The makeover continues at the beautiful old home—one of the oldest on Ocracoke Island—that David has given to Robert, Sally, and their twins. As part of this amazing gift, David has hired Matt and Thomas to renovate the structure. Since his wife's passing, the home where David raised his two sons has felt like too much of a responsibility for him, so he has passed it down to the next generation. But that doesn't stop him from helping out with the renovation. The kitchen and the dining room are almost completed. Today Thomas' cousin, Billy, is working on the stonework on the kitchen fireplace with the help of Robert.

David brings up all the tools he has in his workshop in the basement. Robert walks up the stairs behind him, helping him carry his hammers, mallets, trowels, and paint brushes. "Dad, this is going to be so cool, us working on the house with the rest of the guys. I never in a million years would have thought it would be possible for us all to have moved here," Robert says.

Standing at the top of the dusty old stairs, David pats Robert on his back. "Oh son, you just don't know how happy it makes me to see Sally and you move into this home where we have built so many memories. My heart has finally started to heal after losing your mom. It's been so hard for me to return here but now I can see a whole new future."

Robert clasps his dad's hand. "Oh dad, you just don't know how much this means to Sally and me. Our lives are so blessed, and I can't thank you enough for giving us your home."

After a pause, Robert starts moving toward the kitchen. "I guess I should go give Billy a hand. Thomas and Matt are going to start on one of the rooms upstairs," he says. "I think Sally, Angie, Emily, and Sarah are going to come over at some point to start putting things in boxes for you so that we can see what we to keep, donate or get rid of. Right now, they're taking their morning walk on the beach."

David scratches his chin. "I'm so glad the girls are going through everything in all the bedrooms. I just haven't had the heart to do it," he says. "George has a job on Hatteras this morning but he's going to come by later to check out the AC unit. You know we replaced it about five years ago, but it could probably use some maintenance. I'm going to start clearing out some the boxes in the attic so we can make that it into a playroom for the twins."

After Billy gives instructions on how to safely remove the disintegrating grout without damaging the beautiful gray and rust colored stones. Robert, and Billy get to work on the crumbling mortar that they plan to replace. In the middle of the work, Billy calls out, "Hey guys, come see what I just found!"

Thomas and Matt run down the stairs from the second floor to see what Billy has just found: a key hidden under one of the stones in the hearth.

"It looks like someone liked to use their fireplace as a hiding spot. I wonder what this key unlocks," Billy says.

As the men discuss the key, David hears the commotion and comes down from the attic, where he has been working. "That's so funny. I've just made a discovery, too," he says. "In the attic I came across a door hidden behind some boxes, but I can't get it open—it's locked."

They all laugh as Thomas holds up the key. "Well, let's see if this key will fit that door." After a pause, he adds: "Wouldn't it be cool if we found more hidden treasures behind the door?"

David takes the key and states, "I still can't believe all the hidden gems, jewelry, coins, and other treasures we found when you guys renovated the cottage Evangeline lived in so many years ago. I wonder if there any more of the special coffers like we found earlier this summer."

Matts laughs remembering all the things they found in Angie's home. "Yeah, so far, we've found diamond and gold rings, rubies, gold coins and pearls. I wonder what 's next?"

At that moment, my mother, my grandmother and Sarah's mother arrive at the house. Isabella walks in and sees David examining the key in his hand.

She asks, "What does that key belongs to?"

David shrugs his shoulders. "We're not really sure. They guys found it under a stone in the fireplace. By coincidence, I just came across a door hidden behind some boxes in the attic. Do you ladies want to come watch as we head upstairs to see if this key will unlock the door?"

As we climb the starts to the attic, we hear Evangeline's laughter tinkling in the background. We are all waiting in anticipated suspense. David slips the key into the lock, turns it, and hears a click. He pulls the door open to reveal a small room. Dust mites dance in the dwindling sunlight that flickers through the stained-glass window.

David turns to the others. "This room looks like no one has seen it in several hundred years. Wow, see the heavy wooden chests over there? And look at that easel and all those canvases resting up against the wall. There isn't even any electricity in the room. We're going to need some light in here."

"I wonder how long this has all been shut away," he muses.

"Dad, I'll get a lamp and extension cord," Robert says to his father. "It looks to me like this room hasn't been seen in forever."

As they slowly start to explore the room, Robert moves toward the easel, which is covered with an old burlap cloth.

"Let's see what we have here," David says as he removes the burlap to reveal a painting. Isabella gasps.

Propped on the easel, a spectacular portrait stares back at the group. It is Evangeline sitting in a rocking chair, and she's holding young William in her arms. Isabella's voice carries her awe. "It looks just like Angie—and the child looks like my grandson Jacob," she says, astonished.

They all stare at the picture. Isabella continues to be amazed. "I can't believe Angie's likeness to Evangeline and young William's likeness to Jacob. It's fascinating," she says. "Would you all mind if I take the painting? I have the perfect place for it over our fireplace."

Just as Isabella reaches for the canvas, Evangeline materializes in the dusty room. "Do not be alarmed," the misty image says. "Don't be frightened. I will protect all of you."

Thomas turns to look at the specter and Evangeline winks at him. "Thomas, take good care of Angie and never let her go. Follow your heart, as it will not steer you wrong," she says. "You have truly found your soulmate just as I have found mine in Jacob. Our love that was lost was reunited when you and Angie found our necklaces."

She disappears and the vision fades into the dusty air.

Matt laughs at the look on Thomas's face. He pats him on the back. "Been there and heard that from Evangeline, too," Matt says. "Remember the night I told you all about when she told me to follow my heart about Sarah? She didn't steer me wrong. I have never been happier.

"I can remember, just like it was yesterday," he continues. "I had just come back from telling Sarah how I felt about her and was so worried about our feelings for each other. Evangeline came to me and told me to follow my heart that I wouldn't be disappointed. Boy was she ever right. I have never been happier."

We move from the easel to look at the other paintings—there are about twenty of them—leaned up against the walls of the little room. David uncovers some of the pictures, "Most of these are seascapes, but there several of Evangeline," he says. Then he points to the signature on every one of the canvases: Roger Brown.

"He was an excellent artist. Look how the colors burst off the canvas. He has captured beautiful images of the sea, almost like a real photograph," David says. "It's a shame he was never recognized as a famous artist.

"Wow, look at this one," David continues. "This is a painting of what the original old plantation home looked like over 250 years ago."

Everyone takes one or more of ancient paintings to carry down into the dining room of the house. Robert picks up one and looks at it carefully. "I think we should take some of these to the Ocracoke Historical Society. I really feel the paintings should be on exhibit," he says

Isabella takes the painting of Evangeline and little William and clutches it to her chest. "I think you're right Robert. This island and its residents should be able to enjoy this beautiful work. Maybe you and Sally will want to put some in your house, too."

Robert picks up one of the seascapes, "I think this one would look fantastic over our mantel, but I'll have to get Sally to look at them first."

Isabella turns to Thomas. "What about you and Angie?" she asks. "Do you and my daughter want one for your cottage?"

Thomas studies one of the sunset pictures. "I think Angie would like this one, but let's let the girls decide before we take any of them to the Ocracoke Museum," he says.

Thomas has also found a sketchbook among the things removed from the attic.

"Check this out, guys. There are multiple drawings of Evangeline, William, and Evangeline's other family members," Thomas says. "Luckily, Roger has written the names of all the people in the portraits he drew. What a find! Now we can put faces to the names of everyone."

After a minute, he adds: "Angie is going to love this! Maybe she can use some of them in her new novel."

They decide to take the painting of Evangeline and William back to Shepard's Inn for safekeeping for now. David holds up the canvas, studies it for a minute, and speaks to Isabella.

"That painting of Evangeline and William is going to look very nice over your fireplace. Sally is going to be so shocked when she sees the resemblance between Evangeline and Angie and how much William looks like little Jacob."

Thomas turns to Angie's mother. "Isabella, I agree with David—I think that painting will look nice in your home. It belongs there with you."

David then glances toward the window. "It's starting to get late. Isabella, do you need to head back home?"

Everyone decides it is time to call it day. Thomas takes the sketchbook home with him. "I can't wait to show this to Angie. She's going to love it," he says. "I'm going to take it to the pub. She's working tonight with Emily. I want to show my brother George this sketchbook, too.

When Thomas arrives back at the cottage we share, he smells my light citrusy perfume lingering in the air. He closes his eyes and thinks about how deeply he's fallen in love with me. "It's crazy," he says out loud. "I've only known her for four short months and I'm head over heels in love with her. What am I going to do, Max?"

The dog perks up when he hears his name. The puppy whines then picks up his rope toy and nudges it into Thomas's knees. Thomas reaches down to pet the happy puppy, then he stands up and reaches for Max's lease. "Come on boy. Let's take a walk before we head over to the pub for dinner."

Max barks and excitedly dashes towards the door. Thomas and the dog head out the door and walk down to the beach. They arrive just as the sun is starting to set. Thomas sighs as he watches the glimmering sun dip down below the horizon. The colors tonight are a spectacular display of melon, tangerine, lavender, and purples.

Dusk brings with it a chilly autumn breeze. Thomas pulls up his collar and zips up his fleece jacket. He whistles for Max to come along so he can walk him back to the cottage. Thomas showers and makes his way across the street to the pub.

I'm already into my set when I look up to see Thomas walk into the quaint neighborhood tavern with Max. The dog comes up to greet me while I'm playing and rests his head on my foot. Thomas orders drinks and pizza from Emily. Thomas waves to me and blows me a kiss. I am playing my guitar and singing the lyrics to my new song about Ocracoke.

'Ocracoke, I will always remember your sandy shores
that hold so many memories for me.
I love to watch the pipers and pelicans playing in your surf.
Stunning sunsets dip down into your tranquil sound
and transport me to your gentle realm.
I remember our bonfires on the beach,
so peaceful and mesmerizing.'

There are a handful of people in the bar, most of them locals. Only a scattering of the tourists remain on the island. Most of those at the pub tonight are anglers. Even though it's a small audience, applause explodes when I finish my song. I bow my head and wave to the crowd. "Thank you everyone. I'll be back shortly."

I watch as Thomas recognizes several of the locals and stops by to talk to them. He tells me later that two of the guys that are in the pub tonight graduated from high school with him. I love watching him socialize with everyone he knows on the island.

Thomas eventually makes his way to a table where George, Sarah, and Matt are talking. I head over toward them and wrap my arms around Thomas. I kiss him gently on the lips. "Hi, honey. How was your day?" I love the masculine taste of him and the feel of his soft lips on mine.

He gently kisses me and runs his fingers through my wavy black hair. "Even better now that you're here with me." Then he leans over and whispers in my ear. "I've been thinking about doing this all day."

This time of year, most of the people in the little bar start leaving by 8 or by 9 p.m. This, too, will be an early night. As I start to pull up a chair at the table, I see Emily leave the bar area and head over to join us. At that moment, Thomas pulls out what looks like a sketch book from the pocket of his fleece jacket. "I have something to show you. Look what we found in Robert and Sally's home today," he says.

Emily arrives just as Thomas starts showing us the little sketchbook that had once belonged to Roger Brown. "Look at these drawings," Thomas says. "I recognize a lot of the names from the old family tree in the Alexander family bible. The sketches are of Evangeline's family."

He holds one sketch up for everyone to see. "It's amazing how much you and Evangeline looked alike," Thomas says with awe in his voice, "The other crazy thing is there's also a picture of Emily White from the 1750s. And she looks just like you Emily! It's kind of spooky when you think about it."

Emily stares at the drawing of her ancestor. "I don't think I've ever seen a picture of Emily White when she was my age," she says. "All the pictures I've seen of her were when she was older."

I am looking at one page after another in the sketchbook. "I'll have to figure out how to use some of these in my novel," I say.

Thomas nods. "I thought you might feel that way." Then he yawns. "Angie, I need to get an early start in the morning. I think I need to head home. What about you?"

George points to the bar. "I can help Emily clean up the bar if y'all want to leave."

We get up to go. "Goodnight, everybody. See you tomorrow."

Thomas, Max, and I walk hand in hand across the street to our little cottage. We enter the cottage and Thomas immediately wraps his arms around me. "I have been thinking about you all day. I miss you when we're apart." He lifts me in his arms, carrying me to our bed. "I want you so bad. I love you baby," he whispers to me.

I groan when his soft lips brush my neck. "I love you too," I respond. "I want to feel your body next to mine. I've missed you so much."

Our clothes fall down around us. Thomas takes me into his arms and playfully kisses every inch of my body. I feel the heat rise up between us as his lips reach my most tenders areas and he sends me over the edge. We both explode in ecstasy and gasp out in pleasure.

Thomas kisses me passionately on the lips. "Angie, I love you so much. I know it's only been four months, but my heart is yours."

"I have been in love with you all these months, too," I say, tenderly. "I can't imagine you not being in my life." I gently kiss him on his nose and lips. We fall asleep wrapped in each other's arms, joined together in a lingering lust.

The day dawns with dazzling sunshine rising over the horizon. Thomas has already taken Max out for his walk and returned to the cottage to get ready for work. He kisses me on the forehead. "Good morning, sleepyhead. I'm leaving now. I need to get started on today's job. I'm taking Max with me. Have a great day."

The morning air is as brisk and crisp as an early fall apple when Thomas strolls down the lane with his excited pup. He is enjoying his walk over the cobblestone pathway with the oyster shells mixed in between. Thomas stops and stoops down to pet Max. "I can't believe how happy I am and how lucky we are that most of our customers are dog lovers," he says. He wraps his hands over Max's head and playfully rubs the puppy's ears.

Thomas is thinking of Angie. He reaches up to touch the half-heart pendant around his neck—the duplicate of the one around her neck. He thinks about the day they met. It was five months ago but it feels like just yesterday. It's November. Also, in some ways, he feels like he's known her forever.

Thomas remembers Angie walking into her cottage as he was working to renovate the stone fireplace. He had just found the heart-shaped necklace and he was holding it up to show her. Angie instinctively reached up to touch the very same necklace around her neck, then held her fingers out toward the necklace Thomas was holding.

As their fingers touched, Evangeline appeared before Thomas for the first time. Angie had to reassure him—she had seen the ghostly specter of the island's famous yesteryear resident a few times before.

Thomas thinks about Evangeline and Jacob, of the time in the island's history when they said good-bye to one another. Jacob had to leave to help his family get settled in Williamsburg area, but he vowed to return to make Evangeline his wife.

Thomas remembers the day of the necklace discovery when he and Angie witnessed an apparition of Evangeline and Jacob bidding each other farewell. Thomas still is astounded by the ferocity of the passion that exploded between the two young lovers. How sad, he thinks, that neither Evangeline nor Jacob realized this would be the last moment they would share together.

He wonders to himself that he had never felt that much love and passion—until now. His heart leaps when he thinks about how much he loves Angie. He has decided that he will ask her to marry him. He is impatient and wants to do it now, but he worries that it is too soon.

He continues thinking about Angie as he rounds the corner and get ready to go down the cobblestone driveway. As he does, he reaches up to touch the heart-shaped pendant. Immediately, a spectacular vision of Evangeline and Jacob appears before his eyes. Evangeline tells him, "Thomas, follow your heart."

Jacob adds his own warning. "Thomas don't let her get away. Don't suffer the heartache that I did."

Evangeline seconds the thought. "You have found your true soulmate. Only a few are ever so lucky. Do not let her get away." Evangeline and Jacob fade away before his eyes. Max wags his tail watching the encounter.

Thomas is unnerved by the vision. He continues down the lane to Robert and Sally's home to find that Matt has just arrived, too. Matt takes one look at Thomas and asks, "You, okay? You look like you just saw a ghost."

Thomas tells Matt about his encounter with Evangeline and Jacob. "I was deep in thought when they appeared before me," Thomas says before adding, "I want to ask Angie to marry me. Do you think it's too early?

Matt pats Thomas on the shoulder. "Man, nothing would make her happier. She fell in love with you the day you met. I love my sister and would be thrilled have you for brother-in-law and part of our family."

Matt pauses, looks thoughtful, then continues. "Thomas, sometimes things are just meant to be. I know that you love her. She lived with her previous boyfriend for over four years—and there was no love in the relationship. Larry always put her feelings last. The breakup was hard on her but, really, Larry was an insignificant moment in her life," Matt says. "Remember the diamond ring we found under the old floorboards in Angie's cottage? I think we should ask the others what they think about you giving the ring to Angie. That ring holds a special meaning for both of you. It would be so cool if you could ask for her hand in marriage with that ring."

Thomas's eyes water and he wipes away a tear. "That's so special. She would love that idea, and I know I do, too."

When Matt and Thomas enter the house, David and Billy are busy working. They are almost finished with the kitchen fireplace—and the kitchen looks spectacular. It is a grand combination of the present and the past. Thomas, David, and Matt have refurbished the built-ins. They have also removed one of the walls that leads into the den, leaving a wide-open space that has transformed it into quite a spectacular sitting room. David left the fireplace intact but has added a new gas cooktop to it for cooking. There is also a gas oven and a stove with a grill. The kitchen is one-of-a-kind, and the guys are proud of how well it has turned out.

David is looking at Matt and Thomas. "Thomas, why do you look so serious today?" he asks.

Matt laughs and pats Thomas on the back. Thomas blushes. "David and Billy, I have decided to ask Angie to marry me."

David grins. "I am thrilled. I will love having you as part of our extended family. I have always felt that you, George, and Matt are almost like my sons— and I've gotten even closer to all you guys this summer. I'm not Angie's father, but I consider her just like the daughter I never had. I have watched her grow up into a beautiful young lady. Isabella will be ecstatic over the news."

They all congratulate Thomas and wish him well. Then Matt says, "I told Thomas to propose using the diamond ring that we found. What do you guys think? I think it would only be fitting for Angie to wear Evangeline's ring. I mean after all Evangeline has been encouraging their relationship all along. It's almost as if Thomas and Angie are soulmates."

David heartily agrees. "I think that would be perfect! It's an excellent idea, especially seeing how special it is to them. We will have to ask the others, but I imagine they'll feel the same. We need to keep it a secret from Angie. Boy, is she going to be surprised."

They go back to work and complete the kitchen and the den by the end of the day. They still need to finish renovating the bathroom, and there is work to be done on the master bedroom and the office.

The gleaming woodwork in the old kitchen is breathtaking. The built-ins have been sanded down and refinished to bring out their original luster. The guys finish up for the day and all head back to their homes. It's Tuesday, the day Emily's pub is closed, so everyone has agreed to meet at the inn this evening to discuss the plans for the upcoming trip to Cat Island.

Chapter 10

The Proposal

I'm sitting on the porch, enjoying the day, when Thomas arrives home from work. I have my guitar—I've been working on a new song for Matt and Sarah's wedding.

"I'm impatient to share this new song with everyone," I tell Thomas, "But I want to save it for Sarah and Matt's wedding day so they will be surprised." I play the song for Thomas. He smiles at me and takes my chin in his warm loving hands, then he kisses me on my cheek. His kisses feel like a feather sending me to a wondrous place where only he and I exist.

Max starts barking and running around us in circles. He covers me in wet kisses. Not just his tail, but his whole body wags as he makes sure he is not left out of our attentions. Thomas apologizes to me for Max. "I'm so sorry, Angie. Our boy loves you as much as I do. He gets so excited when he sees you."

Thomas and I sit beside each other on the pretty white glider. I rest my head on his shoulder. "It's okay. I love having him around as much as I love having you around," I say. "I think I'll keep both of you."

I have fallen totally in love with Thomas. My heart swells each time I see him.

"Hey, don't forget we're meeting everyone at the inn tonight," Thomas reminds me. "Yes," I say, "Just let me know whenever you're ready to walk over there."

The gathering is to nail down the details for the trip to Cat Island in early February. Our plane reservations have been made. Sally and Robert will be off from school, and Sarah has hired extra help to take care of the Shepard's Head B&B in her absence. December is a slow time of year on Ocracoke Island and at the inn. Right now, only a couple of guests are booked during the time we'll be in the Bahamas.

Matt, George, and Thomas have been able to clear their schedules, so they won't have any jobs at that time. And Emily has asked Sam Alexander to run the pub while we are away. Sam normally runs the boat taxi in the spring and summer months, and he is very reliable. The rest of the people in our entourage are retired. Everyone is getting so excited about the trip and the upcoming wedding, especially Sarah, the bride.

My grandfather and Jim White went on a fishing trip earlier today, so we'll be having fresh-grilled fish on the patio for a dinner. It's a beautiful fall day. When Thomas and I turn up at the inn, work is already underway for dinner. Paul and Jim have caught flounder and red drum. We watch as Thomas, Jim, and Matt grill the fish. George stands behind them, offering advice. Paul, David, Robert, Sally, and my grandmother, Mary, are sitting next to me on the patio. Emily and Sarah come out on the patio carrying potato salad and a leafy green Caesar salad from the kitchen. They all greet us with hugs.

Thomas turns to me and asks, "Angie, would you mind going back to the cottage to go get the desert?" He continues on. "I picked up a special treat for us at the Fig Tree Bakery, their famous key lime pie. I know it's one of your favorites."

I walk over and kiss Thomas. "Sure, no problem. I'll be right back." I head off to our cottage and wonder why he didn't bring the dessert with him. I laugh to myself. Thomas has such a sweet tooth.

Back at the patio, Thomas wipes his hand over his forehead and turns to my mother and Paul. "Isabella and Paul, I asked Angie to leave because I wanted to ask you both for her hand in marriage."

Thomas is so nervous that his palms are sweating. He wipes them on his jeans.

"I know it's soon, but I can't imagine my life without her. I will make her happy and always take care of her. I promise," he says. "When she was kidnapped, I thought I would go crazy if we didn't find her. It made me realize that I had fallen totally in love with her."

His heart races as he waits for an answer.

The girls squeal, waiting for Isabella to reply. Isabella walks over, smiling broadly, and kisses Thomas on the cheek. "I would be honored to have you as part of our family. I already feel like you are one of my sons," she says. "I know in my heart that you will make my daughter very happy, and I know that she loves you deeply."

Paul grins and hugs Thomas. "Son, welcome to our family. I am also honored to have you as part of our family."

Matt pats Thomas on the shoulder, then turns to the others. "I had this idea," he says. "I think we should give Thomas the diamond ring we found, so he can give it to Angie. What do you all think?"

Everyone loves the idea. "I'll go get the ring out of the safe," Jim White says. "I think it's a grand idea. Angie is like a daughter to me."

He comes back with the ring and hands it to Thomas. "I know Evangeline would want you to have it for Angie," Jim says.

Thomas shakes his hand. "Thanks, Jim. It means a lot to me to have your approval, too."

The girls are ecstatic. They give Thomas a group hug and, in unison, ask: "When are you planning to ask her to marry you? You have to let us know. Maybe we can help you."

Emily perks up. "I'll get you a special wine or champagne to make it extra romantic," she says.

Thomas pulls a little box out of his pocket. "I carved her this wooden box with hearts on it. Our initials are etched into the lid. I want to put the ring in it," he says. "I'm planning to take her down to the beach tomorrow night. I'll hide the box in Max's collar. The plan is for her to find it when we take Max for his walk tomorrow night.

"Hey," he says suddenly. "I think I hear her coming. Not a word, girls. I want it to be a surprise."

They give Thomas one last quick hug and put their fingers to their lips just before I walk back on the patio.

Right away, I know something is up. I could hear everyone whispering before I walk up the steps to the patio. And now everyone is grinning at me, looking happy. "What's up?" I ask. "I feel like I'm missing something."

Sarah shrugs. "I was just telling them about some of our plans for the wedding. I'm getting more and more excited every day," she says. "I have spoken to

Maria, the owner of Shannon's Cove. She went over some of her plans with me the other day. It's going to be so serene and beautiful. I just can't wait."

I nod, but I'm still skeptical. "Okay, but I know that something else is up. I feel like you all were talking about me."

Everyone ignores what I say—they all punt right back to the wedding discussion. The planning is pretty much already organized, but Sarah keeps the conversation on the beach wedding by opening her laptop and pulling up the wedding venue website.

"Matt and I have several different packages to choose from," she explains. "We picked this one two months ago. I think it will make our big day special. We plan to get married at sunset. Matt and I have only invited a few of our friends from Ocracoke, and Matt asked a couple of people from back home in Maryland.

"I also invited some cousins but only five of them will be able to come to the wedding. Most of them are working or are still in college," she says.

She smiles and continues. "Both sets of grandparents will be coming to our wedding. My Uncle Joseph and Aunt Elizabeth, as well as George and Thomas's parents, said they could be there. It's going to be quite an awesome affair. It should be quite a happy gathering."

As I listen to Sarah and see how happy she is, I wonder whether Thomas and I will ever get married.

Sarah continues talking about her plans. She has asked one of her good friends to be her photographer. "Her company is Epic Shutter Photography. Jenni has been one of my friends for years," she says. "Her photography is charming, and she's thrilled to be included in the wedding celebration."

I remember meeting Jenni many years ago, and she did our pictures for Sally and Robert's baby shower and birthday party in the summer. She knows Matt, too.

The evening is ending. David, Thomas, and Matt will be working tomorrow to add finishing touches to the upstairs at Sally and Robert's home. Thomas and Matt have made new dressers for each of the bedrooms and all the furniture for the nursery, even a new crib for the twins. The babies are growing too big for their little cradle. Thomas also made a changing table that he added all kinds of little special features to.

Emily and Sarah are making new quilts for Robert and Sally's new home, as well as for the guest rooms at the inn. Usually in the off season, when the summer crowds are gone, Emily helps Sarah update the rooms at B&B. They went into town earlier this week and bought supplies.

Before I leave, I remember my news.

"I forgot to tell you," I say, "that when I was in Maryland, I had a meeting with my recording agent. My agent called this morning to tell me that two of my songs are moving up the charts. My agent thinks that they might even hit Number One before the end of the year."

Everyone congratulates me. Then Emily tells me to stay right where I am. She dashes out of the room. She comes back with one of her special bottles of wine from the cellar and hands it to me and Thomas. "Here's a bottle of wine to help the two of you celebrate the success on the latest songs," she says.

I see Emily wink at Thomas. "Maybe you can have a special dinner to celebrate—you know, your own little celebration," she adds.

Thomas kisses me on the cheek. "I think that sounds great. I want to plan a very special evening for the two of us. I am so proud of you, Angie," he says. "I love you."

He kisses me again on the cheek. Sally, Emily, and Sarah seem barely able to control themselves. I know in my heart that something is up, but I'm not sure what. I look accusingly at all of them.

"You guys are up to something," I say. They just grin like Cheshire cats when we say good-bye.

Thomas and I leave with Max in tow. Suddenly Thomas stops. He bends down to put the leash on Max and turns to me. "How a walk on the beach tonight? It looks pretty out."

We take Max on the beach and let him off his leash so he can play on the sandy shore. I look up toward the dunes and see Evangeline and Jacob. "It looks like we have an audience," I say as we walk down the beach.

Thomas sees them, too, and waves. The ghostly specters are both grinning from ear to ear, with their arms around each other. They wave, and I wave back.

Max stops running and barks happily, wagging with his whole body when he turns toward the dune. "Wow, I never knew dogs were able to see spirits, too," I say, surprised. The star-crossed lovers then vanish before our eyes in a mist.

Thomas hooks Max back onto the leash, and we start to walk back home. Thomas asks me, "Are you happy living on the island?"

I put my arms around him. "I can't imagine living anywhere but here with you. I can't imagine ever being away from you," I say.

I take his hands in mine and bring them to my lips. I kiss every one of his fingers. "My life finally feels complete with you in it," I add.

He holds me in his arms and takes my chin in his hands and gently kisses my lips. "Oh Angie, you make me happier than I ever knew I could be."

The emotion of the moment sends shivers down my spine, making me tingle all over, and an intense heat rises up in me. Max wags his way up between the two of us. As I looked down, I notice something on his collar.

"What's this?" I ask. "It looks like a heart-shaped box."

Thomas laughs. "I wonder where that came from?" He reaches down to take the tiny box from Max's collar, then he kneels down in front of me and takes my hand in his. "Angie, I love you and I can't imagine my life without you. Will you be mine forever and always?"

He opens the little box and takes out a beautiful, sparkling diamond ring and places it on my finger.

"Please marry me," he says. "I will make you happy and love you always." He kisses all my fingers.

I am so surprised that I am trembling and my whole body is vibrating. "Thomas, I can't think of anything else I would rather do," I say. "My whole life revolves around you. You complete me and I've never been so happy."

I look more closely at the ring. "I recognize this ring. Was this Evangeline's?" I ask. I bring Thomas's fingers to my lips. I kiss them, suckling every knuckle. It sends shivers and goosebumps down his arms.

Thomas stands up and takes me in his arms. "The others know I wanted to propose. They felt it was only right that you should have the ring for your own," he explains. "It's perfect for you."

Thomas picks up Max's leash and turns to me. "Let's go home. I want to feel your body next to mine."

Thomas, Max, and I walk back to the cottage. Thomas opens the door and we walk over toward the fireplace. I feel like I am in a dream because I am so happy. I smile at Thomas. "I love you so much."

Thomas gently holds my chin in his hands. He kisses me gently, then his lips start making their way down my body. Our passion flames and our kisses send an explosion of little thrills into my groin. I lean my body to feel his hard maleness beside me.

We fall to the floor of the cottage landing on the soft scatter rug in front of the fireplace. "I have been thinking about undressing you all day. I plan to kiss every inch of your body," he tells me.

He starts by kissing me on the top of my head, then my forehead, slowly bringing his lips over my neck. It makes me writhe in ecstasy. He begins to unbutton my blouse and slowly moves his tongue over my chest.

I sigh and moan. "I think I have gone to heaven," I whisper to him.

I wrap my arms and legs around him, our bodies intertwined. I feel his taunt body vibrate underneath me. The rest of our clothes cascade into a bundle on the floor. He tugs and pulls me nearer to him, making me moan and sigh as he brings me closer to climax. His tongue trails down my belly as he tastes my skin and makes me gasp and groan. Then he fills me and takes us over the edge. We both explode as we climax, our arms around each other, not wanting the moment or the feeling to end.

Chapter 11

More Dreams

We fall asleep in each other's arms, and I dream about Jacob. I watch him arrive at the bed-and-breakfast. He knocks on the door and Emily answers the door. "Emily, I have come to take Evangeline home with me and make her my wife," he says. "There was no one at her home. Do you know where she is?"

Emily's hand goes to her heart and tears fill her eyes. "Oh, Jacob. Evangeline is missing and is thought to be drowned. She was on the shore and never came back home. We found her necklace, a letter you had written to her, and a letter she had written to you. We searched high and low to no avail."

I watch as the scene unfolds, feeling as if I were in the room. As Evangeline's friend tells Jacob what has happened, her tears fall. "We think that she may have drowned in the sea," she sobs.

Tears cascade down Jacob's cheeks as he listens. I can feel his heart breaking. He hands Emily a beautiful diamond ring. "I planned to give this to Evangeline. I cannot bear to keep it now Give it to her family," he says, crushed. "I will love her always. I cannot believe that she is gone." I watch him walk away with tears streaming down his face.

I wake up in the morning with my heart aching for Jacob. I tell Thomas about the dream. "Jacob returned to Ocracoke after Evangeline was feared dead. He gave Emily a diamond ring that was meant for Evangeline."

I look at the precious ring on my finger. "Could this ring, the one we found under the floorboard, be the one Jacob intended for Evangeline?"

I remain saddened by the dream. "Whenever, I have these dreams, it feels like I am actually there," I tell Thomas. "That's why they have such a powerful effect on me."

Thomas holds me in his arms and kisses away my tears. "I know it must be so hard sometimes," he says. "Evangeline definitely had an awful lot of terrible things happen to her."

I grab my little notebook by our bedside. "I'm going write down this latest dream. These dreams will help me with my novel about Evangeline and our search for Blackbeard's treasure. Her life is really starting to take shape."

He chuckles. "I think it's going to be a great book."

Thomas yawns, stretching his muscular arms above his head. I ask, "What are you doing today?"

"We should be able to finish your sister's home today," he says. "Do you want to bring the girls over later to see our latest progress?"

I can sense how pleased he is with their work. "I am so proud of you guys. The house looks fabulous," I say. "I can't wait to see the finishing touches you've put on it."

He picks up his keys, stuffing them into his faded blue jeans. "We are going to finish work on the attic today. We're making it into a bonus room for the twins. And Robert wanted us to turn the other room, the hidden one that once belonged to Roger, into a studio for your sister," Thomas tells me. "Robert says Sally has dabbled in painting and drawing over the years. You know she has quite a knack for making her paintings look so lifelike.

"The new studio is a surprise for Sally," he continues. "We've been able to use some of the old easels that belonged to Roger to set up the room. We painted it a very pale yellow. It really brightens up the room."

"I can't wait to see the work that you guys have done," I say. "Have you found a house to renovate for yourself?"

Thomas is looking worried. I take his hand in mine, "What's the matter? Did I say something wrong?"

He laughs. "Do you want to get rid of me already? I just asked you to marry me."

I smile, wrapping my hands around his neck. "No, silly. I never want you to leave. I plan to keep you around forever. I guess I should have asked if you'd found a house to renovate for *us*."

He opens the door to leave for the day. "That's good," he says, "because I plan on keeping you."

Max breaks through our mood. He's whining to go outside. Thomas puts the dog on his leash and kisses me good-bye. They walk out the door, leaving me writing furiously in my notebook. I am trying to recapture every moment of the dream. I love it when my words flow freely onto paper.

I finish writing and text the girls. "Hi! I have a big surprise to show you, plus Thomas says the house is almost ready and we should go over to see it. Anyone interested?"

The girls excitedly text me back. "We can't wait to see it and find out your surprise."

Emojis galore appear with lots of hearts and smiles. I suddenly wonder if this was what they were whispering about last night at the inn.

Thomas loves to walk to work leading Max down the stone driveway. He breathes in the crisp fall air, thinking about his proposal to me the previous night. Just as he reaches Sally and Robert's house, Matt pulls up beside him in his truck, rolls down the window, and calls out. "Wow, man you look a million miles away."

Thomas shrugs, grinning. "I asked Angie to marry me last night. She said yes," Thomas says.

Matt parks the truck, jumps out of his truck and swats Thomas on the back. "I can't wait to hear all about it.

"Weirdly, she had another dream last night about Jacob," Thomas says. "I think you are right, Matt, about the ring. It was meant for Angie. I can feel it in my soul. Jacob wasn't able to marry Evangeline, but I will fulfill the promise that goes with the ring."

"I told you that ring was meant for Angie," Matt says.

They both walk into Robert's house and Matt breaks into a smile. "This place looks awesome. I can't believe how beautiful this house has turned out. We restored the crown molding to its original splendor. The built-ins are gleaming. And look how the woodwork dazzles with the sun shining through those windows. The panes sparkle like diamonds in the rough."

Matt points to the windows. "Thomas, I'm so glad you hired one of the local artists to make more stained glass windowpanes," he says. Then he points to the fireplace. "The grand old fireplace looks like it's brand new, but it still holds some of its long-ago mystery."

The golden oak mantel radiates. The fireplace is ready to lure everyone to sit next to its crackling blaze.

Robert and David are in the kitchen, sitting around the chestnut-colored marble island and drinking coffee. Robert wants to help with the work on his wife's room.

"I love the sunny-colored walls and the restorations that you guys did to the woodwork in there," he says.

Thomas grins. "I'm so glad you like it. We only have to finish the floors in the room and it will be complete."

Robert nods. "I'm going to hang up several of the paintings that Roger painted years ago. There's a picture of William, Evangeline's son, that I just can't get over—he looks so much like our own Jacob."

He continues. "Sally has always loved to draw and paint but has never had a place to do it. I just can't wait to surprise her with her own studio."

While the guys are having coffee in the kitchen, David is working on one corner of the attic. His hand rubs against something—a latch—and he notices light shining from under the built-ins. He shouts downstairs for the others to come see what he has found.

"Hey guys, you aren't going to believe this, but I think there might be another secret room!" he says as they enter the attic.

He lifts the latch and opens a door. Inside the secret niche, an eerie light shines through a bronze-colored stained-glass window and falls directly on a painting of Roger, Evangeline and little William sitting on a bench in front of the B&B.

David stares in awe. "I wonder why he left this painting hidden in this room?"

Robert answers. "My guess is that it's because Roger was in love with Evangeline. It was probably his secret wish to make her his wife. Maybe he hid this away for his eyes only?"

Robert's eyes wander away from the painting. "Hey, look. Here's another wooden chest," he says. Robert opens the chest and pulls out a small burlap sack. "Maybe these are treasures from Roger's travels on the pirate ship," he speculates.

"Look! This is a sack full of gold Spanish coins. These look very similar to the coins we found in Evangeline's cottage," he says.

They find other riches in the ancient trunk. Matt picks up some jewelry. "Look at this ruby ring and emerald brooch. And this man's gold ring with a diamond solitaire.

"Hey, Thomas, maybe you can use this one for your wedding?" he adds. "Sarah and I bought our wedding rings."

"Your wedding!" Robert says. "Is it official?"

Thomas nods as the other guys come over to slap him on the back and shake his hand. "Yes. I just couldn't wait any longer," Thomas explains. "I asked Angie last night on the beach and she said 'yes.'"

Thomas looks at the ring Matt has handed him. "This is impressive. I think Angie would really like it if I used it as a wedding band," Thomas says.

There are also old clothes in the trunk. Matt holds up a pair of pants. "Look, I'm a pirate!" he says. "Seriously, I bet Roger wore these when he was a pirate. And look at this cool dagger. It's sharp, even now."

The dirk is adorned with gilded carvings; ruby stones are on the handle. There is also a saber with elaborate carvings and jewels on its handle. As they examine the saber, they find Daniel Teach's name also etched on the handle.

David exclaims, "Wow, I bet that Roger took these with them when he brought Evangeline back home. These need to be in a museum, along with some of Roger's paintings."

There are more of Roger's drawings and paintings in the room, beach scenes from Ocracoke Island and beautiful pictures of golden sunsets. Some of the paintings capture glorious seascapes with the sun glowing over the white-capped surf. One picture has an ominous storm cloud in the distance.

Matt lifts another burlap sack out from the bottom of the chest. "Look inside this sack. There are silver coins, pieces of eight. There's so many. What are we going to do with all these treasures?"

Thomas pulls out his phone. "I'm calling Angie so we can gather the others to come check out our latest treasures."

He finishes his call, then the phone rings. When he gets off the call, he says, "Angie texted the others and they are going to come over to look at the room and our latest finds."

Matt is looking through other items in the chest. He finds a notebook and opens it, reading some of the pages. "I think this must have been Roger's diary," he says. "It was written in 1754. We'll need to give this to Angie so she can use it in her novel about Evangeline."

Chapter 12

The Announcement

As I get to the inn to meet the girls, I am so excited to tell them my news that my heart is fluttering. When we meet outside the B&B, I hold out my hand to show them my ring.

"Thomas proposed," I say.

Emily, Sarah, and Sally are jumping up and down and squealing. Emily grabs my hand. "Oh Angie, it looks even prettier on your finger. I'm so happy for you two."

Sally hugs me. "Oh, little sister, I always knew in my heart that you two belonged together. It was only a matter of time—and fate."

Sarah is so excited that her face is flushed. "Now we can plan your wedding, too. This is so exciting. Do you know when you two are going to get married?"

I look at my beautiful ring. "No, not yet. I'm still in shock over the proposal. We haven't even discussed a date. Maybe we can get married on the anniversary of the day that we met. That would be prophetic."

Emily sighs. "I don't guess I'll ever get married. Always the bridesmaid, never the bride."

I squeeze her shoulder. "You would if you and George would just open your eyes and look at what is right in front of you. He's so in love with you and you're in love with him. Just admit it."

Emily shrugs. "I don't know. We are such good friends. I would never want to spoil that." Then she suddenly changes the subject. "Whatever. Let's go look at this fabulous house of yours, Sally. Thomas says they've found another hidden room?"

I grin. "Yeah. And it sounds like it's a really cool room, too, with more stuff that belonged to Roger, even another cedar chest full of his things. Let's go."

When we arrive at their house, Robert greets us at the door with a blindfold for Sally. "I have a special surprise for you, honey," he says as he places the blindfold over her eyes. "I'll guide you up the stairs. It's in the attic."

Sally is tentative as she walks up the steps with her hands outstretched. "Is the blindfold really necessary, Robert?"

Robert laughs. "Oh, come on, it'll be fun and this way you'll definitely be surprised. We've worked really hard on this."

Sally follows him. "Okay, I can't wait to see what you guys have done."

Robert guides her into her new studio and removes the blindfold. "I hope you like it," he says.

Sally looks around the room, turning in a full circle, speechless. She turns back and throws her arms around Robert, tears glistening in her eyes. "Oh my gosh. It's beautiful," she gushes. "Oh, Robert, you make me feel like the queen of the world. You did this for me? It's gorgeous."

She walks over and picks up one of the paint brushes. "Did you buy all these painting supplies for me?" Robert nods.

She is mesmerized as she looks up at the painting of Evangeline holding William. "Oh, my heavens, that looks just like our little Jacob and you, Angie. Where on earth did you find this?"

Robert explains. "When we were working on the twins' playroom, which is another surprise for you, we found this secret room. We assume it was Roger's art studio. I've been bursting at the seams to show it to you. Look at all these paintings he did."

David waves everyone toward the other corner of the attic and holds opens the door to the other secret room. "And look what else we found," he says. "We think this room was for Roger's eyes only. There's another painting in here of him with Evangeline and William. We think it was his dream for her to be his wife and for them to be his family, and that's why he hid it in here."

We examine the painting signed by Roger. Sally looks from the painting over to me and back to the painting. "Angie, you really do look like Evangeline. And the child she is holding could be our Jacob. It's beautiful. Do you think we can hang it over the mantel, Robert?"

Robert smiles. "I was thinking the same thing. It's stunning, isn't it? It will look great there."

Then he looks over to the rest of us. "Is that okay with everyone else?" We all nod in agreement and tell him that we think the idea is perfect.

Matt opens the chest and starts to pull out the treasures to show us. He holds up the ruby-stoned dagger and sword. "Look at these," my brother says. "We are pretty sure they belonged to Daniel. They sword has his name etched on the handle. We think Roger must have brought these back with him when he rescued Evangeline."

Matt then hands me a man's gold ring. "I think you and Thomas should use this to get married. Sarah and I already have our rings. The others said that they thought it would be nice. "

I hold the ring in my hand. "What do you think, Thomas? It's really quite charming. I think it would be perfect."

Then I add: "I wonder why Roger had the ring. Do you think he planned to marry Evangeline and she declined his proposal? Or do you think it belonged to Daniel?"

Emily looks at the ring. "I guess we may never know."

Matt reaches into the chest again and brings out a worn black leather book and a burlap bag.

"Maybe we *can* find out. I found Roger's diary in the bottom of the chest along with all these gold coins."

We all gasp as he pours out the contents of the sack. The gold and silver coins sparkle in the sunlight that spills through the stained-glass window.

Chapter 13

Roger Brown

Matt hands me the journal that had once belonged Roger Brown. I read out loud what Roger has written.

My name is Roger Brown. I am the grandson of Edward Teach, the man better known as Blackbeard. The year is 1754. My family and several others have left England to travel across the ocean.

My mother passed away during childbirth. I was raised by my mother's sister, my Aunt Mary Dare Brown. She raised me as her own. I have three sisters and one brother. We are really cousins, but they treat me as one of their own.

I was 17-years-old when our journey began. There are many other children on the merchant sloop. We set sail in the early spring. I have become very close to the six other families on the voyage. In all, there are twenty men, nineteen women and eight children on our journey. My closest friends are Jacob Harriot and Robert Alexander. They have become like brothers to me.

May 24, 1754
Today my friends and I are making furniture for the other families for our new homes in the unknown land. Our first job is to make a cradle for one of the servant's wives. The Halls are due to deliver their first child in three months.

Jacob and Robert and I have never built anything before, but we are being taught by one of the deckhands. His name is Jim Davis. He has been working on the sloop over twelve years and plans to join us and stay in the New World once our ship arrives. He bought passage for the woman he loved, Lucy, and brought her on board with him on this journey. He married her on the ship several months ago. He is 28-years-old and already he is balding. He started working on the ship when he was only 16. Jim is a jolly, scruffy character with bright blue eyes that twinkle when he laughs.

July 25, 1754
The days seem to last forever. I am learning mathematics. Robert's sister, Evangeline, is teaching me how to do my numbers. She is very pretty. She has long dark black hair that is dazzling in the sunshine. She is only 16 years old but already she is a beauty. My

heart races and my palms sweat every time I am around her. She thinks of me like a brother. She only has eyes for Jacob. He is one of my best friends.

September 7, 1754
Jacob, Robert, and I went fishing today off the bow of the sloop. It felt great to do something different for a change. The three of us caught several big fish, and the cook let us help grill them for our dinner.

The cook's name is Robert Williams, but we call him Cook. He is a rugged looking old guy with no front teeth. His toothless grin and boisterous laugh fill the room. His shabby gray beard hangs over his big barrel-shaped belly. He is quite a storyteller. He keeps everyone entertained when he spins a tale.

Today is Evangeline's birthday. He loves to spoil her with his special sweet treats. We celebrated into the night. We all had a grand time. My heart swells and my palms sweat when I gaze into Evangeline's pretty, crystal blue eyes that change like the color of the sea.

October 29, 1754
We are sailing the southern route and we arrived today at a place called the Canary Islands. We were allowed to get off the sloop for a little while. Everyone was excited about going ashore. We will dock here for two weeks to replenish our supplies.

Robert, Jacob, and I go into town, and it feels good to walk on the beach and stretch our legs. Emily and Evangeline have been allowed to go into the township with us.

Robert is quite smitten with Emily. Her eyes shine when she looks at him. I often see them sneak away together to hold hands and kiss. Jacob is in love with Evangeline. He talks about how pretty she is and how the color of her blue eyes changes like the tides of the ocean. My heart aches when I see the two of them together, but we are grand friends.

All of us love to sit and share stories of pirates, treasures, and ghosts. They tease me about me being Blackbeard's grandson, but it is all in fun. They tell me that someday I will have to lead them to his treasures.

December 4, 1754
We went into town again today. We went to one of the local taverns for a few pints of ale. None of us had ever had strong drink before and it left us quite giddy and jovial.

Later in the day, we took all the young ones and the girls to the beach to swim in the surf. We had a grand time. The water was a clear, tranquil blue lapping gently on the shore. We floated in the water for most of the day. Our skin turned pink from the brilliant sunshine.

Emily and Robert were caught holding hands today by Emily's father, Jonathan White. He was very concerned about Emily's reputation. They were scolded but Robert held his ground and asked her father for Emily's hand in marriage. Robert told him he wanted to marry her when they reached their new home.

December 25, 1754

We had our first Christmas on the sloop. There were oranges and nuts for treats for all of us. Cook made his special sweet rolls and something he called figgy pudding. The younger ones and the girls all helped him to ice the sweet rolls. We also had fruit cake and a pig roasting on a spit for our Christmas dinner.

Daniel Albright said the blessing and told the story of the birth of Christ. We had hot apple cider. We strung popcorn down the rails of the sloop. We had no Christmas tree, but it was a festive day.

March 3, 1755

I have taken up sketching. I think I am getting quite good at it. Cook lets me use the coals from the fires of his cookstove. My friend Jim has shown me how to make some writing instruments. I sometimes sit at the bow of the ship and draw the sunsets and sunrises.

I have started making sketches of the girls, Emily and Evangeline. They love to pose for me. The captain gave me a journal to keep my drawings in. I have started to sketch pictures of the different families on the sloop. It makes the time go by as the days are so long.

June 24, 1755

My sketches are starting to fill the journal. My favorite is of Evangeline. I feel I have captured her soul in this drawing. The light shines from her eyes and her expression is that of a doe in the springtime. She has really captured my heart. It is sometimes hard for me when she babbles on about my friend, Jacob. My heart longs for her. I only wish she felt the same way.

August 19, 1755

Today is my birthday. I turned 18 years old on this voyage that seems never ending. Cook made me a festive birthday cake. It was quite large. Everyone helped prepare a special birthday feast. We were able to catch fresh fish off the bow of the ship. Evangeline gave me a peck on the cheek for my birthday. I think I turned the color of a bright red apple. I could feel my cheeks flaming. Jacob teased me that she was his girl and that I will never have her.

October 4, 1755
It is getting cooler out. It gets dark so much earlier in the evenings. I do not like this time of year. The nights last so long. The girls and the women are knitting raglans for everyone, preparing for colder weather. Even now, the chill in the air goes straight to your bones. There is a damp cold when the sun dips into the sea at dusk, as if it is melting into the briny deep with brilliant shades of orange, crimson, and amethyst.

My friends and I have been making furniture for our new homes. The Halls had their baby girl over a year ago and she is growing quickly. We were wise to make her cradle a little bit bigger than most. The girls have knitted blankets for the wee one. They love taking her for walks. They croon over her, singing lullabies. I love to watch Evangeline with her brilliant black hair lift the babe over her head, making the two of them laugh heartily. It warms my heart, yet also makes it ache as I well know she will never be mine.

December 24, 1755
I cannot believe we are passing our second Christmas on the ship. Cook prepared more delicious sweet treats and cakes for us. The bairns are excited to help make the bonbons and candied fruits. All our families have become so close. It is like having a very large family. Robert officially asked for Emily's hand in marriage on her birthday in November. Today, he gave her a ring. It is a beautiful diamond that came down from his mother's mother. Emily is impatient to become Robert's wife.

It is nice to see happiness on the ship amidst the hardship and the losses that we have suffered. My heart breaks for the families that lost loved ones to the wretched jungle fever. My poor Evangeline's family suffered the loss of their little baby sister, Anna. Evangeline's mother is still not the same. She has lost herself in grief.

March 1756
It was a very long winter but now the weather is finally starting to break, staying warmer in the evenings. White and gray seagulls gather around the bow looking for handouts. We have reached the shore of North America. We were later told that this land is called Florida.

We docked at a port at the farthest southern tip of this shore. It is a relief to be able to leave the sloop. We had all been getting restless. I went onshore with Robert, Jacob, Emily, and Evangeline. There are many citrus trees on this land and we have tasted a fruit the locals call an orange. It has a succulent juice that drips into our mouths and down our chins. It is like eating a slice of heaven when you bite into this orange-colored fruit.

I met my cousin here on this land. His name is Daniel Teach, and he is a pirate like our grandfather. He has asked me to come aboard his ship and join his crew. I am inclined to do so. My heart aches each time I see young Evangeline. It is becoming increasingly difficult to be around her as my heart tugs with every glance I take. She is more and more beautiful with each passing day. Her eyes, which shine like sapphires, only see my friend, Jacob. It will be hard to leave with Daniel, but I long to spread my wings. I will miss everyone but I know it is for the best that I leave.

June 24, 1756

I joined Daniels crew a mere three months ago and it has been quite a learning experience. I am not sure that I am cut out for the life of a pirate. I am unable to take a life or steal from others without feeling remorse. I cannot understand how my cousin and his men do it.

Despite being a vicious pirate, my cousin has been kind to me. He has tried to teach me the ways of the sea but I have not fared so well. Still, he puts up with me. He has decided to put me in charge of documenting our journey with words and with my drawings. I am also helping him with his books.

Daniel and his crew have pilfered a large quantity of treasure. My cousin has hidden a huge portion of it on one of the nearby islands. The island is named for Arthur Cat. Daniel tells me he was a close friend of our grandfather, Edward Teach. Daniel always refers to our grandfather as Edward Teach, never as Blackbeard. Blackbeard also hid his treasures on Cat Island. When Daniel is in a rum-ridden haze, he loves telling me stories about his treasures are hidden.

December 24, 1756

We have reached Cat Island. A treacherous storm blew us onto its shore. It was such a squall that I thought we would surely perish. But today dawned with a beautiful crystal blue sky and a gentle aqua sea that rolled onto the beach.

We made our way onto the coral-colored sand carrying all the loot we have stolen from others. We ventured into a nearby cavern with a beautiful waterfall and an enticing turquoise lagoon. It is alluring and tranquil. I will have to remember this place. It would be a great place to come to float and relax in its peaceful, calming water.

Daniel tells me this is the secret hiding place for all his treasure. He has come to trust me and he confides in me quite often. He took me behind the waterfall and placed his hand on a ledge on the wall of the cave. He pushed on it and it opened up before us. I am fascinated by this natural wonder, and I helped him hide his fortune behind the wall. He told me to be careful. He has the cave booby trapped so no one can steal his riches.

January 10, 1757

The weather here is perfect. I have had much opportunity to sit and do my drawings. Daniel has allowed me to build a little hut. My little shanty holds a pallet of palm leaves for sleeping and a small bed of coals for cooking the fish I catch.

I thank God that I learned to fish on my journey to North America. The fish here are so delicious and we season them with the juice of the fresh citrus. I enjoy being on the island but know it is only a matter of time before we sail again. I have come to dread our pirating voyages. It is not in my heart to steal or hurt others.

February 14, 1757

We will set sail at the end of the week. I wish I could just stay here on the island. I am neither killer nor a pirate. I do not have the appetite for it, but I have promised Daniel to come along on this next voyage. I think he suspects that it is not in my nature to hurt others.

May 1, 1757

We have reached a beautiful place called Ocracoke Island. We will anchor soon to get supplies. This is where my family and the others on our ship from England were supposed to have set up their homesteads. I hope I will be allowed to visit with them while we are moored here.

I look forward to seeing my family and friends. I especially look forward to seeing Evangeline, who still owns my heart, even if she does not know it. Today we dropped anchor in an inlet called Cockle Creek. It sparkled like crystals and diamonds when we pulled up to the wharf. Too many gulls flew over us, screeching at our heads as they searched for scraps of food from the fishing boats that lined the docks.

May 7, 1757

I visited my family and then continued on my way to visit my good friend Jacob and his family. I was told that they are set to leave on the morrow to settle further inland. It breaks my heart to know that they will not remain on the island.

Jacob met me on the path. I have grown tall and a bit larger since we were last together. I look quite rugged with my scraggly black beard. Jacob laughed and told me I looked like a pirate. He has plans to return to the island for Evangeline once he and his family *are settled in Virginia. I told him how happy I am for him and Evangeline, yet my heart continues to ache for her.*

Evangeline's brother Robert joined us. He told me he planned to wed dear Emily this summer. I longed to see the girls. We went to see them a short while later. Emily has been helping her father a place called the Shepard's Head Inn, which her father purchased before leaving England.

I will be staying with my family while I am here. They love me as their own and I have truly missed them. We reached Evangeline's home in time to see her bending down to pick up one of the little ones from our journey.

She saw me and broke into a smile. She rushed to greet me. She told me how much she has missed me and kissed me on my cheek. My faced flamed red hot, and my heart melted at the sight of her. I had wished that my feelings for her would ebb with time but they're still as strong as ever.

I told them all about my journey and all my adventures with Daniel Teach. I told them we would be setting sail at the end of the next month.

June 7, 1757
We left Ocracoke Island today. Something wretched has happened and I am in a quandary as to what to do. Daniel's men kidnapped my dear Evangeline and Cook. I could hear her screams from my cabin on the sloop. I fear for her life but there is nothing I can do at this time to save her from Daniel. If I intervene now, we will both surely perish. It breaks my heart to hear her sobs.

When I saw an opportunity, I went to her. She was hiding behind the wardrobe in the dirty room where she is imprisoned. Her tears broke my heart, and she clung to me. She is battered and bruised from her capture. I tried to assure her that I will find a way to rescue her and take her home. My heart boils with rage. One day I will get my revenge on Daniel and his men. I must never let them know about my love for her, as it will surely be the end for the two of us.

Later that day, I covered my ears when I heard them drag Evangeline to Daniel's cabin. I can still hear the screams coming from his room. I cannot intervene because it will leave to both my death and hers. It is destroying me that I cannot help her.

July 20, 1757
I sneak into Daniel's cabin to see Evangeline. She is vomiting in a basin and her skin is pale. She is clammy with sweat. A yellowish-blue bruise sits below her left eye. Her lips

are cracked and split. She sees me and tears start flowing down her cheeks. She clings to me, frantically, and asks where I have been. My heart is breaking. I tell her that Daniel has one of his mates guarding her room.

I hold her closely and again tell her that I will get her home one day. Daniel had his way with her violently on the first day, she said, but he has been gentler since that time. She cannot stand the touch of his hands on her.

I tell her we will reach Daniel's Island on the morrow. As I leave her, it feels that my heart it is being ripped from my chest. Her tears start to flow again. She begs me to take her with me. I tell her I will—as soon as there is a way to get her home.

September 7, 1757
Evangeline turns 18 today. Daniel still guards her closely, but I manage to slip into the cabin they share on the island so I could see her. Her belly is swelling with child. She tells me Daniel has been treating her well, especially now that she carries his child.

For her birthday, I gave her one of my sunset sketches. I put it in a small wooden frame. I have hidden some parchment under the drawing so she can write if she wants. I remember that she used to love to write in her journal during our voyage to the new country.

I warn her that I must be careful so Daniel does not become jealous. She shows me an emerald brooch Daniel gave her. She tells me she still longs to be home with Jacob but fears he will not want her now that Daniel has had his way with her. I tell her Jacob will always love her.

Evangeline was unaware that Cook was captured at the same time she was. Cook was always fond of Evangeline and looked upon her like a niece. One day, I told her that he, too, had been taken on the pirate vessel and now is on the island when he is not forced to sail with Daniel's crew. I have spoken to Cook, and he will help me rescue Evangeline when the time comes. She cried when she learned of his capture.

Daniel ordered Cook to make a feast for her birthday, and today he made Evangeline a sweet cake with fresh fruits from the island. Daniel now allows Evangeline to go for walks around the island. She is teaching some of the pirates and their women to read and write.

Evangeline has befriended two of the girls, one who is very pregnant with child. Her name is Katherine Dare. They call her Katrina. She told Evangeline that her great, great, grandmother's name was Virginia Dare. Evangeline thinks she, too, may be distantly related to Virginia Dare. Katrina said Virginia was a baby on a ship of settlers on a journey funded by Sir Walter Raleigh over two hundred years ago. She and the others were left on a place called Roanoke Island to build a colony in the New World. Virginia's grandfather was Jonathan White and her mother was Eleanor Dare.

The settlement was later found abandoned and the colonists had disappeared without a trace. There are stories that they were thought to have been captured by the Croatan Indian tribe, but to this day the mystery is unsolved.

Evangeline said that Virginia's spirit came to visit her when she first arrived on Cat Island, and she found the appearance of Virginia's spirit a great comfort to her. She told me this in confidence, and said she hoped I did not think she had lost her mind. I reassured her that I believed in the afterworld. I still remember stories from when I was a boy of the Lost Colonist group of Roanoke Island. Maybe they were not really lost but were captured.

December 24, 1757

This is my second Christmas away from my family. I am glad Evangeline and Cook are here with me on the island. Evangeline is growing larger with child. Daniel treats her well, but she still longs to be home with her family and Jacob.

Evangeline helped to deliver Katrina's baby last month. The other women on the island have started to come to her for her midwifery knowledge and other skills. Daniel has allowed her to teach the others. Evangeline also visits Cook frequently to help him prepare our evening meals.

Cook made everyone a great feast of a pig roasted on a spit for Christmas. It had a smoky, mouthwatering flavor and reminded me of Christmas on our voyage from England to America. Cook used fresh fruits and vegetables from an island in that feast, too.

Evangeline told the story of the birth of Jesus. Daniel gave her a beautiful pearl necklace. She told me privately that she would trade all the jewels for just one moment with her love, Jacob. For Christmas, I gave her another of my sketches. It is a drawing of the sloop we were aboard during our journey to America. The frame around this sketch contains a hidden compartment.

My crew members got roaring drunk on rum after the Christmas meal. I am glad I have my own small hut. Filled with rum himself, Daniel spun tales for me of where our grandfather Blackbeard hid his treasures. Daniel rarely remembers these talks the next day but I do. I have been using what he tells me to sketch treasure maps that I have hidden in my hut.

I am impatient for the day when I can take Evangeline home, but we must wait until after the baby is born. Daniel and I will set sail again at the beginning of the new year.

Daniel received information that several vessels will be in our area, and he plans to raid them. I find no joy in our pirating, which takes us away on journeys that are so long.

January 17, 1758

We set sail last week and spotted a Spanish sloop to attack. Cook and I do not take part in the attacks. Cook does not enjoy the pirating excursions. He stays hidden in the galley. But I am above deck so I can sketch our pirating escapades, as Daniel has instructed me. I also write in his journal about our attacks. He does not know that I have my own journal that I keep hidden from him and the others.

The vessel we attacked was carrying many Spanish treasures and gold doubloons. The pirates murdered many of the Spanish deckhands and hanged the captain on the mast. It was gruesome to watch and draw. Daniel and some of our mates are very bloodthirsty.

I cannot wait to return to Ocracoke Island to be with my family again. I know there are others in our crew who, like me, find no pleasure in killing. I keep remembering the voyage across the sea with my aunt's family and picture what it would have been like if we had been attacked.

February 12, 1758

Evangeline had her bairn today. Daniel, the proud papa, celebrated heavily after the birth. I was able to go to see Evangeline after she gave birth and she appeared even more beautiful than ever, holding her precious babe in her arms. I took one look at the child and knew he belonged to Jacob. She and I exchanged a glance. She knows I am aware of her secret. Evangeline has named the child William. He has a peach-blonde fuzz on his head. He is a handsome baby. Katrina helped deliver the child. She and Katrina are good friends and that is a godsend.

I tried not to stare into Evangeline's beautiful blue eyes as I sketched her with the babe sleeping in her arms. I gave the drawing to Daniel and Evangeline as my gift. Motherhood becomes her. She allowed me to hold the infant and I was filled with love. I know he is not mine, but my heart belongs to them, and I will protect them at all costs.

June 14, 1758

I have been with Daniel's crew now for almost two years. I know that I will never have the heart of a pirate. We are going on another voyage in pursuit of more treasures. We will be dropping anchor on the mainland of the Bahamas to acquire more supplies. I will try and buy some fabrics for Evangeline.

I made young William a cradle before he was born. I also made Evangeline a rocking chair so that she can rock her child. It makes my heart swell each time I see them. It is hard to believe the child is almost four months old. He has such a gentle and happy personality. He rarely cries, and sometimes I am allowed to hold him.

I whispered to him that one day I will get him home safely. Daniel has been a good father to William. He now treats Evangeline well, and I think she is truly happy at times. But her eyes look sad. She tells me often that she wants to go home. She is homesick for her friends and family.

August 19, 1758
I turned 21 today and the deckhands gave me a celebration with a wench and jugs of rum. My manhood was aroused and satisfied, but my heart and soul still belong to Evangeline. She made me a new pair of breaches and a shirt for my birthday with the fabric that I bought her. I will always treasure them. She even embroidered my initials on the collar of the shirt. Cook made me a special cake with pineapples. It was quite tasty.

January 4, 1759
I have not written in quite some time. Daniel's ship left Cat Island several weeks ago, and we spent Christmas on the sea. My heart aches for Evangeline and young William. She was alone on the island for Christmas, with only William. Luckily, she has many friends on the island. Katrina has become like a sister to her.

Katrina's daughter, Abigail, turned one year old a couple months ago. I wonder if one day she and William will marry. William will be another year older in another month. He reminds me more and more of Jacob. The boy's real parentage is unspoken between Evangeline and me, as I never want to put them in danger. But I am certain she knows that I know.

When we returned from our latest voyage, Daniel gave Evangeline a sparkling garnet hair comb. She is allowed to roam freely on the island, and she loves to take young William to the aqua lagoon behind the waterfall. I followed her one day and watched them floating in the briny water. Her clothes were translucent, and her beautiful breasts showed through them. I tried not to stare but she is so beautiful.

She laughed when she saw me standing on the water's edge and beckoned me to join them. My manhood revealed my lust for her, so I quickly got into the water with them. I took young William as he reached out his tiny little arms for me to hold him.

Evangeline's laughter filled the air, and I was unable to control my urge to kiss her. My lips touched hers and we embraced. My hardness was between her legs, and my body shuddered. I could have taken her then but stopped myself. I told her we could not allow anything to happen as it would put her in danger. I think about her always.

February 12, 1759

Today was young William's first birthday. Cook made him a cake and the child ended up with frosting in his hair and all over his little face. I carved William a little wooden horse. Katrina brought her daughter Abigail to Evangeline's cabin for the birthday. It was cute to watch them playing. Later that day, we all went for a swim. Daniel gave William a tiny tan-colored kitten and a rocking horse. Evangeline has made William a little bear with fabric from our previous raids. The child did not want to put it down.

July 17,1759

The days are long and lonely. We have been sailing for the last two months. I miss the island, Evangeline, and young William. We sailed to the Canary Islands to pick up more supplies. A vicious storm blew in last night. I thought we would all perish. Our sloop rocked up and down and the treacherous waves crashed over the bow. We managed to slip into in a small little inlet and drop anchor. In the morn, we are supposed to go on the island for much needed supplies. I worry when we leave Evangeline for too long. There are even villains out there who are even more dangerous than Daniel.

August 19, 1759

I turn 22-years-old today. We are making our way back to Cat Island. It feels that we have been gone forever. Cook has made me a sweet roll for my birthday. He has become like a father to me. Daniel bought a gold ring Evangeline. He tells me he plans to marry her. I offer my congratulations and try to be excited for him. I continue to draw daily. I'm working on a portrait of Evangeline and William in her rocking chair. I will give it to her for her birthday. I hope she likes it.

March 17, 1760

It has been a long time since I have written in my journal. I have been out at sea with Daniel and his crew. Young William turned two last month. He looks so much like my friend, Jacob. Evangeline is a great mother and my heart aches to be with her. I must keep my distance when Daniel is nearby.

I carved little William another wooden horse but this one is much smaller. Evangeline's eyes lit up with excitement as he played with it. It warmed my dreary heart. Daniel brought her home another beautiful piece of jewelry, this time a jade necklace.

I had a chance to speak with Evangeline alone. She still misses her home and family. I tell her I will try and figure out a way to get her home.

Roger's entries end there. At the inn, we sit quietly as I stop reading and close the journal.

"That was like reading a book that was never completed," I finally say. "It leaves you hanging. You can just feel the tug of pain that poor Roger felt for Evangeline."

Sarah sighs. "There must be another journal somewhere. It can't end just like that."

I am deep in thought. "Remember the dream I told you I had about Evangeline and William's rescue?" I say. "Maybe I will dream more about Evangeline's life. Maybe she will show me in my dreams what happened to them."

"Poor Roger!" Emily exclaims. "He loved Evangeline so much. It must have been so hard for him to be so close to her and never have her as his own."

I frown. "It must have been pure torture for him," I say. "They say that he never married but had many women in his life. There are many stories about him as quite the womanizer, but he clearly had a gentle soul."

"His heart always belonged to Evangeline, just as Evangeline's heart always belonged to Jacob," I add. "Can you imagine what would have happened to her if he hadn't been on the island? She would have never made it home. Our lives would have been so different, just think about it."

We agree to add the journal to the other treasures in the safe at the B&B. Paul examines the sword and the other treasures. "It's a miracle that no one's ever found these."

We decide to go back to the pub for an early dinner. And we talk about the need to eventually share the things we have found with the world. "They will be a great addition to the Ocracoke Preservation Museum," Paul tells us.

I love the evenings we share with our families and friends. My life cannot be more complete. After dinner, Thomas and I walk Max down on the gusty beach. It is very cold tonight and the wind whistles through the seagrass. I pull my hood up over my head, shivering. "Max doesn't seem to mind the cold, does he?" I say.

Thomas laughs. "No, he's a champ. He wouldn't care if it snowed, but you look like you are freezing. I'll hurry him along." He wraps his arms around me and adds, "I'll keep you warm."

I lean into his arms. "Umm, that feels good. I can't wait to get home. Let's build a fire tonight. What do you think?"

I watch a shooting star race across the sky. "Did you see that? You have to make a wish," I tell Thomas.

He kisses me on the back of my neck and whispers, "I already got my wish. I have you."

My heart fills with love for this man who will be my husband one day soon. Thomas whistles for Max "Come on, boy. Time to go home." We walk back and build a crackling fire in our hearth. I couldn't be happier.

Chapter 14

Dreams of Evangeline

I fall asleep in my soulmate's arms. I am deliciously happy. I dream again of Evangeline and William. Evangeline is at the home of her friend, Emily, and her brother, Robert. William is playing with his blocks on the cool wooden porch. Evangeline, Emily, William, and Emily's daughter, Penelope, are enjoying the balmy summer breeze.

Evangeline picks up her little niece, Penelope, and gazes into the baby's face. Emily tells Evangeline, "She has your beautiful blue eyes."

Emily tells Evangeline about Jacob's last visit to Ocracoke, several years ago. She explains that he arrived at the island about three months after Evangeline had disappeared. There are tears in Emily's eyes as she relates how Jacob came to find Evangeline. He had an engagement ring with him. Emily hands Evangeline a beautifully ornate golden filigree ring with exquisite diamonds that sparkle in the sunlight.

Both girls have tears in their eyes as Emily recounts the visit. She tells how Jacob managed after his father passed away from malaria early that first year, leaving Jacob as the man of the family. Jacob had not heard that Evangeline was missing and drowned in the surf. Emily had explained to him that they were unsure if Evangeline died by accident or took her own life. They found her necklace and the letters.

"Everyone knew how much you loved your necklace and that you would not abandon it," Emily says to Evangeline in my dream.

Sobbing, she adds, "Jacob left heartbroken. He left the ring with me, saying that if he could not give it to you, he knew you would want me to have it."

Tears stream down Emily's face as she relives that day. "It was like losing you all over again."

Evangeline holds the ring up to her heart then places it on her ring finger, never to be removed until she is an old woman. I can feel Evangeline's heart breaking as Emily tells her that Jacob has married a girl from Williamsburg. Emily heard it was an arranged marriage.

"Jacob's brother, Walter, came to visit the island last year," Emily says. "He said Jacob has three children. He has resigned himself to being married to his wife, Mary." Evangeline's heart is being torn in two. I can feel her anguish. She whispers, "One day, maybe not in this lifetime, our souls will be reunited." I wake up with tears flowing down my cheeks.

Thomas holds me in his arms. I gaze at the ring he has given me. "I wonder if we helped them to be reunited in this lifetime when you found the other half of the heart pendant? It's so awful. Can you imagine how she felt to finally make it home only to discover that he had moved on with his life?

I start crying again as I add, "Evangeline knew he would never betray his new family. It just wasn't in his nature."

I look at Thomas. "I'm so happy that I will be your wife forever."

Thomas kisses my tears away and gently strokes my hair with his fingers. He cups my chin in his hands. He passionately moves his lips over mine. Our fire is rekindled, and I wrap my legs around him making us one. He breaks away, laughs, and picks me up. "I need to get to work, but I have plans for you in the shower."

The warm water flows over us. He lathers my body and caresses me until we moan in ecstasy together again. I tell him how much I love him.

He heads off to work with Max in tow. He is going to David's house today. They are almost done with the renovation. They already have another job lined up on Howard Street at one of the original homes of the island. Ocracoke Realty has hired the guys to renovate the house.

I hear a knock at my door. Emily and Sarah rush in, anxious to talk about wedding plans. I show them my diamond ring again.

"I dreamt again last night about Emily and Evangeline. I can't help but think she has been guiding me to this time. Emily gave Evangeline the diamond ring from Jacob. My heart goes out to her, never being able to share her love with Jacob," I say. "Daniel and his crew robbed her of the life she wanted. In the dream, I felt like I was there. The pain was so real. Jacob left Ocracoke heartbroken, believing that Evangeline had drowned at sea.

"It was just awful. He married another woman, and when Evangeline made her way home, she knew he would never leave his new family. So, he never found out that little William was his son. He never even got to meet him. Can you just imagine?" I continue. "Their last time together was when their son was conceived, and she kept that secret forever. She wore his diamond ring until the day she died. So sad."

I wipe a tear from my eye.

After a minute, I compose myself again and smile. "On a good note, Thomas wants me to come to look at a house that he is interested in. This is happening so quickly. It's exciting but a little bit scary. He said it was a cute little bungalow with a wraparound porch."

As Emily, Sarah, and I leave to meet the guys at the house Thomas found, I explain, "The house hasn't even been put on the market yet. The guys won a bid to renovate it and when Thomas saw the place, he wanted it for us."

Chapter 15

Our New Home

The house is right down the street from the Shepard's Head B&B. You can see Silver Lake from the home's crow's nest. Its pillars reach out to welcome us, and the veranda holds a charming white swing and several white rocking chairs. The wind chimes waft in the warm Carolina breeze as we walk up the steps.

Thomas greets us at the door. He's all smiles and takes my hand in his. "I'm so excited for you to see the house. I think it would be perfect for us. I hope you like it."

He picks me up and carries me over the threshold. "I'm just practicing since we might make this one our own," he says.

He sets me down in the parlor of the old home. I can't help but laugh because he is so excited. His green eyes are sparkling, their gold flecks dazzling as he shows me around the old dwelling. The parlor leads to a curving stairway. He explains, "I want to keep the stairs as they are. They're just so charming."

Emily and Sarah follow us into the large living room which holds a massive gray-and-tan stone fireplace with charming built-ins on either side of the mantel. Matt comes into the room from where he is working. Emily says, "Why don't you two go look at the house together alone."

I grin, holding Thomas' hand in mine, turning to the girls. "Are you sure you don't mind?" I ask. Sarah nods, saying, "I think it is something that you two should do together. It's fine. We'll get the tour a little later."

The ornately adorned oak of the mantel and built-ins have been painted white. The gray-and-tan stones cover the length of the wall. I spot some crumbling mortar that will need to be fixed, but it is so gorgeous that I am in awe. I sigh. "It's beautiful," I say.

Antique pane windows frame either side of the built-ins. Thomas brings me in through an elaborate doorway. "This kitchen is ancient. It hasn't been renovated since the sixties," Thomas explains. "The widow who lived here finally decided to sell it to the realtor. She didn't like newfangled things, so she kept things unchanged. She especially loved the charm of the old fireplace. I want to make it into a working fireplace for cooking like we did at Robert and Sally's home."

He continues, "The oak cabinets are original to the house, which was built in the 1700s. This home once belonged to the Brown family. Roger Brown's adoptive father acquired it before moving to the states."

Thomas points toward the other room. "Matt and I plan to extend the kitchen into the living room. We really like the idea of having an open floor plan. We are going to transform the dining room, office, and den into a bathroom, dining room, and combination laundry room and mud room."

Thomas lays out the blueprints and shows me the plans that he has made for the home, wanting to get my approval. "Well, what do you think so far? Do you like it?"

I gently kiss him on the lips and circle my arms around his neck. "Like it? I love it. It's what I've always dreamed of. I'm so excited. I can't wait to see the rest of it and to watch your plans come to life."

Thomas leads me up the creaky old stairs. "Well, if you liked what you've seen so far, you're going to love this bit that comes next," he says, before adding, "I'm definitely going to need to fix these creaks."

As we climb to the second floor of the home, he points up. "What do you think about these stained-glass windows?"

Shining prisms of sparkling light shine through the windows and down onto us as we walk up the steps. "There are four bedrooms and here is the old bathroom that hasn't been touched since the seventies," Thomas says. "These olive-green fixtures will definitely have to go. The plumbing was added to the home in the early 1900s."

He places his hand on the tub. "Look at this antique clawfoot tub. The bathroom is charming but definitely needs a lot of work. What do you think? I want to add a massive walk-in shower with double shower heads but keep the tub."

I run my hand over the tub. "I love it," I say.

Then I whisper in his ear. "I can just picture us soaking in the tub together." I grin at him.

The massive master bedroom overlooks Silver Lake. Doors from the room open onto a private veranda that leans over the old porch. I start to move toward it but Thomas stops me. He warns, "It's too rickety to go out there safely. We are going to buttress it so that one day we can sit outside and gaze at the stars and the moon shining over the water. Can you see it, Angie? It's going to be so cool. Several of the bedrooms have fireplaces that are still in working order."

One of the quaint bedrooms has a door with an antique brass key in its lock. The door leads up into the forgotten attic. The narrow stairway precedes an old, hot, and dusty room that holds the promise of many treasures yet to be found. All the old homes on the island have secret passageways, and I'm betting this one will, too. I think to myself, Thomas loves to find the hidden latches that lead to the secret lives of ancestors from long ago.

Thomas shows me around the cobweb-riddled room. "I know it doesn't look like it now, but we are going to make this into your music sanctuary, the place where you can create your music," he says. "I want to build in an alcove with a large stained-glass window and a window seat so you can look out over Silver Lake. I have a vision of you in my mind sitting in the window seat playing your guitar. "

I hug him. "The longer we walk around this old house, the more I feel at home. I just love it and everything you and Matt are planning to do," I say. "Look at Max laying on the hearth on the cool stones. He's such a sweet boy—he's already picked out his spot.

"I think Emily and Sarah are going to be as excited as I am," I add.

My heart is so full of love for Thomas. I am holding him by the hand when I absentmindedly reach up to touch my necklace. Evangeline and Jacob appear before all of us. They are both smiling.

Evangeline looks at Thomas and me and exclaims, "We are so happy for you two. Your love was meant to be and written in the stars. You will have the love that we were not able to share."

Jacob holds her closely with a look of so much love in his eyes. "We will be guarding you all and keeping all of you safe," he says.

Then Evangeline again gives us a warning. "Be careful in the caverns on Cat Island. Daniel has placed many booby traps to protect his treasures." The two evaporate into thin air as they wave good-bye to us.

These appearances by Evangeline and Jacob are always unexpected and leave us a little excited and jittery. When we go back downstairs, we tell Sarah, Emily, and Matt about the vision. Emily asks, "What type of booby traps is she talking about?"

Matt replies, "Most pirates were known to keep their treasures safe by adding spikes that would fall on unsuspecting treasure hunters. You've watched all the Indiana Jones movies. So, something just like that."

Emily grimaces. "That's scary. We're going to have to be very careful when we're treasure hunting."

Everyone laughs nervously, thinking about the danger we might encounter if we are not mindful of the traps.

Thomas pulls me aside to kiss me. He takes my face in his hands. "I will keep you safe," he assures me. Then he adds, "I can't wait to make you my wife."

The group teases us, and Emily adds, "You two will have plenty of time for that later."

Sarah checks the time on her phone. "I need to leave and get back to the inn," she announces.

"Emily and Angie, what time are you opening the pub today? Has the pub started its fall schedule yet?" Matt asks.

Emily nods. "We aren't opening until after 4 p.m. I guess we need to leave to get to our jobs, but I'm really glad we came to see the house. I really love it, Thomas," she says. "I can see you and Angie growing old here."

The girls and I walk down the old stone road back to the B&B and pub. Along the way, Sarah asks me, "So when are Thomas and you going to be getting married. Have you set a date yet?"

I laugh nervously. "We haven't had time to discuss it yet. I am still a little in awe by the proposal. I never expected to fall in love after breaking up with Larry last year. It's just something I never thought would happen to me," I say. "I can't believe how strong my love for Thomas is after such a short amount of time. I guess it was just meant to be, the two of us finding each other."

I wonder to myself what would have happened if I had met Thomas sooner. "My dad told me that Evangeline said the time was right for us to meet," I say. "I guess we both needed to get to this point in our lives for our relationship to grow and blossom."

Chapter 16

Wedding Plans

Thomas and I are meeting tonight with the others to discuss our trip to Cat Island and get our airline tickets purchased. We are the last to arrive at the inn, and I can tell that Sarah is bursting to tell us all the latest planning details.

Sarah turns to me and my sister, Sally, to show us the Bahamas pamphlets. "I'll have to show these to your mom and Grandmom when they come over later after their pedicures," she says.

"So, here's what I have figured out so far from looking at the arrangements that Shannon's Cove Resort has made for us," she continues. "We will be taking Billy's plane to Cat Island and stay at Shannon's Cove Resort, which is also catering our wedding."

She opens up her computer, "From looking at all the brochures and on the website, Shannon's Cove Resort has several bungalows available for us to rent. We've been working closely with the resort owners. One of them, Maria, has been very helpful organizing and coordinating all our wedding plans."

The guys—Matt, George, Thomas, and Robert—all nod. Thomas laughs. "I like how you have this all figured out, Sarah. I think it's going to be great."

I read one of the blurbs on the pamphlet and begin laughing. "The mosquitoes must be like the ones we have here on Ocracoke Island because one of the reviews of the resorts says, "Don't forget your bug spray or Skin So Soft from Avon."

I turn to my brother. "Matt, do you remember the day when we were kids, we got covered in welts from all the mosquitoes? That was a crazy vacation. We looked like we had chickenpox."

Matt laughs. "Yeah, I remember that day. The mosquitoes came out in swarms. We had to run back to our minivan."

Sarah is animated and excited as she talks about the wedding. "I have plans for us every day, from the day we get there until the day we leave," she announces. "The day that we arrive, we are going to meet with Maria, and she'll show us photos from previous weddings to help us decide what we want. It's a shame Jenni isn't going to be able to make it to do our wedding pictures. I was really worried that I wouldn't be able to plan our wedding remotely, but Maria has been great about everything, even hiring a photographer for us."

I look again at the brochure for Shannon's Cove. "The pictures of the resort and the island look like a heavenly paradise," I tell the group.

My mind wanders back to when I told Thomas that I really didn't know what we should do for our wedding. It is still surprising to me because I never expected him to propose so soon. I'm ecstatic but a little nervous about the when's and where's. Before we headed over to the inn, I also confide in Thomas about something that is troubling me. I told him how I am concerned about Emily.

"I'm worried because she has been so quiet when we're discussing Sarah's plans. She told me she thinks that she will never get married," I say. "I have been trying for years to tell her that George is in love with her, but she doesn't believe me."

Thomas nods. "Time will tell," he says. "Just be patient. It will happen eventually."

After we talk about the wedding, we agree to meet in the pub later for an early dinner. The guys leave to go back to do some work at Robert and Sally's house. Sarah and Emily's mom, Sally White, has something she wants us to do after dinner.

"Girls," she says, "let's go up in the attic to see if we can find something special for Sarah and Matt's wedding."

Sarah nods in agreement and turns to my sister. "I love to explore our old attic and look at all the treasures! Sally, do you think you can come over to the B&B to help us later tonight?"

Sally, my sister nods and speaks. "Absolutely, I wouldn't miss it for the world."

At dinner we celebrate with a little wine, and we start reminiscing. We continue the conversation until we head upstairs to the attic. The guys tell us to meet them in the den when we're done. They're heading into the den to watch a little football. My sister, Sally, gets up and points upstairs.

"I need to go home and check on the twins and pick up Mom and Grandmom after their pedicures. Then I'll come back to join you," she says.

"Do you remember when we were all little girls and how we used to play in your old attic?" I ask the girls as we climb the attic stairs. "Remember we would spend our days in the early summer playing dress up and braiding our hair on rainy days. It was so much fun and so magical."

We're all lost in thought for a minute, then I quietly ask Emily, "Do you ever wonder if you and the old Emily are linked together, like I am to Evangeline? Do you ever dream about her? I was just wondering."

Emily nods. "That's so funny that you're asking me today because I had a dream about her last night. It was about the day that Jacob came back to collect Evangeline and take her home with him to become his wife," she says. "In my dream, Emily kept telling him that she didn't believe that Evangeline was dead, that she could still feel her soul. When Jacob left, he gave Emily the diamond ring that he had planned to give Evangeline, saying that if his love couldn't wear it, he knew that she would want Emily to have it. It was so sad."

Emily pauses and looks thoughtful. "Sometimes I think you and I are linked in some deep-in-the-past way, Angie," Emily says. When you were kidnapped, I could feel your terror. I never told you, but I dreamed that you had been captured."

I shake my head. "Wow, that's so crazy. I can't believe you never mentioned it before."

Emily shrugs. "I guess I was so happy and relieved when they found you that I just forgot all about it."

I think to myself how blessed I feel to be with my friends. I am so lucky that we continue to share in each other's lives and make so many new memories.

I remember suddenly. "Oh, I forgot to tell you guys, my mom has decided to come and help us explore tonight in the attic, along with my grandmother, Mary. They'll be here in a little while."

We are going over Sarah's plans again for the wedding as we head into the attic, then everyone starts teasing me about my wedding to Thomas.

I just laugh. "I really want our wedding to be casual, with just a few friends and family. I want to hold our reception on the beach of Ocracoke Island," I say. "I want my wedding gown to be simple but elegant. I will know my wedding dress when I see it."

We climb the dusty stairwell and step into the past. The dust mites sparkle and float in the air as the sun shines into the forgotten space.
"I didn't realize there were so many old trunks up here," Sarah says. "Mom, didn't you tell me most of the things up here are from the 1700s and haven't been touched?"

At that instant, before her mother could answer, Evangeline appears before us. "Look into the trunk against the wall, Angie. It belonged to me when I was but a girl. Some of the things in it even belonged to my friend, Emily."

The image of Evangeline evaporates into the air, and we walk toward the wall she indicated and pull out the ancient trunk. I feel my hands and arms tingle as I help open the trunk. What's inside is absolutely amazing: a beautiful, pale ivory wedding gown embellished with pearl beads around the neckline. It is very simple but elegant.

I pull out the gown and sigh. "This is exactly what I have been dreaming about," I say in wonderment. "This is it. I just love it. What do you think?" I hold it up to my body.

Everyone is in awe. Sarah hugs me. "It looks like you just found your wedding gown."

Inside their attic is an antique mirror. I walk over to the frosty mirror to the gaze at myself. "I don't know what you guys think, but it's so pretty. I can't wait to show my sister, Sally, Mom and Grandmom."

I quickly try on the gown. My dark hair flows over the beads that have been so intricately sewn onto the fabric.

"I don't know how but this fabric looks brand new," I marvel. "Look! There's a note attached to the dress. It says, 'This is the trousseau of Evangeline Alexander, to be worn on my wedding day. I sewed the gown with the help of my friend Emily White. Please give this gown to my descendant one day so that my love can be rekindled with that of Jacob.'"

I feel goosebumps up and down my arms and legs.

We stand back, dumbfounded. I wonder aloud, "Do you really think that I was meant to find this gown for my wedding? Do you think my love for Thomas is real—or is it being guided by Evangeline? I'm worried what if it isn't real?"

Evangeline appears before us again. "Angie, what you have for Thomas is real. I only guided you to him. He will make you happy. His love is true, and he will be good to you.

"He's a good man," she continues. "Don't doubt the feelings you have for each other. The feelings are real. You and Thomas have unlocked the past so that I can be reunited with my Jacob. Be happy and remember I am here to protect you."

Evangeline again vanishes as quickly as she appeared. She leaves me with tears streaming down my cheeks. Sarah wipes them with the corner of her sleeve.

"Angie, believe in Thomas's love for you. He's a wonderful guy and will make a great husband," she says.

Emily hugs me. "I've known Thomas all my life and he has never loved anyone the way that he loves you. Don't be afraid. Open your heart up to him. He will make you happy."

I feel so emotional. "I just don't know what I am supposed to do. I've never felt this way before even when I was with Larry. My love for Thomas is so strong. It's overwhelming. What if it isn't real?"

Emily shakes her head. "You were always meant to be with Thomas. He's your destiny. Remember what your dad said when he revealed what Evangeline had said to him about the 'time being right?' Remember when he gave you the necklace? Maybe that was why your paths never crossed until now. You both had to get to this point in your life so that you could be together now."

I smile with big tears glistening down my cheeks, hugging the gown to my chest. "So, what do you guys think about my new wedding dress?" They all laugh and gather me up in a big bear hug.

Even though Sarah is managing the B&B, I turn to Emily and Sarah's mom. "I guess we're going to be planning another wedding?" I say, tentatively. Then I take Sally hand in mine and ask, "Do you think we can get married in the B&B? I have always dreamed about walking down your stairs into the parlor on my wedding day."

With tears in her eyes, Emily and Sarah's mother enthusiastically nods her head. "Oh honey, I would just love to have you and Thomas get married here! I've always dreamed about one of you girls getting married in our home. I remember when you four used to play dress-up. It seems like only yesterday."

Sarah looks sad. "Mom, would you rather that I get married here, too?"

Sally White hugs her daughter. "Sweetheart, I love your wedding plans with Matt. I can't wait to see you in your wedding dress on the beach. It only seems fitting that you two would get married on a beach. Don't you remember when you and Matt were kids, you two would chase each other down the shore. I have always known in my heart that you would marry him one day."

Emily laughs. "That's so funny, Mom. I always felt the same way. I knew Sarah and Matt were meant for each other."

Sarah smiles. "I always dreamed about getting married to Matt. I dreamed he would be my husband even when I was a little girl."

"Well, now that that's established," Sarah adds, "we should keep exploring these old trunks. We have a lot more trunks to look through."

Inside the trunk that held my wedding dress, we find all kinds of old treasures. There's a sapphire bracelet and another brown leather journal containing letters that belonged to Evangeline from her time on the island. "I can't wait to read more about her life," I say.

In one of the tiny wooden boxes is a little note in Evangeline's handwriting. I start to read the note aloud. "If you have found my blue sapphire bracelet, it was given to me by Daniel when I was on Cat Island after I had William. It holds a key to his treasures. It really is perfect for your 'something blue.'"

Sarah squeals. "I know, Angie, I just love it! I will treasure it always. She has the bracelet on her tiny wrist, and we look more closely at it.

I reread Evangeline's note.

"Wait a minute," I tell the others. "It's so funny that we discovered the key, because I remember in one of my dreams Evangeline said that Daniel had hidden the key to unlock his treasure in a gift he gave to her." I recite what the note in my dream said:

"A treasure you will see when you use the key.
Look to the caves to see, a treasure lost to me.
Daniel's love was strong. He thought I could do no wrong.
He hid the key in a gift he gave to me."

"Wow, look at this book. It has Evangeline's name on the inside cover. I think we just found one of Evangeline's other journals and look at all these notes and letters in it." She hands it to me.

I hold the book in my hands, "I can't wait to read them. This must've been when she was on the island with Daniel."

Emily looks over my shoulder at the book. "That should help you with your new novel." She looks back at the contents of the trunk. "There are also some old baby clothes in here that must have belonged to William. It's like going back in time 200 years, like opening a time capsule to look at all these ancient items.

"Look Angie. Here is a letter from Evangeline, the one that must have never been sent and was found on the dunes when she disappeared."

The letter reads:

My Dear Jacob,

I miss you dreadfully. My heart aches for you. I am so sorry to hear about your Poppa. He was a lovely man and so kind to our family. I can't wait for the day that you will come for me to make me yours. I long to hold you in my arms forever.

Please hurry. My heart is breaking waiting for you.

All my Love,

Evangeline

Sarah sighs. "Oh, that's just so sad. Can you just imagine how she was feeling back then? She was pregnant with William and the man she loved was miles away. She couldn't tell him. It wasn't like today where you can pick up a phone and call someone."

Sarah hands me the letter. "You really should have a great love story when you finish your novel."

Emily finds another trunk in the corner of the room. "Where was this? I've been coming up into the attic for years and never remember seeing this one," she says.

She opens it. Tucked inside its lining at the back of the trunk is a charcoal portrait. It stares back at her.

"Oh, my goodness! This must be Emily's trunk. It's like looking in a mirror," she says, as she waves her mother over. "Mama, I never realized I looked so much like the old Emily White."

Emily's mother stares at the picture.

"Wow, you're right. I never knew it either. I'm amazed at the likeness between you two girls," she says. "I haven't seen many pictures of Emily when she was young or your age. All the ones I've seen are when she is older, holding one of her grandchildren.

"Look here," she adds, excited. "In the bottom corner of the picture is the signature of Roger Brown."

I gaze at the sketch. "Oh my gosh. It is like one of the pictures that we found in his books in his secret room."

We continue searching inside the trunk and come across an album with more charcoal sketches. There is a note in the front of the book that says:

For My Dear Friends, Robert & Emily,
Please enjoy these pictures of all your friends and family. I am so happy to have been among them.

It is signed by Roger Brown.

I think to myself how amazing it is, the likeness of the past Emily to our Emily and Evangeline to me.

Emily reaches into the trunk and pulls out an old hand-carved mirror. There are tiny pearls and garnet stones inlaid on the handle and the back of the mirror. "This is so pretty," Emily says. Then she adds, "Do you think I am linked to Emily from long ago, maybe like you and Evangeline? If so, maybe that would link you and me, too."

I question Emily. "What do *you* think? You said you dreamed of the old Emily when Jacob gave her Evangeline's ring."

Emily thinks for a minute. "All my life I've had dreams about a woman dressed in old clothes from the 1700s. I have never able to see her face, but it is as if I have been watching her life through my dreams," Emily says. "It reminds me of some of your dreams about Evangeline. So far, though, she's never come to me in a vision like Evangeline has to you."

Sarah looks at both of us. "Maybe it's because you haven't needed her to yet, Emily. Just think, Evangeline didn't start speaking to Angie until last year when the time was right to guide her toward Thomas."

I nod in agreement. "When I went to our old home in Ripley, my father visited me. I never finished telling you the whole story. I'm still trying to process it. I still miss my dad so much that it hurts."

After a pause, I continue. "You know, Dad told me he has been here the whole time. He told me he was even there when Sally gave birth to the twins. It's funny now, how I can feel his presence."

Emily asks, "Do you think that Emily is watching over me, too?"

I answer, "I am pretty sure that our ancestors are here protecting us. They're our guardian angels. Evangeline had an ancestor that visited her when she was on Cat Island. Her name was Virginia. I think she might have even been the one and only Virginia Dare. One of my dreams was about how she came to Evangeline and told her that her colony had been abducted by a Spanish fleet and taken to Cat Island when Virginia was a baby. In the dream, she was dressed in clothes from the 1500s.

"And in one of my other dreams," I continue, "Eleanor Dare, Virginia Dare's mother, came to Evangeline in a dream. It was a like a dream inside a dream. In that dream, Eleanor was giving birth to Virginia."

Sarah grins. "Angie, your grandfather would love to hear about that dream. Maybe when we go to Cat Island, we can find out more. Maybe Virginia will even come to you when we go to the island."

Emily turns to her mother. "Hey, Mom, do you think I can have the mirror and the picture album? Sarah, would it be okay with you?"

Sally White hugs her daughter. "Of course, honey. You girls are welcome to have anything in these trunks."

We hear footsteps coming up the stairs to the attic. My mother, Sally, and my grandmother walk in through the door.

"What did we miss?" my mom asks. "You all look so serious."

I twirl around in the wedding dress that I had found in Evangeline's trunk. "What do you think about my new wedding dress?"

There are tears in her eyes as Mom embraces me. "You look so beautiful, Angie. I can't wait to see you in it on your wedding day."

Grandma just smiles and takes my chin in her hand. "Oh honey, you look so pretty."

Then I show them the note that was attached to the dress in the trunk. "Well, what do you think?"

My sister squeals, "Oh, Angie. It's perfect for you. It's just how I imagined it." I hug her back and point to Sally White. "Sally said that Thomas and I can be married in the inn."

My mom can't contain her emotions and tears start welling up in her eyes. She embraces me and straightens my hair. "I can't believe my baby is going to get married," she says. "Time is just flying by."

Sally White wraps her arms around her dear old friend. "Isabella, I know how you feel. Our girls are all growing up. Before long they will all be married with children."

Emily frowns. "Almost everyone."

Her mom grins as she takes her daughter in her arms. "Your time will come, honey," she says. "You and George need to open your eyes. It's so obvious he's in love with you. Just wait until he sees you in that bridesmaid's dress."

Then Emily leads my mother and grandmother to the chest that once belonged to the old Emily White. She opens it. "Look at this. It's a picture of the old Emily."

They gasp in shock then look from the picture to Emily and back to the portrait again. They are amazed at the resemblance.

My Mom looks closer at the picture. "Oh my, I never realized that there was such a likeness between you two."

We show them all the other things that once belonged to Evangeline and her little son, William. We also show them the picture album that was in Emily's trunk. Names are written on the back of each charcoal drawing to identify the subjects of the portraits.

My sister is excitedly flipping through the old sketch book. "I can't wait to set up my art studio so that one day I can paint these pictures." We can only smile, remembering the surprise room the boys and her husband, Robert, have made for her.

Emily thinks for a minute then says, "I think that would be great to see portraits of all our people from the past. Mom is it okay if Sally takes the sketchbook so she can do pictures?"

Sally White agrees. "I think that is a lovely idea."

We finish exploring and start to go back down to the parlor to meet with the guys to discuss our treasure hunting and Sarah and Matt's wedding plans. I remove the wedding dress, changing back into my clothes, and Sarah takes it from me.

Bitsey Gagne

"We can't let Thomas see this. It's bad luck. I'll tuck it away somewhere safe," she says. "You go ahead—the guys are already in the parlor. Don't forget that you need to tell your grandad about your dream about Virginia."

Chapter 17

More Plans

The football game is over and the guys are all gathered around the large dining room table when we come downstairs from the attic. Paul is telling everyone about his latest finds at the library and on the Internet.

"I've been doing research on Cat Island. It looks like we really might be able to find Blackbeard's treasure," he says. "As you are all aware, Blackbeard was grand friends with Arthur Cat, for whom the island is named. There are many hiding places we can search. There are numerous caverns and underwater caves that would be a perfect place to stash a treasure."

He points to an area on one of the maps. "One of the spots that we definitely will need to explore is a place called the Mermaid Hole. I heard years ago that whenever there was a bad storm, the locals would go to hide there to be safe from the storms. Can you imagine being caught in the grip of a hurricane in a grass hut? I reckon the caves were quite a sanctuary against the elements for the locals if a hurricane was coming."

Robert chimes in. "I read about that in some of your old history books. It's really quite fascinating," he says. "People didn't have weather forecasters. They just had to watch for signs of bad weather approaching. I can't wait to explore those caverns. I'm going to bring my small metal detector with me."

I nod in agreement. "I really want to explore Mermaid Hole, too," I say. "Along with the caverns, there are supposed to be blue water holes. I wonder if this is where Evangeline used to take her little William swimming back when she was on the island?"

We all start talking about the things we want to do in the Bahamas.

"I heard that the snorkeling and scuba diving down there is awesome. Shannon's Cove Resort has a company called Shannon's Cove Diving," Robert says. "Sally and I took scuba diving lessons at our local college several years ago with Matt and Thomas. Who would have thought we would get to use our scuba diving skills to hunt for pirate treasure?"

Matt turns to me, Sarah, and Emily. "You girls should really think about taking a scuba class before we go to Cat Island. It might come in useful for our trip. George took a dive class at Roanoke Island Outfitters and Dive Shop around the same time we did. At the time, we been talking about going on a scuba diving trip one day.

"Now it looks like our first dive trip is going to be searching for Blackbeard's treasure," he continues. "How cool is that?"

George nods in agreement. "Yeah, they have a really neat class. I highly recommend it."

Emily raises her eyebrows. "We've always wanted to try it. You would've thought we would have done it already by now," she says. "Sarah and Angie, what do you say we take a scuba class so we can go diving with the rest of them?"

We agree that it's a really good idea. Emily opens her phone to look up the class schedule.

"We need to sign up for a class later this month before it gets too cold," she says. "How's next weekend sound?" We agree, and she registers us for the lesson.

"So, that's all settled. I signed us up for a class," she says.

Paul and Robert show us other places on the map we need to explore while we are on the island. Robert points to a specific spot. "We should try kayaking on Orange Creek while we are there," he says.

"Oh, and we need to see Bennett's Harbor. It has a famous hiding place used by pirates in the 1600s and the 1800s that we should check out. The pirates would hide in the port waiting for unsuspecting ships to pass by.

"The harbor has quite a fascinating history. It was also important for producing salt later," he adds.

Emily has been reading about the Bahamas in preparation for the trip. "I was reading a book by Kim Heinbach," she says, "and in it, she talked about Obeah. Sounded spooky, a bit like Vodou that you hear about in New Orleans. Apparently, some locals think the practitioners are responsible for witchcraft."

Isabella and David interrupt to ask in unison: "But where is the wedding going to be held?"

Sarah excitedly answers. "Shannon's Cove Resort. They have a restaurant right on the resort that will be catering our wedding," she says. "I asked one of the resort's owners, Maria, about local photographers to take our wedding pictures. She emailed me examples of the work of one of the photographers who seems to do a very good job."

"What about your friend Jenni?" Isabella asks. "I thought she was going to fly with us and do the wedding photography."

"Yes, that was the original plan, but now it looks like she can't leave at that time of the year," Sarah explains.

She turns to give Matt a kiss on the cheek. "I can't wait for our special day," she tells him.

My sister, Sally, stifles a yawn. "Excuse me. Sorry, the twins had me up at two in the morning. They're teething right now and they're quite a handful," she says. "Thank heavens for Georgia. She has been a lifesaver, but sometimes they just want their mama."

Isabella hugs her daughter. "I remember those days. Maybe we should all call it a night."

Thomas taps Robert and David on the back. "We have news. Your house should be almost done by tomorrow. I know it's been a long time. We really hope you are going to love it."

David winks at my mom. "Isabella, do you want to share our news with the others, or would you like me to tell everyone?"

My mother blushes. "David, you go ahead and tell everyone."

David grins. "As all of you know, I've been staying in Isabella's home during the renovations at my place. Well … Isabella and I have decided to make it permanent."

He puts his arm around my mother and kisses her on the cheek. "I've fallen deeply in love with your mom. We want to be together."

Isabella pulls out a gold chain that is around her neck. The light catches the dazzling diamond solitaire strung over it.

David moves behind Isabella, unhooks the necklace and removes the ring. He then steps in front of her and bends his knee. "Isabella, please be mine forever."

My mother takes David's hands in hers. "Yes, I will be your wife."

We all start clapping and cheering. There are tears of joy and happiness as everyone celebrates this happy news.

I kiss my mother. "Oh Mom, I'm so happy for you and David. He's such a special man. So, does this mean we're going to have another wedding on the horizon"?

Isabella grins. "It certainly looks that way."

David turns to Sally, Matt, and me and asks: "May I have your mom's hand in marriage? I really love her and want all of your blessings."

We laugh, nod, and the room erupts again in congratulations, hugs, and kisses. Paul and Mary, our grandparents, call out their approval of the union, too. I can feel my dad's presence and, for a flash, I catch a glimpse of him. I don't say anything—I don't want to interrupt the moment—but I smile and wink at him.

Thomas sees and asks, "Did you just see Evangeline?"

I hug him and give him a quick peck on the cheek. "I will explain it to you later."

Jim White laughs. "Well, this has been quite a happy night. I can't wait to see what the future holds. What a great way to end an evening."

We help to gather up all the treasures and clues so Jim can lock them back in the B&B safe. Then we say good night to each other.

Thomas and I stroll back to our cottage, hand in hand, grinning at each other. We take Max out for his nightly walk on the beach. Autumn is closing in on us and the air is becoming chillier with each passing day. Most of the tourists have already left; only a few fishermen linger about the island.

Thomas exhales. "You know I can't decide what time of year that I love the most on Ocracoke Island," he says. He wraps his arms around me and kisses me on my neck. "Angie I'm so glad that I moved back to the island and even happier to have you here with me. I love you so much."

I feel like my heart will burst. "I hope we always feel this way," I say. "And I'm so happy for Mom and David, too.

"I've been wanting to ask you something," I continue. "Do you think it's okay if we get married at the Shepard's Head B&B?"

I explain what happened when we went looking around the attic. "I found the dress that I will wear when we get married," I tell him. "It's beautiful and it once belonged to Evangeline."

Thomas looks thoughtful. "I really hadn't thought so far ahead yet, but it all sounds great," he says. "I can just imagine you walking down the stairs with your long dark hair flowing. You will look like an angel." He squeezes my shoulder.

I lean back into his arms. "We really haven't talked about when, where, or how we wanted to get married. Do you have any ideas of what you want?"

Thomas thinks for a moment. "No honey, I'm just anxious to make you mine. I never thought I could love someone as much as I love you."

I feel the tears welling up in my eyes.

"You have made me so happy," I tell him. "I never thought that I would feel this much love in my heart. It's kind of crazy, you know.

"Now that we have the 'where,' we just need to figure out the 'when,'" I add.

Thomas nods. "I say we get married a year from that fateful moment when we met. Do you remember that day? You had just arrived on the island. I'll never forget it. It was June 5th. I think it falls on a Wednesday next year, so how about the following Saturday?"

I agree. Then I add: "I don't want anything, too elaborate. I want to keep it simple, just family and a few friends."

Thomas laughs out loud. "Well, between our family and friends on the island, it will still be quite a large wedding."

Thomas whistles. "Here, boy. Max, let's head home." As we walk the dog toward the cottage, Thomas slips his arm around my waist, and I tell him, "You make me so happy. I can't imagine my life without you."

When we get home, I show Thomas the journal holding the letters from Daniel that we found in Evangeline's trunk. I explain, "Maybe it holds more secrets that will lead us to the treasure."

Chapter 18

A New Beginning

The boys have already packed up most of the furniture to take over to Sally and Robert's new home by the time Sarah, Emily, and I get to my mother's home. The twins are being fed. I tickle little Evie on her belly.

"I can't believe how much they have grown in the last month. They are both so alert, but I think Evie is the more curious of the two," I say. "Watch how her little blue eyes follow you around the room but William, also, watches everything that is going on, too, so I guess they are both curious. He's so cute and his curly blonde hair tickles your nose when you hold him."

Since Sally and Robert have been living in my mother's home with her while work is underway on their house, most of their belongings are still in boxes. Emily, Sarah, and I plan to help them unpack all the boxes. Mom plans to stay behind with Georgia. Sally is so organized. Every box is labeled so we know which room it goes in.

"Your mother is going to help me watch the twins while you help Sally and Robert move today," Georgia tells me. "I'll bring them over later today when you call me. David and Isabella offered to drive us over to the house once you've set up the babies' room."

Emily pulls up in George's truck, and we pack all the boxes in the back of it. It is going to be a gorgeous fall day. The crystal blue sky is cloudless. It is cool enough that we need to wear long sleeves.

If I were still in D.C., there would be frost by now. I don't miss that about D.C.—I used to hate having to come out in the mornings and scrape my car windows—but I will miss the leaves changing colors. I told Thomas the other day that we should plan a trip up to the mountains soon.

With all the boxes packed into the truck, we head over to Robert and Sally's new house. It is only about two miles from my mother's home.

Isabella is tearful. "I am going to miss waking up and having you all around every day." Sally's laughter fills the air. "Mom, we're only right down the lane.

You can come visit us anytime, every day, if you like. I'm sure Georgia would love to have your company and your help with the twins."

When we get to the house, Robert rushes out. "Wait, Sally, I want to carry you over the threshold." She is giddy with excitement as he swoops her up. Once inside the house, he sets her down but adds: "I have something to show you before we get started unpacking."

We are all grinning from ear to ear. Sally smiles. "What is it that you've planned?"

He leads her upstairs to the attic. "It's a surprise."

We all follow them up the newly refurbished stairs. Sally shakes her head. "I can't understand why you are taking me to the attic. Once upstairs, Robert hands her a set of keys and points toward a door.

"Wait. I don't remember seeing this door before. Where does this lead?" Sally asks. She slips the key in the lock, unlatches it, and opens the door.

We all yell, "Surprise!"

There are tears in my sister's eyes as she enters the room that once belonged to Roger. It has turned out perfectly. Robert painted the walls a pale yellow. The oak floors gleam.

Sally is astonished as she walks around looking at all her painting supplies. Robert mixed some of the old easels in with Sally's easels. The antique stained-glass windows frame an old stone fireplace. Above its beautifully stained oak mantle is a painting of Evangeline holding little William in a rocking chair. Her beautiful blue eyes stare out at us.

Tears are prickling Sally's eyes as she kisses Robert on his flushed cheek. "Oh honey, thank you so much for this special gift. It's perfect," she says, emotion in her voice.

In a mist Evangeline appear before us. She turns to Sally. "I hope you enjoy this room as much as Roger did. He loved to escape to this room and make magic in his paintings and drawings." Then she disappears as quickly as she had appeared, leaving us all open-mouthed.

Sally wipes joyous tears from her eyes, "I just love when they come to visit us. It's like having our own guardian angels."

The rest of us decide it is time to let Sally and Robert have some private time. As we walk out of the room, I turn to hug my sister. "Take your time and enjoy this special moment."

It always amazes me how much Sally and Robert still love each other. I hope Thomas and I will be as happy as them in our life together.

Thomas, Matt, and George start setting up the furniture that they helped Robert build for the twins. In the nursery, the golden oak mantle glows in sunlight that streams through the old plate glass windows. The nursery is painted a pale green. Sally has added murals of seashells, seahorses, and sand dollars.

Thomas and Matt have made two rocking chairs for the twins' room. I can just imagine Robert and Sally in the room together, each one rocking a baby to sleep. Emily and Sarah have made cushions for the window seat. Matching curtains with the same sea seashore theme frame the cozy room.

Sally and Robert come into the nursery just as we've finished setting the room up. Sally's cheeks are wet with happy tears. Sally blubbers, "It's so beautiful. Thank you, guys, so much. I have no words to describe how I blessed I am feeling."

Robert looks around. He has tears in his eyes, too.

Then Sally sighs, wistfully. "I only wish dad could have been here to see all this."

I hug my sister. "He is probably watching us right now," I say. "Remember I told you that he came to me at our home in Ripley? He told me then that he is always with us and will be here to protect us. He was with you at the twins' birth, but he didn't make his presence known because he didn't want to take away from the moment of the day."

As I say this, my father appears before us. There are tears in his eyes. "I'm so proud of all of you, and I am so happy for you. Your home is beautiful. You boys did a wonderful job—the woodwork and the furniture are magnificent."

Sally places her hand over her mouth. "Daddy, I have missed you so much. I wish I could hug you."

He reaches out to brush her tears away then kisses her on the cheek. "I must go now. Kiss your adorable babies for me. Please know that I will always be here for all of you."

Then he vanishes.

None of us move. We all stand staring at the spot where he appeared. Then Matt and I hug Sally while she cries in our arms. She whispers, "It was so good seeing Dad. I finally feel like I have been able to say good-bye to him. He passed away so suddenly. There has been a hole in my heart ever since he died. I couldn't let him go."

Sally wipes her eyes, shakes her shoulders, and takes a deep breath. "Enough with the tears. We need to unpack these boxes and set up this house."

Robert takes Sally in his arms and kisses her gently on the lips. He brushes her tears away. "I love you, Sally. I can't wait to begin our lives together with our family in this home."

"Well, let's get started unpacking all the boxes in the kitchen," I chime in. Matt nods in agreement.

"Thomas, George, and I are going to finish unloading the furniture. We'll see you downstairs in a little bit." We leave Sally and Robert in the nursery. Sally is trying to be brave.

Emily, Sarah, and I start unpacking boxes in the kitchen. We are unwrapping the dishes when Sally joins us. "I can't thank you guys enough. The nursery turned out beautifully and is so special to Robert and me," she says. "All the things that you girls made are so unique and gorgeous. We really appreciate them."

Robert and Sally's everyday dishes are rust-and-tan colored, and the gray-and-tan tile backsplash accentuates the colors of the plates. The dark gray granite island and countertops have splashes of tan and rust splattered throughout in an explosion of color. The spicy scent from the Bath & Body Works cinnamon and cloves wallflowers' fragrance fills the air. Sarah runs her hand over the beautiful island. "I can't believe how well these tiles match our stoneware and kitchen. The guys did an amazing job."

With so many hands working, we finish organizing Sally and Robert's kitchen in less than an hour. Sally puts on some hot water. "How's about I make us all some tea?"

Then she smiles and glances around the room again. "It's so pretty. I just love how it's turned out," she says. "But I'm feeling chilly." She looks toward the fireplace.

Robert pulls out a log to lay a fire. "I was just thinking the same thing. It will take the chill off this old place," he says.

Before long there is a fire blazing in the ancient stone fireplace. Meanwhile, we continue working and the living room starts to look as if it were lived in, not just being set up today.

Sally beams. "Look how the wooden oak built-ins gleam as the sunlight filters through the stained-glass windows and reflects off the wood. It reminds me of an old country home. It is so quaint."

Sally had helped the girls make rust-and-brown pillows and curtains. The walls are painted dark tan and the accent wall —where the fireplace is—is a pretty maroon. It reminds me of autumn. The dark brown leather couch, loveseat, and easy chairs are positioned around the fireplace. There is a splendid painting of a sunset over Silver Lake mirroring golden, orange, and tangerine bursts of color above the water.

The painting is signed by Roger Brown. Robert found it in Roger's studio. He felt it would give the room a special touch and be a nice way to honor the memory of his ancestor, Roger Brown.

The dining room opens off the cozy kitchen. Here the walls are mustard and warm pumpkin. There is an ancient mahogany china cabinet built into the walls. We found a note inside—signed by Roger Brown—that says the wood was "brought over by me when I traveled the seas as a pirate."

Robert and Sally's china pattern, with its golden-framed pearl-colored plates, matches the colors on the room's walls and trim. The centers of the plates have small orange and blue flowers.

"I'm so happy and proud of the way our house is shaping up," Sally announces, beaming with excitement.

There is a tiny powder room off the kitchen. It is decorated in pale baby blue, and its sand-colored border frames the ceiling with seashells and turtles. Everything in the petite bathroom has a beach theme.

Next to the powder room are a combined mudroom and the laundry room. The guys have lined the mudroom and laundry room with pretty white cabinets. They've thought of everything, even a laundry chute to carry clothes from the second floor to a basket in the laundry room. There is an area to hang clothes and organize all the laundry supplies.

The mudroom has a sink big enough to give a pet—or a baby, if needed—a bath. The hall tree with a bench will be handy when putting on and removing shoes. The boys even made a space to store boots and shoes. The mudroom door opens to the yard, where a stone walkway leads to an outdoor shower. The guys thought it would be perfect for after a day at the beach.

We work to unpack all the boxes my sister has organized when she packed their things earlier in the year. Sally and Robert have only a few more belongings left in their home at Clements, Maryland.

"I want to unpack the things for the master bedroom next," Sally says. "I have a lot of things I'm going to throw out, but you guys don't need to help me with that."

The master bedroom is painted a pale green with a sage accent wall that makes the old stone fireplace pop. A decorative white mantle sits like an eyebrow above the beautiful stonework. Thomas and George's cousin, Billy Alexander, was able to use all the old stones when he rebuilt the fireplace. The stones are in hues of pearly powdered gray, oyster, and khaki.

The room is welcoming. Sally, the girls, and I made pillows, curtains, and a quilt for the room in sage, moss, and olive and the overall effect is charming. The massive king-sized four poster bed gleams in the light streaming through the old windows. Two other bedrooms upstairs have a similar theme. Each contains some of Robert's dad's old furniture.

We are still working on the curtains and quilts for those rooms. Sally runs her hand over the quilt on her bed. "I really love all the quilts, curtains and pillows that we have made."

She turns to me. "Angie, it's your turn next. The house Thomas found for you two is going to be so beautiful. I can't wait to see what they do to it. It sounds like he has all kinds of ideas on how he wants to renovate it."

I sigh. "It's like being in a really great dream," I say, adding, "I have never been so happy and at ease since I met Thomas. I feel like I have known him all my life—even though it's only been five months since we met."

We are all tired by the time we finish moving Sally and Robert into their new home. David and my mom go to pick up pizza from Sorrell's and to bring the twins to their new home. Their pizza is always so good, and we are all starving since we didn't stop to eat lunch. Robert pops open some chilled white wine, compliments of Emily for their homecoming.

Soon David and my mother are back with the pizza and twins, and we're settled in, ready to eat.

Sally grins. "Our first meal in our new home," she declares. She is radiant as she wraps her arms around Robert and the two cuddle their beloved children. The adorable twins are wide eyed, taking in all of their new surroundings, but it isn't long before they start showing signs that it's time for a much-needed nap.

David holds up his glass of wine and toasts the group. "Bless this home and all our family and friends," he says. "May everyone who enters here always be healthy and happy."

One of Sorrell's special pizzas is called the "greenhead." Pesto swirls add to its flavor, and the cheese melts in your mouth. The guys love the Hawaiian pizza with its succulent pineapple, ham, and bacon.

The home's floorplan has a spacious living room, and Max, Ace, and Skippy have staked out spots to lay in front of the roaring fireplace. We join them, as we all sit back with our full bellies and relax in Sally and Robert's new home.

Chapter 19

Evangeline's Life

Thomas is the first to get up, and he grabs Max's leash. Max wakes up when he hears the jiggles of the lead. His tail wags. Ace and Skippy rouse from their spots in front of the fire. They want out for a walk, too.

I pet them, my mother's dogs. They wiggle their little bodies and butts, squirming in delight.

"Mom, I'll take Ace and Skippy. Where are their leashes?"

Mom points to the mudroom. "I hung them up on the hall tree. Thanks, guys."

Thomas and I step out into the frosty autumn air. I zip up my royal blue ski jacket and we take the puppies for their walk. The oyster shell driveway crunches under our feet as we make our way down the driveway.

The town is pretty much deserted as all the tourists have gone for the season, although there are still a few fishermen still left. The locals love it when the island comes back to them so that they can enjoy its beauty. The light has dwindled, leaving a glowing orange sunset.

"I will never get tired of the sunsets here. They are so beautiful and enchanting," I tell Thomas. "It is always magical when the sun melts into the Pamlico Bay. The colors seem to explode into awesome slices of magenta, tangerine, and so many different shades of pink."

Thomas pulls out the rope toy that belongs to Max. The dog's whole body wiggles in joy. The dogs run free on the beach. Max catches the toy and plays tug of war with the other puppies.

The shoreline glows with the fading sun, and sandpipers are busy feasting on coquinas in the waning light. Thomas hugs me and kisses my cool cheek. "Hopefully by this time next spring, we will be in our home," he says. "I can't wait to show you the plans I've started working on. It's going to be awesome. Matt and Billy are going to help me design it."

I smile up at him and kiss his lips, nuzzling my mouth on his chin and his warm neck. I feel so at home when he is near me. "You make me happy," I say. "It's hard for me to believe I could ever feel so much love. My heart feels full when you are near."

Our passion is erupting as our lips meet. Thomas grins. "I think we should head home or I'm going to take you right here on the beach," he says.

He whistles for the pups, and they come running to meet us. The temperatures have fallen, and the air is frigid. The weather forecast calls for it to go down into the fifties tonight as a cold front approach the Carolina coast. I am forever grateful to be away from the frosty Maryland winters. It rarely gets too cold here on the island although always feels colder on the coast.

We head back to Sally and Robert's home and, when we open the door, warm air from the fireplace envelopes us. We know it is time to go back to our house. I see that Sarah and Matt are getting ready to head home, too. It is going to be an early night. All of us are tired. Thomas and I start to stay our good-byes.

The twins are up from their nap. They are so alert as they look around their new home. Then suddenly, I sense Evangeline and Jacob before I see them watching my niece and nephew. Little Evie, cooing, reaches toward where they are standing. Little Jacob's eyes are on them, too, watching intently. Max's tail begins to wag when he looks in the direction of the ghostly figures.

Robert laughs. "It never gets old seeing the two of them. I feel like they are protecting us."

Evangeline and Jacob disappear as quickly as they arrived, a signal for us to hug and kiss everyone good-bye. David and my mom, Isabella, leave with us. David hugs Robert and Sally. "Enjoy your new home," he tells them.

The cold hits my mother in the face when we open the door. "Oh, my goodness," she says, "the temperature has really dropped." David wraps his arms around her. "I think we need a fire in our fireplace, too. This was so cozy."

They walk toward David's brown Ford SUV, holding hands, then wave as they pull away. I am so happy that Mom has found David to take care of her. I was so worried about her when my dad died. Sally and Robert are standing outside their front door, waving good-bye.

"Thank you, guys, for all your help," they call after us.

Matt and Sarah walk with Thomas and me down the lane covered in oyster shells. The shells crunch under our feet. Max races ahead. He sniffs at the ground and marks his territory.

"I got some more information from Shannon's Cove Resort," Sarah says, excitement in her voice. "Angie, do you want to come over tomorrow and go over everything? We'll make it a brunch with my mom and Emily. I picked up some scrumptious croissants from the Ocracoke Coffee Company."

I think about the buttery croissants and how they melt in your mouth. Sarah's blonde hair is blowing wildly in the chilly November night. She is smiling from ear to ear. I laugh. "I wouldn't miss it for the world. Maybe I'll get some ideas for our wedding," I say, looking at Thomas. "I haven't even begun on that front."

"Then, we'll have to start on that tomorrow, won't we?" Sarah agrees. "I'll see you in the morning. We're planning to meet around 9:30."

My brother turns to Thomas. "I guess I'll see you in the morning, Thomas. What time did you want to go fishing? High tide is at 7 a.m.," he says. "I heard they're catching some killer puppy drums on the point. I picked up some bait earlier today. They say they're also tearing up the fresh mullet."

Thomas pretends to cast out a line. "Sounds like plan to me, man. I'll see you in the morning."

When we reach the B&B, Matt walks up the steps with Sarah. I giggle to myself. It is so sweet to see how happy my brother and Sarah are.

Max whines, wanting to pull us down onto the beach again. The briny, blustery breeze is whipping the sand down on the dunes. My nose tingles when the cold air lashes at us when we take Max for a quick walk on the beach. The raging waves shatter and crash on the shoreline, yet it is eerily quiet.

As he zips up his flannel lined brown hoodie, Thomas whistles for Max to come back. "Time to go home, boy," he says. Max follows us back to our cottage with his whole body wagging.

We enter our cozy cabin. The toasty aroma of cinnamon fills the air. "How about a little fire in our fireplace? I think it will help take the chill off the place," Thomas says. "And then a hot shower. I can even give you a massage."

He is grinning from ear to ear as he snuggles his whiskery beard into the crook of my neck, sending chills up and down my body. I turn to face him, taking his juicy lips in mine. I giggle. "If you keep that up, we will never make it as far as the shower."

My muscles are sore from helping Sally and Robert move but my groin yearns to feel Thomas's body next to mine. Passionate kisses lead to our clothes dropping to the floor and our bodies exploding in unison, like a fire ignited by a spark. My body responds to his erotic touch. He leaves kisses down my body. My nipples stand erect as he suckles them, leaving me craving for more. Our lovemaking is better each time we unite. We lay in front of our old fireplace on the fluffy tan-colored rug. My heart and soul completely belong to Thomas.

Thomas lies on top of me. "Whenever I think it couldn't get any better, it does. Oh Angie, my love, I'm so glad you came into my life," he says. His green eyes are sparkling with gold flecks. I feel like I can see into his soul, and he can see into mine.

I run my hands through his wavy blonde hair. "I was thinking the same thing."

He rolls off and then pulls me on top of him. I tremble realizing how chilly the cottage really is as goosebumps erupts over my body. Thomas playfully swats my bottom. "I think a hot steamy shower is in order. I still owe you a massage."

We stand up and then he lifts my aching body in his brawny arms. His chest hair tickles my nose as I rest my head on his bare chest. He carries me into the shower where steamy hot water cascades over our tender bodies. Thomas massages my body. My hands lather his muscled arms and chest. Our passion is reignited, and we are left panting in delight as suds flow over our bodies, stimulating our desire.

Thomas laughs. "If we keep this up, we're not going to be able to get up in the morning."

I giggle and, dripping wet, let Thomas dry my body. He gently strokes my chest, back, and bottom. I shiver as he wraps the soft yellow towel around my body. And then I yawn. "This girl is ready for bed," I tell him. "I don't know about you, but I'm whipped."

Thomas kisses my chilly nose. "Me, too. Guess we will have to just keep each other warm in bed."

We fall into bed and are both asleep before we know it. I tumble into a deep dream about Evangeline.

In the dream, Evangeline is standing on the bow of the sloop with young William in her arms. She cradles his curly blonde head in the crook of her neck. Her raven-colored hair spills over his little shoulders. He is sucking his thumb and whining. Tears are falling gently down his cheeks. "Where is my Papa? Why are we leaving, Mama?" he asks.

She takes his little face in her small hands. She whispers in his ear. "Your daddy has gone to heaven." Her heart is breaking for him as Daniel is the only father he has known.

"I'm scared, Mama," he whimpers.

The child doesn't understand why they are leaving the only home he has ever known. He has never been off the island. Evangeline holds him tightly.

"Oh, my little man, I am taking you to my home to be with our family," she says, tenderly. "My papa, your grandpapa, will be so happy to meet you. You have aunts, uncles, and probably cousins by now. Don't be afraid. Everything will be just fine. I'll protect you."

She pats his tiny body, and he relaxes in her tired arms. Tears from her crystal blue eyes roll down her cheeks. She is happy to be going home to her family but also surprisingly sad at the loss of Daniel. She shakes her windblown head, runs her fingers through her hair, and wipes the tears from young William's cheeks.

Roger soon joins them on the bow of the sloop. He takes the now sleeping child from her arms and rests him against his brawny chest. Evangeline knows of Roger's love for her and William and finds comfort in him. She wraps her arm around his waist, and he wraps his other arm around her. She rests her tasseled head on his shoulder. "Roger, I can't believe we're finally going home.

It feels like a dream," she says. "William is so upset about his papa. I'm so glad you are here with us."

Roger smiles sadly. "Oh, Evangeline, I just wish I could have taken you home sooner."

She snuggles up against him. The salty air is brisk and the three of them look like a young family. Roger aches with desire for her, but he knows her heart belongs to another. She will never stop loving Jacob. He has decided he doesn't care. "I will always be here for you two. I only wish that you were mine," he says, quietly.

Evangeline takes one of his burly hands into her dainty ones and brings it to her lips. "Roger, I only wish I could give you my heart, but I fear I will never stop loving Jacob. It isn't fair to you. You deserve so much better, my loyal friend. You belong with a woman who can give you herself freely and totally, one who can give you her heart and soul. You deserve an unwavering love that belongs only to you."

Roger sighs. "I will always be here for you and your little William. I will always protect you." There are tears in Roger's chocolate brown eyes as he says those words. I can feel his love. The golden sun dwindles into a tangerine horizon.

Chapter 20

Sarah's Plans

I open my eyes and find the bed beside me cold. Thomas and Max have managed to sneak out without waking me. I stretch my sore arms over my head and rub my tired eyes, feeling sad tears as I remember my lonely dream. The room is nippy, and I snuggle under the warm covers. When I rise, a dazzling sun is shining through the rose-stained windows and making prisms of color on the walls. It looks like it will be a glorious fall day.

I dress in one of my favorite deep blue sweaters and old worn blue jeans. I love this time of year when the autumn air is brisk. I crunch along the oyster shell driveway toward the white pillared porch of the B&B. I can't wait to hear Sarah's plans for her wedding. The wind chimes are tinkling in the salty Carolina breeze as I open the ornate front door into the opulent parlor. I stand and look up at the magnificent stairway, imagining myself waltzing down the stairs in my ivory wedding gown.

My heart aches when I remember that my father will not be able to walk me down the aisle to my new life with Thomas. Then I feel a whisper of a touch on my face, and my father appears before me. "Oh, Angie, I will be here with you. I promise," he says. "You must ask David to accompany you. I will be there, too. You will see me."

He vanishes before my teary eyes. I grasp my chest where my heart aches just as Sarah comes out of the den. She takes me in her arms. "What has happened? Why are you crying?" she asks. She looks at the tears in my eyes and wipes them from my face.

I try to stop crying. "I was just imagining myself coming down the stairs on my wedding day," I say. "I realized my dad wouldn't be here with me, and it made me so sad. Then he appeared and assured me that he would be there and that I would see him. He asked me to have David walk me down the aisle."

I can feel the tears welling again in my sapphire blue eyes as Sarah hugs me. "I know I'm not your dad, but I'm here for you always," she says.

I take a deep breath, shake my shoulders, and sadly smile. "I'm so sorry. This is your day. I'm okay," I tell her. "It just took me by surprise. Let's get on with the day. We have a lot of plans to go over."

Sarah wraps her arm around me again. "I know Angie, but always know I'm here if you need me."

I sigh. "Let's not tell the others about this," I say. "I want this to be a happy day. I don't want to spoil it for you."

I wipe my eyes and plaster a smile on my face. Everyone is already seated in the bright and cozy sunroom off the family den. Brunch is laid out on the patio table, and the smell of smoky bacon makes my mouth water. Then I catch the aroma of fresh buttery croissants from the Ocracoke Coffee Company. I breath in deeply. "Yum, everything smells heavenly," I say.

Evie is sitting with my mom and has her pretty blue eyes on me when I come in the room. I can't resist picking her up and snuggling her against me. I love the way she smells like baby powder. She looks like a little cherub with her tiny pink lips and I adore the way she coos at me. As she reaches for my hair, her wee brother, Jacob, resting in Emily's arms, watches intently. Then he holds out his arms to me. He is a little bundle of joy, always wanting to be cuddled. I can't resist tickling his tiny belly. He squeals in delight.

Sally beams, so proud of her babies. She is such a good mother. Emily bounces Jacob on her lap. He is such a happy child. My mom, my grandmother Mary, Sally, Sarah, Emily, and her mom are all watching the babies' interactions. Then Mom asks me, "Angie, what ideas do you have for your wedding?"

"I was just asking her the same thing," Sarah says. "It's so exciting that each of us is getting married around the same time."

Emily laughs. "I can't wait to see you both in your wedding dresses. You're both going to be such beautiful brides," she says. "We need to go back up to the attic today to see if we can get some accessories for your weddings."

Sarah exclaims, "But first, I must show you all the pictures that Maria from Shannon's Cove sent me from Cat Island." The pictures show beautiful bridal parties posed on the island's gorgeous coral-colored shores. Sarah is so excited, imagining what the pictures from her wedding with Matt will look like. She shows us where she plans to have their wedding ceremony.

141

"Matt and I want a sunset wedding with a luau-style barbecue," she says. "Maria says that their chef makes a scrumptious pig that he will roast on a spit for our meal. We want it rustic and things to be down to earth." Sarah babbles on, "There will be delectable juicy local fruit. Maria hosts these types of celebrations all the time."

With tears of joy in her bright green eyes, Sarah sighs. "I can see it all in my dreams. I can't wait to be married to Matt. Somehow in my heart I always knew we would be married."

My sister, Sally, hugs her. "I guess that will make us all sisters. She turns to embrace Emily. "You, too, will be part of our family and nothing could make me happier."

We toast to the happy union of two souls whose love began when they were just children. We laugh and Sarah hugs herself. "We will grow old on this island and watch our children grow up together," she says.

They ask me again about my wedding. "I really want to keep it simple," I say. "Our wedding plans will be centered around Ocracoke Island. Thomas and I want to get married in the inn. I will walk down the stairs into the parlor to marry the man of my dreams.

"But today is for planning Sarah's day," I say. "We'll plan my wedding with Thomas at another time."

Emily picks up her phone. "I don't mean to change the subject, but I got an email to confirm our scuba diving classes before it gets too cold. Maybe I should call now to confirm it?"

I agree. "Sounds good, Emily, why don't you give them a call to confirm it for this week? I'm glad we planned for Tuesday since the pub is closed that day."

Emily punches in the number to the diving center. "That sounds good. I'll call them while you have your brunch," she says. "The croissants are heavenly, especially with some of the veggie scrambled eggs and bacon."

I sit down to eat, my mouth watering. The smell of the smoky scent of the bacon fills my nose and the buttery croissants melt in my mouth as I devour them. "Some things are just plain ole good," I declare.

Evie reaches for my breakfast and tries to get a bite of it. I pinch off a wee piece of croissant and give it to her. Her little hands reach out for more and she is cooing in delight.

We finish eating and clear away the pretty antique plates that Sally, Sarah, and Emily's mom, has put out for us. She holds up one. "I just love these old plates. I was told by Jim that they are original to the home. He told me that they once belonged to Emily and Robert White. It is said that they were a wedding gift from Robert Alexander, Evangeline's father."

The antique pearl-colored plates are delicate and beautiful, with small pink and coral flowers on them. My sister, Sally, looks at them carefully. "They remind me of our plates, except our flowers are orange and blue cornflowers. They really are quite stunning. We very rarely use ours. We were told that they once belonged to Roger Brown's family and have been passed down in Roger's family over the years."

Emily laughs. "We're surrounded by treasures! It's time we head upstairs to see what other wonderful things we can find. You never know what might be hidden away," she says.

Sarah leads the way up the dusty servant's staircase that winds into the musky old attic. I always remember how, as little girls, we would play dress-up in the attic, rummaging through Sally's grandmother's trunk of old dresses. Some of the gowns were beaded with matching headbands. They were from the 1920s. Emily loves the old styles. "If I ever were to get married, I want to wear my great grandmother's gown," she declares.

We pull out her great grandmother's old trunk and begin searching its contents. Sarah finds a lace-and-pearl handbag. She cries out, "What do you think? This purse looks like it was made for my gown. It will look great and match my dress perfectly."

She continues searching. "I still need to find a veil for my dress," she explains. "I can't wait for Matt to see me in my wedding outfit."

Emily reaches deeper into the chest and pulls out a package wrapped in tissue paper. "I wonder what this is?" she says as she unwraps the wrinkled tissue paper to reveal a beautiful lace-and-toile veil.

"You mean you need a veil like this?" she asks her sister.

Sarah gasps in pleasure. "Oh, my goodness. It's like it was made for me," she says. "I love it!"

She places the veil on her head and gazes at herself in the old attic mirror. Tears glint in her eyes.

"Do you think maybe our great grandmother had this made specially for her? It's perfect."

Emily hugs Sarah. "She might have, but you know that back then most people designed their own wedding outfits. She might have sewn it herself. We'll have to ask Grandmom and see what she thinks."

Emily looks down into the bottom of the cedar chest and spies another wrapped package. She pulls it out and carefully unwraps it.

"Wow, look at this cape, Angie! It looks almost identical to the gown that you found in Evangeline's chest," she says.

I wrap the cape around me and look into the mirror. "It's beautiful, Emily, but it belonged to your grandmother. Wouldn't you girls rather keep it for someone in your family?"

Sarah smiles, embracing me. "Angie, you are part of the family. You have always been like a sister to us, and your brother will soon be my husband, so that makes us related. Besides, the cape matches your dress perfectly and looks heavenly on you," Sarah says. "If you want, it can be your something borrowed."

I can't be happier with my new find. "Thanks so much. I can't wait to see what the dress and cape look like together."

Emily closes the lid on her great grandmother's chest, "I want to have another look in the cedar chest. I can't help thinking that I'm missing something in there that's important," she says. "I dreamed about Evangeline's Emily—Emily White—last night, and she was trying to show me something in a false bottom to the chest. I just must check."

Emily opens the chest and her face stares back at her. She reaches out and touches the portrait of the long-ago Emily. "It still amazes me, her likeness to me," she says. "Now let me just empty out this chest and see what's at the bottom." She reaches the bottom of the chest and explains: "In my dream, there was a button about right here."

Her finger grazes a button, and she pushes on it. It pops open to expose a stack of dusty letters and a note written by Emily. It says,

If you ever find these letters, you will need to search for more clues to find Blackbeard's treasure. Evangeline brought these back with her when she returned from Cat Island. I have kept them hidden so that you may be aided in finding the treasure. You must have found the treasure maps for these letters to benefit the cause.

Happy Treasure Hunting.
Yours genuinely,

Emily

Emily hands me the six parchment letters that were hidden in the chest's false bottom. I examine one of them. "I recognize the handwriting! It's Evangeline's."

As my hand touches the first letter, Evangeline appears in a mist before us. Her beautiful raven hair flows over her shoulders as she proclaims, "These clues will help you in your search." Then she turns to Emily. "You must be very careful, or you will find yourself in peril."

A new vision appears before us as the old Emily White becomes present before our eyes. My friend Emily gasps, lifting her hands to her own face. She stares back at the vision before her and exclaims, "It's like looking at myself! But why are you here? How am I in danger? I must know."

The spirit of Emily White whispers, "Never fear, we are here to protect you all from harm. We will be with you on your journey. It is in the cave that there are hidden traps to prevent those from finding the treasure. For your own sakes, heed our warnings."

The two spirits vanish before our eyes leaving Emily standing open mouthed. "She is just as she appears in my dreams, except now I can see her face. I guess I really am linked to her."

Sally, Emily's mother had come up to the attic just before the visions, and she now places her arms around her daughter Emily's shoulders. "It looks that way, doesn't it?" she says. "I have to say, it makes my heart and soul feel safe knowing that they are protecting us from harm."

Sarah is holding up the letters. "Are we going to read the letters now or do we want to wait for the guys?"

Sally shrugs her shoulders. "I think we need to keep searching through the chest to see if we can find more baubles for your weddings," she says. "Let's look in Evangeline's chest again. Maybe she has a hidden compartment in hers as well."

I open Evangeline's cedar chest and the scent of the cedar fills my nose as we empty the reminders of Evangeline's life. I smile when we pull out the old clothes that once belonged to young William. A silver hairbrush made with a shell and bristles of horsehair is accompanied by a note from Evangeline. "William received this as a baptismal gift when he returned home with me from Cat Island," the note says.

There is also a cream-colored silk blouse with pearls woven into the collar and matching long-sleeved cream-colored gloves. The clothes are in surprisingly good shape. There is a tortoiseshell comb.

The black medical bag that Evangeline used as a midwife is in the bottom of the trunk, along with a sapphire bracelet. "I remember dreaming about when Daniel gave it to her along with its hidden key," I speak.

I hand the bracelet to Sarah. "Here is a something blue that you can wear on your wedding day, too," I say to her. "We need to give some of these items to the Ocracoke Preservation Museum, especially Evangeline's old medical bag."

Sarah spots a small cream-colored lace handbag. Pearls are intricately woven into the silk fabric. Sarah hands me the purse. "You should use this for your wedding handbag," she says. "It will look really cute with your dress.

"I wonder," she continues. "Do you think Evangeline planned to use this bag for her wedding? Emily had one in her trunk, too."

I examine the pretty handbag. "Probably Emily and Evangeline made all their wedding attire by hand," I say. "Look how these beads are sewn. In one of my dreams, I saw the two girls sewing their wedding trousseau."

We continue emptying out the contents of the hope chest. "It's like looking into a time capsule, like looking into the past lives of Evangeline and Emily," I note. "It's just so sad that Evangeline's dream of marrying Jacob never happened."

I pick up some scanty-looking clothes. "These must be what she wore during her days on the pirate sloop and on Cat Island. It reminds me of pictures I've seen in books about the pirate Anne Bonny," I laugh. "We can use these for costumes for your annual Halloween party. It's so cool looking into the girls' past lives."

The chest also holds two small ivory-colored christening outfits and a brown teddy bear that must have belonged to Evangeline's son, William. My sister Sally holds up the christening gowns. "How beautiful are these?" she says, impressed. "I wonder why there are two of them. Maybe she made two thinking that one day she could give them away."

I look at the gowns. "Why don't you use them for Jacob and Evie's christening?" I suggest. "How fitting would that be?"

Sally sighs. "I'd be afraid that they would be ruined," she says. "I think we should build a little shadowbox and frame them."

I disagree. "I'm sure Evangeline would love for you to use them and afterwards we can frame them. When are the twins being christened?"

Sally grin. "Hopefully within the next month or so. I need to talk to the pastor this Sunday," she answers. "I'll let you all know when we have it scheduled."

She pauses then adds: "I was thinking it would be cool if we could have you and Thomas be their godparents."

I am delighted at the idea, and I give my sister a big hug. "Really, that's such an honor. I know Thomas will love the idea. He just adores your babies."

We finally empty out both of the chests in the attic. Emily examines another parchment paper that turns up. She opens it to reveal a drawing with a map of a cave. "Look. There is a sun symbol with the triangle pointing down in a circle in the center of the triangle. There is also a dagger."

Sarah points to the symbols. "Don't you remember what your grandfather said? I recognize that from the research he did with Robert. It's a Jesuit symbol. He said the triangle pointing down stands for water and the circle inside is supposed to be a cave. The dagger symbolizes danger.

"This is so exciting," she continues. "Do you think this is the same place that Evangeline used to take William to swim?"

We speculate about that as we continue looking. Then we find other drawings and another letter with this riddle:

If you have found the map then you must go to a land without wind and snow.
A paradise you will see, but first you must find the key for a treasure for to see.
You will need to look to the cave for its bounty. You must be brave
for you to use the key. Look to the place to see
where the fresh meets the salty sea to find a treasure that was once lost to me.
Daniel's love was strong. He thought I could do no wrong.
He hid the key for me in a gift he found at sea.

Evangeline appears before us. "You have only to ask. I am here to guide you on your way," she tells us. "Roger and I were never able to return to the island to find the treasure as it was too dangerous a time.

"But I have another clue for you: Look for something blue and you will find the key." She vanishes before our eyes.

We all turn toward her and remember the delicate sapphire bracelet sparkling on Sarah's petite wrist. "Oh my, look how the silver design is encircling the pretty blue stones," she says. She pushes on the tiny silver clasp and a little skeleton key falls into her hand.

Emily picks up the tiny key. "Wow. Now all we must do is find the lock that belongs to this key. I can't wait for the guys to see this."

Sarah looks sad as she fingers her sapphire bracelet. I turn to Sarah and ask, "What's wrong? Why do you look so sad?"

"My bracelet looks so different without the key," she says. "It takes away some of its beauty with the key missing."

I smile to reassure her. "Don't worry, Sarah. We can put the key back in the bracelet. What a perfect hiding place for the key—and what a great way to get a treasure key to the island without anyone realizing. No one will ever guess, and the bracelet is yours to keep forever and to wear on your wedding day."

Sarah nods then jumps to a new subject. "Didn't Evangeline swim with William behind a waterfall with a lagoon? Maybe the fresh and saltwater from the spring and Atlantic mix there. When Emily and I went to Cancun several years ago, we snorkeled in underground cave, and you could see where the saltwater and the freshwater were mixing."

My brain is racing. "We need to call the guys and get the gang together so we can go over these latest clues," I declare.

Giddy with excitement, I look at one of the drawings. "This looks like the lagoon in my dream, the one where Evangeline used to take William to swim and relax. We definitely need to take our scuba diving lessons. I can't wait to go check it out."

Emily holds up her phone. "Remember, I confirmed the lessons for us for this Tuesday. The weather looks like it's going to be an Indian summer coming up. The guys at Roanoke Island Outfitters and Dive Shop say it was no problem as they aren't busy this time of year."

Sarah has an idea. "Let's get all the jewelry out of the safe," she says. "We need to look at all the jewelry Daniel gave Evangeline to see if we can find any other keys."

Emily texts her father. "I'm going to ask Dad to have everyone meet in the parlor room for dinner tonight. Matt, Thomas, and George went fishing today, so maybe we'll have fresh fish. In the meantime, let's take all our treasures down to the parlor. We are getting quite a collection."

Isabella lifts Sarah's the necklace and looks at the bracelet. "I think you girls should wear some of these things for your wedding. That emerald broach will look perfect with Emily's dress," she says. "Let's go through the jewelry and match pieces to your dresses."

149

Bitsey Gagne

As we make our way down the rickety stairs and into the parlor, I remind them: "We only have a few more weeks until we leave for Cat Island. I can't wait for Tuesday, when Emily, Sarah, and I will go to take our scuba lessons. But I think we have more prep we need to do. Let's go over all the clues we have again tonight."

Chapter 21

Scuba Lessons

Thomas and I walk Max down to the shoreline. The temperatures have dropped, and the damp breeze bites my nose and chills me to the bone. Max runs along the shore, seeming not to notice the cold. I have come to really love our walks with him on this deserted sandy beach. Some nights we see Evangeline and Jacob sitting on the dunes watching us. I no longer feel any fear connected to their presence because I truly believe we are under their protection as their gaze washes over us from their perches.

Later that night, I dream of Evangeline. She is watching young William playing with his toys and his small black cat. He looks to be about two years old. As he leans forward, his curly blond hair drapes over his sparkling green eyes. He looks so much like the pictures I have seen of his father, Jacob.

Evangeline is telling William how much she loves him and how one day she hopes to take him to her home. In her petite hands, she holds one of the paintings that Roger has given her. She pulls out the tiny journal Roger has hidden for her in the painting frame. She loves being able to write in her little book, but she must hide it from Daniel as it holds all her secret thoughts. She slips it back in the hidden panel before Daniel arrives home.

I see Daniel coming into the room. He carries a fuzzy brown teddy bear for William. He also holds a dazzling emerald broach. He kisses Evangeline and hugs young William, who climbs up into his arms. Daniel swings the boy into the air, making the child squeal in joy and delight. They seem like a happy family.

When I wake up in the morning, I write down my latest dream. I think how bittersweet it must have been when Daniel perished at sea. I vividly remember the brooch and the teddy bear. I feel as if Evangeline is reliving her life in my dreams.

I jump out of bed, remembering that today we have our scuba lessons. I have always wanted to learn to scuba dive, and I am looking forward to the lessons. Our local scuba instructor does the training over two classes. Today we will learn the basics of scuba diving, then tomorrow Emily, Sarah. and I will go scuba diving in the Pamlico Sound. The weatherman has forecast an especially warm weekend for this time of year.

The girls and I will need to make our way down the long highway to the ferry. We need to be at Roanoke Island Outfitters and Dive Shop by eleven this morning. I have my camera with me so I can take our pictures as we embark upon this new adventure. I love to learn new things and this one has been on my bucket list for many years.

I race across the driveway toward Shepard's Inn. Hearing the oyster shells crunch under my feet makes me nostalgic, bringing back happy memories of so many childhood summers on the island. I am wearing the heavy pink sweater my grandmother knitted me for Christmas last year.

I climb the stairs that lead into the old inn and feel again like I am coming home. My hand touches the doorknob and, as I turn it to enter, I hear traces of the past—Evangeline and her friend Emily are laughing at the top of the stairs. They watch me as I come into the house. Then they warn me, again, to beware of the caves before they disappear into a mist. It is comforting in some ways when they appear to me. It makes me feel protected.

The girls are in the kitchen with their mother. Sally White hands me a mug. "Angie, have a cup of coffee and one of your favorite buttery croissants."

I plunk down onto one of the stools at the end at the kitchen island and tell them about last night's dream. "I think Daniel may actually have been a good father to young William," I say. "In my dream, he is sweet and loving to the child."

Sally shakes her head in agreement. "From the stories I've heard, Daniel ended up being good to both Evangeline and William. He really loved them both despite holding them captive on the island. He was extremely possessive of them both and didn't want to share them with anyone."

Sarah looks a little wistful. "I wish I was linked to one of the spirits like you guys are. I feel kind of left out," she says.

Emily smiles. "Sarah, I really feel like they're protecting all of us. I don't think they will let anything happen to us," she says, before adding, "Maybe you do have a link to one of them, but it just hasn't happened yet."

Sarah nods. "Yeah, I know." Then she stands up, "Hey, I guess we really need to get going so we can get to our class on the mainland. I hope we can get right on the ferry."

I agree with her. "Yes, we need to head off. It will be nice today—I think the temperature is supposed to be in the high 60s," I say. "I can't wait to learn how to scuba dive."

Emily picks up her aqua colored beach bag. "It's great that we get to take the class, and maybe even do our first dive all on the same day. It's supposed to be a really good class from what I understand," she says. "When I spoke to Timmy, the instructor, he said he thought we could probably be able to dive today since he knows we are all good swimmers and have all been snorkeling before."

"This is so exciting," I say as I stand up from the stool. "Just think of all the scuba trips we can take once we learn how to dive. Let's go!"

We make our way out of the comfort of the warm kitchen with its aromas of coffee and butter. I breath in the heavenly scent and think again how grateful and happy I've been since coming back to Ocracoke Island.

Emily grabs the keys to her bright red jeep. "I'm driving," she announces, then laughs. "We might even get to take the sides down today. I can't believe it's almost November. What's happened to this year?"

The sky is a bright blue and there are puffy white clouds dotting the horizon. The air is brisk, reminding me that colder weather is on its way.

When we reach the ferry, there isn't much traffic. "Looks like we might even be able to catch the nine o'clock ferry," Emily says.

There is a chill in the air as the ferry chugs away from the old graying dock. The sun shines brightly over the choppy waters, starting to warm the air. We make our way across the peaceful sound to the quiet mainland. Seagulls are squawking, looking for a handout. Pelicans fly in unison over the water and dive into the wake to grab their breakfast of fresh fish.

"I don't think I'll ever tire of watching all the birds on the coastline," I tell the girls.

After we dock, we have an uneventful ride down Highway 12 to 158, which leads to Roanoke Island Outfitters and Dive Shop, which is right across from Jockey's Ridge.

Emily looks at her coral-colored Fitbit. "I hope we get to dive today. How exciting is this going to be."

Sarah smiles. "Wow, I know. I can't wait. I heard that they sometimes take people in their lessons out to some of the old shipwrecks," she says. "Did you know that this area is supposed to be one of the worst areas for shipwrecks because of the shoals and the current? There's a good reason that it's called the Graveyard of the Atlantic."

We pull into the parking lot of the dive center. I take a deep breath. "I am so thrilled that I can barely breathe," I say.

As we step out of the Jeep, the fresh salty air whips my hair around my face. "It feels exhilarating," I say. "I feel like we're opening a whole new door in our lives by taking this class."

Emily pulls open the door to the dive shop. "Here we go girls," she says. Our dive instructor is waiting for us. Emily steps over to hug him, then kisses him on the cheek. "Hi, Timmy. How have you been? We haven't seen you lately."

Timmy Walton is one of Emily's frequent customers in the pub. His grandparents have been living on Ocracoke Island all their lives.

He hugs her back. "That's so funny, Emily. I was planning on coming over to see you tomorrow. I heard Angie's playing tomorrow."

Emily steps back and turns to us. "Girls, you guys remember Timmy?"

Timmy used to join us on the beach when we were younger, so of course I remember him. He flashes a warm smile and embraces me. "Angie, I'm so glad to see you again. I'm definitely going make it over to the pub to hear you play," he says. "My grandparents saw you play on the 4th of July and loved your songs. I'm so sorry I missed it. This place has been busy, and I haven't had much time off."

He turns to Sarah and plants kisses on her rosy cheeks. "And Sarah, I hear that congratulations are in order. I heard that Matt finally told you he loves you and popped the question? It's the talk of the town," he says. "I remember how, as kids, I used to tease Matt about you when I visited my grandparents. I'm so happy for both of you."

Sarah blushes. "I know. Can you believe it? I've been in love with him my whole life," she says. "The wedding is going to be in the Bahamas. We are getting married on one of the little islands—Cat Island—at a resort I found online. And that is why we need scuba lessons. The island is known for its beautiful coral reefs and scuba diving excursions."

Timmy nods. "Yeah, I've heard of that island. Good ole Arthur Cat, a known friend of Blackbeard." He laughs. "Maybe you'll find Blackbeard's treasure."

We all freeze then sneak glances at one another. Emily swats Timmy on the back. "Don't we wish," she says, "but it's probably all hidden here on one of the islands of the Outer Banks."

She quickly turns her head because she knows her eyes will give her away. We busy ourselves looking over the dive equipment. None of us looks directly at Timmy.

Timmy picks up one of the diving regulators. "Well, are y'all ready to learn about scuba diving? The classroom is down the hall on the left. There's coffee in the pot and cream and sugar if you're interested before we start. We try to keep things really casual," he says. "We will do class for a couple of hours and then go diving if the weather holds. There's a shipwreck right off the coast that is really cool and great for beginners."

The class flies and by the time it is over, the three of us feel ready to try out our diving gear. Timmy and one of his assistants, Bobby, help fit us into our gear.

"Normally, I'd have you go in a pool first, but I know all of you, and I know you're all strong swimmers. Plus, all of you have been snorkeling," Bobby says. "We'll be going out of Oregon inlet. The water is super calm today. We should have a great dive."

Timmy and Bobby load up all the equipment. Sarah, Emily, and I head out of the building in our wetsuits.

"The last Nor'easter we had uncovered another shipwreck. We will be diving there today," Bobby explains. "From what I understand it's an old Spanish galleon. A couple of people have found gold coins at the site."

As we climb aboard the dive boat, I can feel my palms getting sweaty. "It's exciting, but I'm also a little nervous. It's been a couple years since I have been snorkeling."

Bobby gives me a reassuring smile. "Don't worry. Timmy and I will be at your sides the whole time."

I nod in thanks. "That makes me feel better."

When we finally reach the dive site, the air is a little brisk but, surprisingly, the water doesn't feel icy. Bobby slips his hand in the cool water. "The water temperature is 74 today," he says.

We splash off the back of the boat, directly off the dive platform. The initial shock of the cold hits me as I plunge under the water. But that quickly passes, as does my fear, as we dive under and around the shipwreck. I am fascinated the structure is still pretty much intact. With the regulator in my mouth, I breath in the oxygen. I am amazed at how all the pieces of the shipwreck have somehow remained intact, despite the vicious breakers.

I can see the rust-colored anchor submerged beneath the sand and I swim around it looking for gold doubloons. I laugh to myself because my mom is always searching the shoreline for them. The dive is over before we know it.

Sarah swims over to where we are floating by the back of the dive boat, smiling from ear to ear. "I don't know about you, but I thought that was awesome."

Emily surfaces next to me, all grins. "Wow, that was so cool. I can't wait to go diving in the Bahamas. Did you see all the cool barnacles and coral on the sloop? Bobby, do they know what year that ship was wrecked?"

Bobby nodding says, "From what I understand, this was a ship from the early 1800s, maybe even the late 1700s. It's really neat though to see how time has pretty much stopped. The ship is pretty much preserved."

I am surprised. "Really, I just can't even imagine it staying so unbroken."

We cruise back to the dock and help the guys gather up the dive equipment and pile it into Timmy's truck. Then we make the short trip back to the shop.

"You girls did great and you should be fine to dive in the Bahamas," Timmy says. "But if you want to come back again, just give us a call."

"The water in the Bahamas is much warmer water," Bobby adds. "You're going to love it."

Bobby and Timmy give each of us a hug good-bye. Timmy adds, "Take lots of pictures. Tell all the others I said 'Hi.' And tell Matt I can't wait for the bachelor party!"

Sarah smiles, her cheeks pink with emotion.

"I'll let Matt know," she says. "As for today, all I can says is 'Wow!' That was a lot of fun. I can't wait to go diving on our honeymoon."

As we head toward Emily's jeep, Sarah reminds her: "Emily, don't forget that we need to stop and pick up our dresses at the bridal shop today. They should have finished altering them by now. It's time for my final fitting."

By the time we arrive at the bridal shop, Sarah is flushed with excitement. She tries on her wedding gown. The satin flows down over her petite body, fitting to perfection.

"It doesn't look like you'll need any further alterations. It fits you like a glove, "Emily tells her sister. "You look so pretty. I can't wait for Matt to see you."

We gather up our dresses to take them home. All they'll need when we get to the Bahamas is to be pressed. Sarah looks radiant.

"Just think, in six weeks, we will be on Cat Island and Matt will make me his wife," she says. She is giddy with joy, and we swoop in for a group embrace.

"I'm so glad my brother and you have finally found each other," I tell her with emotion in my voice.

The drive back to the ferry and across the sound flashes by. As the ferry moves over the water, the crystal blue sky shifts first to orange and then to tangerine while the sun slowly sinks into the silky sound. I snap a few awesome shots of the glorious sunset. It makes me smile. It is always so peaceful on the ferry ride.

Back at the inn, we race up the front steps and Sally White greets us at the door. "Come on in, Angie, and join us for dinner," she says.

She turns to Sarah, wrapping an arm around her. "I can't believe my baby girl is getting married." After a pause, she adds, "Thomas and the guys are already in the parlor waiting to hear about your diving excursion."

I laugh. "You should take a lesson, too. You would really love it."

Sally shakes her head. "No thanks. I'll stick to snorkeling."

As we move in the direction of the parlor, some amazing aromas greet us.

"I made a pot roast for dinner and the guys caught some bluefish," Emily and Sarah's mother says. "Are you girls hungry? We can eat whenever you're ready."

Emily rubs her belly. "I'm famished. All that fresh air has made me feel like I am starving," she says. "And look what we've got to eat! I love your pot roast, Mom. It's one of my favorites, along with freshly caught bluefish."

Sarah grins. "Me, too!" she says. "It's so great having you back home, Mom. We've missed your dinners.

"I'll meet you in the parlor," she adds. "I'm going to run my dress upstairs first so Matt doesn't see it."

I hear laughter as we make our way into the room. The guys are sitting in front of the TV watching reruns of Carolina Panthers football. They turn around when they hear us come in. As I walk over to where they sit, Thomas reaches up, takes my hand, and pulls me into his lap. He kisses me on my neck, making my heart flutter. I feel all warm and cozy inside and my cheeks flush as I snuggle up next to him.

Matt looks around. "Where is Sarah? Have you left her in the crab pots in the sound?" he asks.

Emily laughs. "Ha-ha, very funny," she replies. "We picked up her wedding gown after our scuba class and she just took it upstairs. She didn't want you to sneak a peek until the big day."

Matt is beaming. I am happy to see my brother so excited about his wedding to Sarah. "I can't wait to see her in her gown on the beach," he says. "Can you believe it's only a few weeks away? Thanksgiving will be here before we know it. We need to finalize all the plans."

George agrees. "Yeah, but I think everything is pretty much set. I guess before we leave, we will have to go over all the clues again. I think the main place we will need to check out is the cave behind the waterfall where Evangeline used to swim with little William. Evangeline keeps warning us to beware of the caves. She keeps saying that there are booby traps and that we will need to avoid the traps. That makes me think we'll find something important there," he says.

As we sit in the Whites' large dining room eating our dinner, I am thinking about our upcoming treasure hunt. "Maybe Evangeline will have me dream about where the treasure is hidden before we leave," I say. "Or maybe while we're there she will give us more clues."

I wipe my mouth and turn to Sally. "Dinner was delicious, as always. The pot roast, carrots, and potatoes just melted in my mouth." Sally made her famous butter biscuits as a special treat for everyone.

We finish the meal, and everyone heads home. For Thomas and me, the evening ends with our usual walk to the beach with the dog. Max runs down the beach and chases the sandpipers in the surf. I love watching him entertain himself, dodging the waves as he runs. When Thomas whistles for him to come back, Max dashes up to us and shakes his drenched body, soaking us with the salty sea.

Thomas wipes the sea spray from his forehead. "Oh, Max, now we're going to need to give you a bath. I knew I shouldn't have let you off your lease," he says.

We laugh. Thomas is rubbing Max's head with a towel. Max follows that up by brushing his damp head on my jeans. The air is cool but refreshing today. The salty air tingles my nose. We make our way back to our cottage and towel Max down again—this time really well—when we get back on the porch.

"Thank goodness you guys equipped our bathroom with a large tub. It works well when Max needs a bath," I say.

Thomas leads Max right into the bathroom. Max knows what is coming. His ears flatten against his head and his tail is hidden between his legs. Thomas lathers him up and by the time he is done, both he and Max are soaked. Thomas rubs the dog down, but not before Max shakes himself all over the bathroom.

I watch as Thomas strips out of his soggy clothes. His muscles ripple over his chest and abdomen. I walk over to him bare-skinned and caress his naked body. He reaches out to take my breasts in his hands and caresses my nipples. He pulls my shirt over my head then his mouth suckles my breasts, making me squirm in delight. Our clothes are left disheveled on the floor as we walk into the shower. Our bodies gleam with water and suds as he enters me, sending us both into ecstasy as our bodies shudder in orgasm.

Thomas laughs. "I love it when you surprise me that way. Our bodies seem to fit into one." As we towel off, he continues running his hands over my body. I reach down to rub his manhood. Soon it stands erect again, and he brings his body up against mine.

"You keep that up and this is going be a long night," he whispers.

He takes my hand and leads me to the bedroom. We fall into bed naked with our legs entwined as we ride another wave of ecstasy. He lays on top of me, taking my face in his hands. He kisses my forehead, both cheeks, my nose, and my mouth.

"Do you know how much I love you?" he gently asks. "You are my life. I never thought I would ever fall in love, Angie. But you came along and that changed everything."

My heart bursts with love for this man who will one day be my husband. He rests his head on my shoulder and I rub my hands over his broad shoulders. "Last year at this time, I was living with a man who always put his needs above mine. I had given up on finding love," I tell him. "I didn't know what love really was until I met you."

I look into his eyes, overwhelmed by the emotions I feel. "I wasn't looking for a relationship when I met you," I say. "And now I can't ever remember being so happy or at peace."

Chapter 22

Another Dream

Time is speeding by, and I can't believe it is already November. We fall asleep nightly in each other's arms. Tonight I dream of Evangeline, again. I can feel the intensity of her love for Jacob. My heart breaks when I see her pining for him after he leaves with his family to move inland.

In the dream, I also see her later on the pirate island with Daniel and young William. Daniel loves her and always brings her new jewels or trinkets when he returns from his marauding. I sense her feelings for Daniel shift to accept him, but I know she can never love Daniel—or anyone else for that matter. Her heart belongs forever to Jacob.

Evangeline begs Daniel to take her back to see her family. Daniel tells her he cannot—he does not want to share her with anyone. Tears well up in her eyes when she realizes she may never see her family again.

Next in my dream, Roger is visiting Evangeline when Daniel is away. Roger promises that one day he will bring her back to her family. I see his love for her reflected in his chocolate brown eyes. He holds her tenderly when she cries over the loss of her family.

"Evangeline, I will get you and William back home to Ocracoke Island," Roger swears to her. "Keep hiding the jewels that Daniel has given you in the hems of your dresses. When we leave, we will have to move quickly. It could be very dangerous."

Roger hands her a map and shows her where he helped Daniel hide the booty from the pirates' raids. Evangeline conceals the map in the picture frame where she keeps her diary. A shiny sunset gleams from the canvas of the painting.

I wake in the morning with the sun streaming through the windows. I reach for my journal and write down my latest dream. Thomas and Max are already up, and I can smell the earthy aroma of freshly brewed coffee. I wrap my warm pink fleece robe around me and wander into the kitchen, where I see bacon sizzling in the frying pan.

Thomas is standing at the stove, and Max is sitting behind him, waiting for morsels of food to be dropped. I rub my eyes and breathe in the heavenly scents of the morning. Thomas turns to me and kisses my forehead. I wrap my arms around him and rest my tousled head on his shoulder.

I tell Thomas about my latest dream. He hands me my phone. "We need to call Sally and Robert to see if you can recognize the painting from your dreams," he says. "It's probably among all the art in the studio where Roger did his drawings."

I shrug, unsure. "I don't know. I feel like Evangeline was given it as a gift from Roger. Maybe it's in her chest or somewhere in the inn," I say. "We will have to ask Jim and Sally White if there are any more things that belonged to Evangeline."

Thomas agrees. "Let's eat and then swing by the inn when we finish breakfast."

I agree. "I will text Sarah to tell her we're coming over. I'll let Emily know, too. Can you see if George wants to join us?" I ask. "I wonder if Robert and Sally will want to help, too. I'll call them after breakfast and see if they're free. Maybe Georgia will watch the twins for them.

"We can use all the eyes we can get to find the map from my dream," I add.

I think of how the time has flown by. We only have another month before we leave for the wedding on Cat Island.

The breakfast is just what I needed. The bacon melts in my mouth and the vanilla coffee tastes like heaven. "I love our Saturday mornings together," I tell Thomas.

We finish eating and each take a cup of coffee over to the sofa. Max lies at my feet. Thomas rests his head in my lap. I slide my hand through his wavy blond hair. It always feels so silky. I breathe in his manly scent. I wonder for the millionth time, how did I get so lucky?

I pick up my phone to text Sarah and Emily, and then I call my sister. Sally answers the phone, and I can hear little Evie cooing in the background. I tell Sally about my latest dream.

"Do you remember seeing a small painting of a sunset in a wooden frame?" I ask her.

She laughs. "Do you know how many of those Roger made? I think sunsets were one of his favorite things to paint. He reminds me of you and all the sunset photos you have taken over the years."

I concede that I may favor sunsets over other themes. Sally says she'll ask Georgia if she can watch the twins. "If she can, we'll be over in about half an hour to help you guys look," my sister says, "but you might want to start looking in my studio first. I've been trying to figure out what to do with all of Roger's paintings. I have hung several in our house, but you should come and take some for your place, too."

I tell Sally that she might be right about Roger's studio, but I believe the little painting we're looking for is more likely at the inn, where Evangeline once lived. "This was a gift to her from Roger, so I feel like it is with her things in the attic.

"Anyway, I love going through Evangeline's old things. It's like a mirror back into time," I add.

Sally agrees. "Okay, see you in a bit at the inn."

Thomas and I arrive just as everyone else is showing up. Sarah has set out coffee and pastries in the parlor. My mother and David have even come to help us look for the little painting. Sally White leads the way to the attic. The only thing we have ever been through is Evangeline's cedar chest, so there's no telling what we'll find.

Sally White asks me, "Do you remember what the painting looked like, Angie?"

I think for a minute. "It was a picture of a beautiful sunset. The landscape didn't look familiar. I'm thinking it's from Cat Island. I'll know it when I see it."

Our whole group is there. Even my grandparents, Mary and Paul, have turned up to help. We agree that after the attic search, we'll look at the maps we found earlier and review the clues we have.

We search through everything but cannot find anything new to help us with our quest for Blackbeard's treasure. I rub my hands over my face and shrug.

"Oh well, it was worth a shot to look in the attic," I say. "I guess we should just go over what we have at this time."

We all head back downstairs to the parlor to review the maps and clues.

"I'm so glad everyone is here. We can go over details for our trip to Cat Island, too," Sarah says. "I was thinking about the map we have, the one that is made up of different pieces of paper that fit together like a puzzle. Maybe we could each take a piece of it in our carry-ons?"

Emily concurs. "I think that's a great idea. I was wondering how we could get the maps down to the island without anyone noticing them or bringing attention to them," she says. "Oh, and Sarah, you can probably even wear your bracelet with the hidden key."

That reminds me of something I've been meaning to tell Emily. "Hey, Emily, I think you should wear the jade necklace in the wedding. It will match the color of your eyes," I explain. "We should all wear the jewelry we found. I don't think Evangeline would want it to stay hidden."

George frowns. "Aren't you worried about the wrong person seeing the jewelry? That could cause problems," he says.

I shrug. "I think as long as we keep the treasure maps a secret we don't have to worry," I say. "But it does make me think of another issue. What happens if we find the treasure? What and how are we going to get it back home?"

My grandfather steps in. "If we find the treasure, we're going to have to notify the local authorities because it is considered part of the history of the Bahamas."

"Can you see the security guard if we tried to bring back the treasure chest?" Matt says, as he hands map pieces to each of us. We all start laughing at the thought.

My grandfather, Paul, grins. "I can't believe we are getting so close to finding the treasure. It's always been a dream of mine—of your father's, too," he says to Sally, Matt, and me. "Angie, you said Evangeline even saw Virginia Dare's spirit on the island. What if we can solve the mystery of the Lost Colonists, too? That would be so neat."

I tell everyone again about the dream of Virginia Dare. "Evangeline said Virginia's spirit came to her, too. Maybe Virginia will come to us on the island," I say.

When we finish the inventory of jewelry and clues, we are surprised by how much jewelry Evangeline managed to bring with her to Ocracoke Island. We each have pieces of jewelry to wear.

With that, we sit back while Sarah reviews the wedding plans. She is excited. She goes over every detail.

As I've mentioned before, everything will be casual. The wedding will take place as the sun is setting, and we've only invited family and a few friends so there will no more than 20 people," she says. "We will be having a luau-style reception with roasted pig on a spit, steamed shrimp, and freshly grilled fish and fresh vegetables."

Sarah pulls up a picture of the type of food that will be served at the reception. She smiles. "And look at this wedding cake! It's small, but the chef uses fresh fruit and pretty orchids to decorate it. It's just perfect and what I have always dreamed about having at our wedding.

"We told our bigger circle of friends that we will have a big party at the pub later in the month to celebrate our marriage," Sarah added.

"Hey, and when you're packing," I laugh and tell everyone, "don't forget the mosquito spray!"

Chapter 23

The Trip

The day has arrived.

It's time for all of us to leave for Cat Island. We are packed and ready to go. Sarah, Sally, Emily, and I have pieces of the map in our carry-on bags. Sarah has hidden hers with her wedding planning book. I slid my part of the map between the pages of the novel I am writing. Sally put her portion in the twins' diaper bag while Emily has secured hers in a hidden compartment in her carry-on bag.

We have it all planned out.

We are so excited. Sarah epitomizes the image of a blushing bride. She is floating on air. Matt just keeps smiling. "I can't wait to make you, my wife," he tells his bride-to-be. "It's just a matter of days before we will be one."

Thomas and George's cousin, Billy Alexander, has a small airplane we'll be using for our trip. First, we will fly to Miami and go through Bahamian customs in order to fly directly to New Bight Airport on Cat Island. The staff from Shannon's Cove Resort has arranged to pick us up with their van at the airport.

It is absolutely beautiful flying over the Bahamas, dazzling with coral-colored sand against the aqua-colored water. When we get over Cat Island, we are mesmerized. "I can't wait to get my feet onto that tropical beach," I tell the others as we look out the windows of Billy's small plane."

When we land, we step out into glorious weather. Sarah beams, ecstatic to be here on the island. Evie and Jacob are so alert and a big hit with the airport staff. Sally and Robert are the proud parents as the airline workers awe over their precious twins. It is December 14th, and they turned five months old this month.

I sense and see Evangeline watching over us in the airport. We breeze through customs, gather up all our belongings, and head out of the airport where we easily find the van waiting to take us to the resort.

The resort owner, Gregor, is behind the wheel. He is a jolly fellow who welcomes us with open arms. He and his wife, Maria, only recently purchased Shannon's Cove Resort. He already feels like part of our group even though we have just met him.

The views are spectacular as we drive along dusty dirt roads lined with tropical flowers. When we arrive at the resort, Maria greets us in the restaurant. We have our lunch on the veranda, which has breathtaking views of the Bay of Shannon. The heavenly aroma of fresh steamed seafood and grilled fish fills the air. My mouth waters. A tropical fruit salad of pineapple, mango, and coconut—grown right on the resort's property—awaits us.

As we eat, Maria reviews the agenda with us. Sarah and Matt look so cute holding hands and kissing while she goes over the details.

Once our bellies are full, Maria and Gregor show us to our cozy bungalows. The pathway leading to the cottages is linked to a beautiful tropical garden. The heady scent from the floral blossoms fills my nostrils. The fragrance is an ambrosia.

When Thomas and I step into our cottage, we find rose petals on our bed and charming little swans made from hand towels. The owner has thought of everything. We have a reed basket of tropical fruit and a bottle of chilled champagne on our kitchen counter. We step over to the windows. Our view of the bay is spectacular.

Thomas and I are to meet with the rest of the wedding party later today for the rehearsal dinner. Thomas wraps his arms around me as we look out at our heavenly views. Then he presses kisses on my forehead and trails his lips down my body. "I can get used to this," he says.

I lean back in his muscular arms. "Me, too," I say.

"Hey, how about a walk on the beach and maybe a swim?" I say. "That water looks so inviting. I can't wait to float in the crystal blue sea."

Thomas agrees. "Let's get our suits on and go for a swim."

We quickly throw on our swimsuits and head down to the beach. On our way, we meet up with Emily and George, who are also on their way to the water.

They are sharing a bungalow with George's parents. Then Matt and Sarah run up to us excitedly chatting.

"We just love this place! It's absolutely gorgeous," Sarah says. "We're definitely going to have to become regular visitors here."

Sarah is staying with her parents the night before the wedding but for now is staying with Matt

Matt takes Sarah's hand in his. "Only two more days before we get married. I guess tomorrow we need to do some exploring. Maybe we can even do some cave diving. I'm so glad you girls took scuba diving classes before we left."

George tells us, "In our cottage I found a few history books on Cat Island. We'll have to get Paul to look at them."

We walk down onto the cotton-candy pink sand and all the stress we have been carrying vanishes. I breathe in the bay breezes; floral aromas mix with the briny air. I strip off my white beach cover-up and I race into the surf. "Last one in has to buy the first round of drinks," I call out as I run.

I am laughing as the warm water rushes up to greet me before I dive into the surf. The others aren't far behind. They race into the bay and soon we are all floating atop the calm waves. The water is so clear that we can see the tropical fish swimming below us. Conch and other seashells pepper the ocean floor. I am awed by the glorious sights of this island. My mind wonders back to Evangeline, and I wonder what she must have thought about this place when she lived here.

The afternoon cannot be more splendid. Eventually, all our family joins us for a swim. The twins look so cute in their colorful bathing suits and floppy white hats. I can smell the coconut-scented baby sunscreen that Sally has slathered on them, turning their little bodies pasty white. Evie's bright blue eyes sparkle in the sunlight as she floats in Sally's arms, splashing water with her tiny hands. Jacob, the more mellow of the twins, rests in Robert's arms. His little body is lounging in the aqua colored water.

Isabella and David are really enjoying their swim. Mom is floating on her back. "I just love that I can actually get in the water without being knocked over by the waves," she says.

Sally White, nearby, smiles in agreement. "I know. This is heavenly," she says. "We might have to make this is our new annual vacation spot."

Even my grandmother, Mary, is in the water. This is her first swim of the year.

The resort owner brings out pitchers of a fruity tropical drink for everyone to enjoy. Matt pours himself a glass. "Maria, you're spoiling us," he tells her. "You may already have several visitors who plan to return to your resort."

Maria laughs. "The more the merrier. We would love to have you come back," she says. "Oh, and by the way, I just got a call from the airport. The rest of your wedding party has arrived. They said to tell you all that they would be down later. I only wish I had more room so they could have stayed here with you."

Maria looks at her watch. "Dinner is at 6:30 p.m. so you all have several hours," she says. "Everything here is casual. I put some snacks out for you on the beach. Please let me know if there's anything else that you need."

Sarah's grandparents, William and Anna White, are the first to arrive at the resort. Matt's college friend, Brian, is the next to show up. He is here with his girlfriend, Sandy. According to Sarah, Sandy used to date Matt, but it was a long while back during his freshman year of college.

I vaguely remember Sandy other than the fact that she is a saucy blond with very little filter when it comes to flirting.

Sarah isn't really sure how she feels about Sandy coming to the wedding, but Matt says it was just a fling with Sandy and it never meant anything to him. He assures us that Sandy won't cause any problems.

Little does he know.

The twins are taking a nap on the peaceful beach under the shade of the coconut trees. When they awaken from the siesta, their cheeks are rosy and their eyes look sleepy. Jacob rests his head in the crook of his grandpa David's arm, cooing in delight at all the new sights. Meanwhile, Evie—attempting to wiggle out of my arms—tries to put the gritty sand in her mouth. My niece, with her crystal blue eyes, has me wrapped around her little finger.

The twins are close to starting to crawl. It is only a matter of time before poor Georgia, Sally, and Robert will have their hands full.

We are having a lovely time at the resort. Maria, our hostess, has thought of everything. She has laid out several large tarps with soft terrycloth blankets for us to lounge on, in addition to several bright orange beach chairs. The seashell wind chimes tinkle softly and a mix of floral fragrances waft by in the balmy breeze.

We are all relaxing on the beach when Sandy and Brian come bouncing down the sandy path. Sandy's bleach blonde hair swings in the breeze and her miniscule bikini top barely covers her large fake breasts. The guys can't take their eyes off her.

When Sandy takes off her wrap to reveal a bright pink thong bikini bottom, everyone gasps.

Emily laughs as she swats at George, whose mouth is hanging open. "Down boy. Better be careful or you'll catch some flies with that mouth," she says. George blushes and looks away.

Sandy and Brian continue playing before us, eventually jumping into the ocean. My grandfather's eyes bulge out of his head when Sandy comes out of the water in her now-wet see-through bikini, which leaves little to the imagination. The sun catches the water glistening over her bronze goddess-like body.

My grandmother, Mary, pokes Paul. "What? I'm not dead," he replies. The whole beach explodes in laughter.

Sandy looks up and starts to laugh with us, oblivious to the origin of the laughter. Brian suddenly realizing what is going on, quickly wraps a towel around Sandy and mouths, "Sorry, guys."

Robert grins. "No problem, man." Sally ruffles his hair then says, "On that note, I guess we better get back to our bungalow."

Before dinner, we'll do a practice run of the wedding ceremony when the sun is setting over the bay. For Sally and Robert, getting ready for anything now takes a lot longer because they have kids. Sally picks up the diaper bag. "I'm so glad Georgia came to the island with us," she says to me. "We left her sitting by the pool. She said she's not into getting all sandy at her age."

As Sally and Robert head off with the twins, my sister turns and calls out, "See you guys at dinner!"

Sarah nods and reminds her: "The photographer will be here tonight to get some rehearsal dinner pictures."

Brian and Sandy start to follow my sister and Robert down the path, then Brian stops to talk to Matt. "We need to go back to our room at Orange Creek Inn," Brian says. "Luckily, we rented a golf cart to get around—it's just up the path. Do you guys' plan to go sightseeing tomorrow or go one of the guided tours? Sandy and I are going sightseeing tomorrow."

Matt, with his arm around Sarah, explains that we're going scuba diving. "We have plans to scuba in the blue hole and in the underwater caves around that area. The girls took a scuba diving class before we left Ocracoke," he says.

Brian smiles and says, "Okay. We'll see you guys later for dinner." We watch as he and Sandy make their way to their golf cart, jump aboard, and speed away down the dirt road.

Emily flexes her muscles, pointing at Sandy as they drive away. "Wow, she's a handful. I can't wait to try out our new scuba diving skills. The water here is so clear compared to the Pamlico Sound," she says. "I was looking at some of the pictures people have posted on the Shannon's Cove Instagram website. Man, the photos are spectacular with all the tropical fish swimming around the coral. All this—and maybe even a little buried treasure."

I sigh. "I'm so excited to go down in the caves. I'm also curious to see if the waterfall and the lagoon in my dreams are the same as the one here on Cat Island. It was so beautiful in my dreams—I can see why Evangeline liked to take William there," I say. "You know, I'm surprised I haven't seen Evangeline yet. I can feel her presence here. Maybe I'll dream about her tonight."

Thomas wraps his arm around my slender waist. "Yeah, you haven't had any dreams in the last few days about Evangeline. Whether you see her or not, she said she would help protect us, and I'm sure she will. We just need to keep our treasure hunting a secret," Thomas cautions. "No one can know that we have the maps. We should bring them with us to the caves and study them right there as long there isn't anyone is around."

We tell Thomas that sounds like a good idea. "I think we need to look at the Blue Hole," I chip in. "We're lucky that Gregor is letting us borrow his van to take all our gear to the caves. That will help us keep it all quiet."

George stretches. "Yeah, the Blue Hole sounds like a good place to start. Evangeline could have walked there from this end of the island. From what you have said, Angie, it sounds like she was around this area where the resort is."

I say out loud what I've been thinking. "I wonder if Daniel ever knew about her secret hiding place. We know Roger knew after reading their journals," I note. "Can you imagine being ripped away from your family and home? It must've been terrifying. Thank goodness she had her friend Roger here with her. She would never have returned home if not for him.

"And just think, Thomas, if that had happened," I add. "We might never have been born if Evangeline and little William hadn't returned to Ocracoke Island."

Thomas laughs. "Or we could've been here but with different names if William had stayed on the island. "All of our paths might never have crossed. It's really crazy if you think about it. If Daniel hadn't gotten drunk and fallen into water, we might not have existed. Sorry, Daniel, but I'm glad you met your maker that night."

I wrap my arms around Thomas. "I know. Have you ever thought about how one thing can change your life? If I had stayed in D.C., I would have never met you. My life seems so full now. It looks like you were the piece of the puzzle that was missing in my life. And, hey, we might never have found the treasure map."

Thomas nods in agreement. "Look at all that has happened since you came to live on Ocracoke Island. Your whole family has moved there. The twins were born there. Matt and Sarah found their way back to each other and he finally proposed to her."

Emily turns to me. "I'm so happy that you, my best friend, is here with me. I'm so glad you moved to the island. I was always so sad whenever your family left each summer to go back to your life in D.C. It's like you came back home when you came back to our island."

I smile. "Oh, that's so sweet, Emily. I know what you mean. Whenever I left, I always felt the same way. I never really had a true friend at home. I just had a lot of acquaintances and my sister, Sally. I was always so busy playing in the pub. I never took the time to get to know other people."

Thomas looks at his watch. "I hate to break this up but it's almost 5:30. We need to be at the dinner in an hour. We got to fly." He turns to Sarah, "If we're late, you will have our heads."

Sarah holds up her phone, "Don't you worry about that. I have an alarm set on my phone."

We run down the path to our bungalows. I giggle. "You're right. We better be on time and be gorgeous. Emily, are you wearing that new sundress you showed me the other day? It is really pretty on you."

George grins. "Wow, a dress, really? I don't think I've ever seen you in anything other than shorts and jeans. This should be interesting."

Emily blushes and punches him in the shoulder. "I'm only doing this for Sarah. It will probably snow, or we will have an earthquake or something. Stop teasing me. I'll see you guys at the restaurant."

I think to myself how I can't wait to see the dress on her—or the look on George's face when he does.

Chapter 24

Rehearsal

The time passes by quickly as Thomas and I hurry to get ready for dinner. The little bit of time we were in the sun has made my cheeks rosy. I pick out a royal blue floral dress to wear. It makes my eyes turn a sapphire blue. Thomas teases me. "I think you're going to be prettier than the bride, but don't tell her I said so because I will deny it."

I kiss him, blushing. "Well, I definitely won't tell Sarah that. She would be devastated, even if you are biased."

We hold hands as we stroll down the path to the restaurant. Glowing tiki torches light our way along the thatched pathway lined by tropical vegetation, including white and pink orchids. Our walk feels almost dreamlike.

We meet up with George. Joe and Liz Alexander—George and Thomas's parents—are with him. Thomas's mother takes my hand. "Oh, Angie, you look so pretty."

I look up at Thomas. "Not as handsome as Thomas is." I look around and then ask, "Where is Emily? I figured she'd be with you guys."

George shrugs. "Oh, she's still primping—but don't tell her I said that or she'll kill me," he says. "She said she would be over shortly."

"Do you think I should go help her out?" I ask him.

George nods. "I'm sure that she'd love that. She never wears makeup or curls her hair."

I kiss Thomas. "I'll meet you guys over there in a little bit. Tell Sarah that we won't be long."

I run down the path to Emily's bungalow and knock on the door. I am almost run over by Emily coming out the door. My breath catches as I see her transformation. Her skin is glowing, and small freckles sprinkle her petite nose. Her eyes are the color of the bay and match perfectly with her aqua sundress.

I grasp my chest, teasing her. "Wow you clean up nice. I love how you've done your hair."

Emily turns a bright crimson red. "Come on. Do you think it's too much?" she asks. "I'm so not used to wearing makeup. I feel like a clown."

Emily's eyes shine brightly. They catch the reflection of the tiki torches, reminding me of the sun setting over the aqua-colored bay. I stare at her in disbelief. "Oh no! You look fabulous. George is going to drop dead when he sees you. He'll be falling all over you in that outfit."

Emily touches her the pretty jade broach that she is wearing and pushes the tendrils of hair from her face. "Do you think Sarah will be happy? I was trying to look nice for her wedding pictures. You know how much this all means to her. She's been dreaming of this day since she was a little girl."

After a pause, she adds, "And George and I are just friends, nothing more. You know that."

I hook Emily's arm in mine. "I think Sarah will be ecstatic with your look, but if we don't get there soon, she's going to freak out. We're supposed to be doing a practice run after we have dinner. She said it'll be quick, along with photos."

We hurry down the beautifully exotic pathway that leads to the restaurant. George and Thomas are both ogling Sandy, who is wearing a lowcut pale yellow sundress. Her boobs are falling out—you can almost see her nipples. She is flirting with both brothers.

Emily's green eyes glow jealously, and I hear her hiss. "Really, that little twit is such a flirt. I just hope she doesn't upset Sarah," she says. "How can Brian stand to be with her? He's such a nice guy. Girls like her are just eyepieces. He hasn't found the right girl yet. Look at Matt."

We made our way over to the guys. Sarah sees us and squeals. "Oh, my goodness. Look at you two. You both look like tropical goddesses," she gushes. "Emily, that outfit is so pretty. It's perfect on you. You and Angie both look gorgeous."

George turns when he hears Sarah. His jaw drops and he catches Emily's eyes. There is love and admiration gleaming in his sparkling blue eyes. He comes over and twirls Emily around, teasing her. "Oh, look at you, girl. You are beautiful."

Emily blushes so deeply she is as red as the cherries on top of an ice cream sundae. She curtsies to the group. "I really feel ridiculous. Look at Sarah, the bride," she says." If anyone is beautiful, it's her."

Sarah smiles and hugs her sister. "Yeah, but so are you, Sis."

Matt just beams at us with his arm around Sarah, who looks like a princess. Her flowing blonde hair is piled up on her head and tiny ringlets of curls frame her Ivory face. Her rosy cheeks say it all: "This is what I've always dreamed of. It's perfect."

My attention shifts to Robert and Sally who enter the restaurant with their cherub-cheeked twins. The babies are wearing adorable outfits. Jacob has on a forest-green short set with a matching bib that makes his pretty green eyes sparkle. Evie is wearing a royal blue dress that makes her sapphire-colored eyes shimmer—the color of the dress matches mine. Her curly chestnut colored hair is as fiery as her personality.

"I just love my little niece and nephew. You guys make such a beautiful family," I tell Sally, with her auburn hair and bright blue eyes, and Robert, who is as tall, dark, and handsome as they come.

Sarah is thrilled by the twins. "We need to take the pictures while they are so alert and bright," she says, urging us to gather around the deck.

The deck is decorated with orchids, and the sun, dipping into the bay, provides a tropical backdrop for photo-taking. I can see why Roger had painted so many fabulous sunset scenes while he was on the island. The photographer is very interactive, taking candid shots of all of us all evening. I have my camera with me and I am thrilled to catch some awesome family pictures, too.

My mind wanders back in time to when Evangeline was on the island. It's almost like a vision or waking dream that plays out for me. I see Evangeline, with Roger carrying young William, and some of Daniel's crew taking

Evangeline and Roger's belongings down a path to a port where Daniel's ship was docked.

About twenty people are rushing to board the pirate sloop. I think I hear Roger say, "We must hurry before others in the area discover that Daniel is dead. They will come and to steal his belongings and all his treasures if we don't get away quickly. We are all be in danger."

The vision vanishes. Thomas nudges me. "Where did you go, you looked like you were a million miles away?"

I nod, saying to him, "I just had a vision of when Roger, Evangeline, and the others escaped the island on Daniel's ship. It was so weird. It was like I was there. I could even smell the ocean and hear the seagulls squawking overhead as the ship sailed out to sea.

"Evangeline must be trying to tell me something. I could feel her heart beating madly as they scurried down the path, and young William's eyes were wild with fear," I continue. " He was whimpering, his tiny arms wrapped tightly around Roger as he cried, 'Mama, I'm scared. Where's Poppa?'

I paused for a second, then continued. "Evangeline was telling her boy that it was okay, that they were going home. She had tears in her eyes and was patting his back to comfort him.

Thomas leans over to whisper to me. "Please be careful. The bartender might overhear you," he says. "We'll have to look through the history books in George's bungalow to see what ports were open here in that time. Maybe we can figure out where they lived and find out more clues. I wonder if their house is still standing today. That didn't even occur to me until just now. We'll have to ask the others what they think."

I nod. "You're right. I didn't think of that either. Evangeline may have left more clues there, and that's why I am having this vision. Maybe we can ask the resort owners if there are any homes still standing from that time."

Thomas agrees. "We'll ask Paul to investigate the history books. In the meantime, I'm starving. How about you? Looks like they are serving dinner now before we rehearse. I guess everyone else was starving too," he says. "We better be more social or Sarah is going to wonder what we're doing."

I kiss Thomas on his cheek. "It's all this fresh air. I'm hungry, too. Yum—local seafood and vegetables. Can you smell that grilled shrimp and fish? It smells heavenly."

At that moment, Matt stands and clinks his glass. "I want to thank everyone for coming to our wedding and making these days so special for us. A toast to all of you. Thanks for coming." Cheers erupt from the small dining hall as everyone toasts the happy couple.

Sarah stands up next. "As all of you know, I have dreamed of marrying Matt ever since we were kids. It's not very often that you have your dreams come true," she says. "Thanks, everyone, for sharing with us as we start our new lives together. It means so much that all of you can be here."

My mom and Sarah's mom both have tears in their eyes as they watch the happy young couple. My mom walks over to Sarah and Matt and smiles. "Sarah, you have always been an important part of our family, and I'm so glad that you will be my daughter-in-law soon," she says. "I wish you both all the best."

David has his arm around her, and he kisses her on her cheek when she finishes speaking. I am so happy that my mother has let David into her life. Sally White is standing close and she nods. "I totally agree. I already feel like Matt and your family are a part of our family. Now it will be official," she says. "Sarah and Matt, I love you both so much. I'm so happy for you."

The evening continues and the weather can't be more perfect. Matt and Sarah along with the wedding party rehearse for the wedding after dinner, as the sun melts into Shannon's Bay. There is music playing and drinks are flowing. Everyone is so happy and enjoying themselves. Before the evening is over, we discuss our plans for the next day.

Maria has told us that breakfast is served between eight and ten. We are planning to meet at eight so we can go diving at the Blue Hole at nine. Gregor has made all the arrangements for us. We are picking up our diving equipment at Shannon's Cove Dive Shop and borrowing Gregor's van to drive over to the Blue Hole and Bain Town.

The next morning, Thomas and I rise early and take our juice and coffee down to the beach to enjoy the cool early morning breeze. Birds are singing and playing on the shoreline as a mellow wave chases them in and out of the surf. We walk back to the resort to meet the others for breakfast. You can feel the excitement in the air as we anticipate our morning dive. On the way to the dive shop, I tell everyone about last night's vision of Evangeline, Roger, and William leaving the island.

"Somehow, I think Evangeline is trying to tell me something."

Thomas agrees. "We should see if we can find out where Evangeline lived on the island. Maybe there are more clues."

Everyone concurs. We all wonder if Daniel and Evangeline's house is still standing. We will have to ask some of the locals. According to the history books, there is an inn near a town where the local reverend might be able to help us. We decide to pay him a visit after our dive.

When our group arrives at the Blue Hole, we decide to start in the area closest to the road. Emily, Sarah, and I wrestle a little bit with the scuba gear, but we are ecstatic about making our dive.

Thomas and George are the more experienced members of our group, and they guide us down with them into the depths of the Blue Hole, which is also known as Mermaid Hole. I think about the folklore that mermaids would scare away children to keep them from drowning. We dive down some twenty feet and see several stone shelves lining the sides of the cave. We swim into one of the blue chambers and it leads us down into a tunnel. We use dive lights to illuminate the way.

The bottom seems endless, and my heart beats faster as we make our way through the crystal-clear chasm. At the end of the chamber there is an opening. We come up to the surface and see a waterfall at the entrance and a hidden stone shelf lining the cave.

We climb out of the water. I stand, staring in awe.

"This is exactly what Evangeline showed me in my dream. This is where Evangeline and William used to come to swim when he was a wee one," I say. "I remember her laying on the stone shelf to dry in the sunshine."

I shake my head in disbelief. "Oh my gosh, it's happening. We're so close," I say. "We need to follow this out behind the waterfall to see if we can find the path she took to get here."

Emily points. "Look. There's a path over there hidden behind some vines. This must be where she came from."

All of a sudden, Evangeline and her friend Emily appear. "You have found my special hiding place and the treasure is near," she exclaims. "You must fear the caves or they can be your peril. Walk gently and watch your step. There are traps set by Daniel to prevent his treasures from being stolen. Beware, too of the pirates that still roam the island. We will try to protect you as best we can."

Then they vanish.

Emily pushes her way through the vines to the overgrown path we believe Evangeline must have used. The ground is so thick with foliage that we can barely make our way through it. Soon we comes into a clearing that is just a short jaunt from Shannon's Cove Resort where we are staying.

Thomas points. "Look, there's another well-worn path that looks like it leads into the forest."

We follow that path to its end, where there are several run-down cabins. Some are the size of a small hut but there are several that are the same size as our bungalow. We decide to walk over and explore these later.

We head back down to the path toward the waterfall. Emily stops to play in the cascading water. "I can see why Evangeline loved to come here. This is so peaceful," she says.

We slip back under the water, explore another blue hole, and then finish our dive. As we pull off our wetsuits, Thomas explains, "We should keep it a little shorter since these are your first dives."

I shake my head in acknowledgment. "I'm loving this, but I also know you're telling the truth. Besides, we need to head back," I say. "We still need to take all our gear back to the dive shop. And I think it would be a good idea to go to Orange Creek Inn to do some research. We might be able to find out more about Evangeline's stay on the island."

Chapter 25

The Search Continues

Maria greets us when we get back. "I can serve you lunch on the beach if you want. We have fish tacos, salad, and fresh pineapple, along with frozen margaritas and planter's punch."

We have all worked up quite an appetite and, after freshening up at our cottages, we meet her on the beach where others in our families are already lounging. Paul, Jim, and David are swinging on the hammocks in the shade. The twins are with Sally, my grandmother, and my mom, splashing in a baby pool that Maria has set up for them.

"I swear it sounded like both Evie and Jacob just said 'mama' and 'dada' when they saw Robert and Sally come down the walkway," I say, laughing. The twins' little arms are flailing as they smack the water in the pool. I'm glad I brought my camera.

"They are so cute with their floppy white hats and precious little bathing suits," I say. My soul stirs as I sit and watch them, wondering if motherhood is in my future.

Eventually, we find ourselves all sprawled out on comfortable beach chairs. We tell the others about our diving adventure, including our discovery of the path that leads behind the waterfall. We decide that after lunch and a swim, we'll all go for a walk so we can explore the area around the waterfall.

The water is warm as we swim in the bay; waves lap gently at the shore. Everyone is enjoying the balmy water. Yellow tangs and minnows nibble on our feet and legs as we float in the surf. It is both surreal and peaceful.

The tart margarita tickles my tastebuds. What a thirst quencher. "This drink is making me feel even more mellow," I declare, holding a plastic cup while I lounge in the water.

Thomas wraps his arms around me, and I float aimlessly, savoring every moment. Georgia comes down to gather the twins to take them for their afternoon nap, but Sally tells her to sit with us for a bit first.

"Relax a while, Georgia," my sister says. "Maria carved out a little spot for the twins to rest on the beach. Why don't you stay and enjoy the beach, too?"

She nods. "Thanks, Sally. It surely is beautiful here. I just love the pink sand and the tranquil water. You guys go exploring. I'll stay here with the kids. It's so peaceful here."

I turn to my grandfather. "I had a vision yesterday about where Evangeline lived," I tell him.

Paul lights up. "There's a good chance Evangeline could have left other clues in her old cabin," he exclaims.

After a wonderful lunch, we walk down the path to where we saw the rundown huts. One of the houses is still pretty much intact except for a small hole in its roof. The walls are made of bamboo, coconut trees, and cedar. Paul points to one of the sturdier cottages.

"I think we should look in this one," he says. "It is better built than all of them, so chances are this once belonged to Daniel since he was the captain."

He pushes open the door and we all step into the eerie space. It's as if time has stood still. Some of the furniture is still in place. There is even an old broken-down rocking chair in the corner by a dilapidated bedframe. I reach down and touch the rocking chair. Evangeline appears before our eyes.

"You have found my old home on the island. This is where I bore young William all those years ago."

Then she adds, "My ancestor, Virginia, is here with me."

With that Virginia materializes before us.

"I know people have been trying to find our colony of Roanoke Island for centuries. I was but a babe when a Spanish fleet captured us. I was brought to this island with my mother, Eleanor Dare. We lived out our lives here," she tells us. "The Spanish captured all the women and children and some of the men. The other men they slaughtered. We were made to be slaves and indentured servants. I fell in love with one of the boys who was kidnapped. I raised three children here."

Virginia points to a stone beside the fireplace. "My husband made this carved stone tablet for me." Etched into the stone were these words:

Virginia Dare Kercher, Born 1587
Married Kenneth Kercher, 1602
Bore three children Mary, David, and Elizabeth in the year 1602, 1604, and 1605

Virginia turns to my grandfather. "Now you know what happened to some of us," she says, quietly. "There were twenty of us captured. We were never able to escape."

My grandfather is speechless. He holds the stone tablet in his hands, hardly believing his luck. "Amazing. After so many years of research I have finally found the answer to where the Lost Colonists had gone—or at least some of them," he says, incredulous.

With that, the two spirits vanish, but not before Evangeline warns us, "Beware the caverns." Then she adds, "I will leave you to one final clue. Look beneath what has weathered the time. It gave me warmth when the days grew cold."

We are quiet for a minute, then Thomas points to the fireplace. "It has to be the fireplace. She probably hid another clue like she did in her cabin on Ocracoke Island."

George jumps in. "You guys check the right side; we'll start on the left side. We'll meet in the middle."

The guys probe around the fireplace and have almost given up hope when Matt kneels on one of the stones and it loosens underneath him.

"Bingo!" he says as he pulls the stone up. In the hole underneath is another one of Evangeline's boxes. Matt hands the box to me. "You open it."

I pull open the lid and peer inside.

"Look it's a rolled-up parchment, like the others," I say as I flatten the paper to see what is written on it. "It's a letter from Daniel to Evangeline." I begin to read aloud.

Evangeline,

If I should leave this earth before you, know that you will be able to find my treasure that I have hidden here. Look for the cascade of water, where the sea meets the fresh, on a shelf of stone, but beware of the traps in the cave.

All my love,
Daniel

Sally excitedly says, "Well, at least we're looking in the right place. Now we must figure out where in the cave he hid it."

I can tell that Paul is thinking about something. "There must be a hidden chamber somewhere behind the waterfall. We should go look while we're here. It sounds like a great hiding place."
We walk down the twisting path hidden behind the vines. We search the caverns and behind the waterfall but to no avail. We can't find hidden pathways or shelves anywhere in the cave.

Sarah raises her hands in despair. "Don't worry guys. We didn't get this far to not find the treasure," she says. "We'll have to try in the morning and do some more diving before the wedding."

Thomas reminds us that we are scheduled to dive at 9 a.m. tomorrow. "We can dive until noon. After that, it's wedding time," he says, swatting Matt on the back and giving Sarah a little hug. The soon-to-be-newlyweds are beaming like the sunshine.

Sarah looks at her watch. "I can't believe it's already three," she says. "Maria has another seafood feast for our dinner tonight at six. Brian and Sandy are supposed to come back by then to join us for dinner."

Sally checks her rose gold Apple watch and tells Robert, "We should go back and relieve Georgia. Then we will have to get ready for dinner."

Robert agrees and takes her hand. "So long for now. See you all at dinner."

Paul holds up the stone that once belonged to Virginia Dare. "I guess I'll take this back to our bungalow. We will need to document it with the local authorities," he says. "Hopefully they will allow us to take it back to Roanoke Island so they can put it in the museum, though I suppose they may want to keep it here on Cat Island."

I laugh. "I guess it's a good thing we flew in on Billy's plane. I'm thinking about how we'll have to take that through customs!"

George turns towards Emily. "I don't know about the rest of you, but I'm going to take a dip in the pool. We still have another two hours before we need to get ready."

Emily wipes the sweat from her brow. "That sounds good. It amazes me how warm it is here in December. Must be 80 degrees today." She asks us, "Who's in?"

Thomas pulls off his sunglasses. "I'm in. What about you, Angie?"

I smile. "Absolutely. That warm water looked so refreshing when I dipped my toes in earlier today."

As we head back to our bungalows to regroup at the pool, we push along the path overgrown with vines and small branches that reach out to snag us. We have to push them away to get by. "No wonder this has stayed hidden for so long," I say.

"Even so," Thomas replies, "you would think the locals would have come here to swim, too. It's so peaceful. I can see why this is where Evangeline brought William."

I sigh. "Can you imagine being torn from your home and taken by pirates? In some ways, I guess she's lucky she stole Daniels's heart. In all my dreams, too, she has really good friends here on the island. Some even went back with her to Ocracoke Island.

"Thank God for Roger," I add. "He was her saving grace."

Emily clears her throat. "It's funny, the last few week, I've been dreaming about the old Emily, too. It's as if she's reaching out to forewarn me, like she's trying to tell me that I need to be careful," she says. "It gives me goosebumps."

Sarah steps over and hugs her sister. "We aren't going to let anything happen to you, Emily." Then George playfully punches Emily on the shoulder. "Definitely not, Emily. You should stop worrying and have some fun."

I think for a minute about what Emily has said. Why was she singled out for a warning, I wonder?

Finally, we push our way out of the tangled foliage and follow a path back to the resort. To get to our bungalows, we have to pass the pool—where everyone else is lounging—and it looks just too inviting. It is heavenly to dive into the crystal clear water.

As we splash in the pool, Maria arrives with refreshments. "Here guys, have some cold drinks," she says. "You need to try our special tropical rum punch."

I want to float aimlessly in the water forever. Then I take a sip of the rum punch, which is served in cute plastic margarita glasses that we can take into the pool. "Oh! I feel like I've died and gone to heaven," I proclaim.

It isn't long before Sarah stands up to make an announcement. "I guess we better get ready for dinner," she says. "I can't believe we're here. It's like a dream." She steps over to Matt, wraps her arms around him, and gives him a gentle kiss on the lips. "Only one more day then we'll be one," Matt says.

Sally smiles. "I never imagined that my little brother would become such a romantic soul," she tells the rest of us.

The dinner that evening is a success. The drinks are flowing, and the atmosphere is happy. Brian's friend, Sandy, is the only distraction as she flirts with all the guys. Her voluminous breasts billow over her low-cut dress. George is eating up the attention Sandy is paying him. I feel bad for Emily, and I can sense her pain as she watches Sandy flirting with him.

I really wish Sandy had never been invited, but there is nothing we can do about it now. Luckily, Brian and Sandy are staying at another resort and they don't hang around for long after dinner. As they make their good-byes, they tell us that they are doing some more sightseeing tomorrow.

When they finally leave, I can't stifle myself anymore. "What a relief," I say. "She's a handful and really annoying."

Everyone laughs. George agrees, but he playfully teases Emily. "I kind of liked the attention," he tells her with a laugh.

Emily, aggravated by his comment, abruptly stands up. "I'm going to call it a night," she says before leaving our group.

I turn to George. "You need to be nice and start telling Emily how you feel about her." George shrugs in reply. "Emily and I are just friends and that's the way she's always wanted it to be," he says, before adding, "but I'll always be here for her."

Thomas laughs at his brother. "Boy, both of you are so blind. It's so clear to everyone that you two belong together. Open your eyes, man."

George disagrees. "She's never told me that I was anything but a friend." Then he shakes his head, wistfully. "When we stayed together last year it felt like we were married. I sure do miss not waking up in the same house."

I nod. "Have you ever considered that she's waiting for you to take the first step. She's convinced you think of her as a sister."

George shrugs again. "Maybe one day I'll get up the nerve to tell her how I feel. I just don't want to face rejection. Plus, I don't want to ruin what we have together now. She's like my best friend."

Thomas shakes his head. "I don't think you'll ruin anything by saying what you feel. She's so in love with you."

Sarah takes Matt by the hand. "We're heading back to our cottage to get some rest. We have a big day ahead of us tomorrow. We'll meet you all at nine, right, so we can do some more exploring and diving."

We say good night to everyone. Thomas takes my hand in his and leads us back to our room. The hibiscus and orchids smell so sweet, and their fragrance lingers in the breeze that blows through my hair. I feel so calm and happy.

Inside our bungalow, Thomas nibbles on my ear. "How's about a nice warm bath in our Jacuzzi tub?" He runs his lips down my neck, which gives me goosebumps, and I feel the heat rising in my body. We slide out of our clothes and into the Jacuzzi. The bubbles tickle my nose as we touch one another and the passion between us starts to rise. Soon we are wasted in ecstasy.

I lean back into his arms as the water bubbles around us, and I soak in the love we feel for each other. "My heart is bursting with happiness," I tell him. "And I feel a contentment I've never felt before now."

Thomas agrees. "I'm so in love with you," he says, "and I've never been happier." We soak together for a few minutes longer and then Thomas says, "My beautiful lady, we better call it a night. We have a busy day tomorrow. It's still hard to believe that Matt and Sarah are getting married tomorrow."

"I know this sounds so weird," I reply, "but I always knew the two of them would marry one day. They've been in love with each other since they were kids."

Thomas shakes his head in agreement. "I know. I can remember playing with them in the surf when we were kids. Matt used to tease her mercilessly, and vice versus, but you could always feel their fondness for one another."

"I'm just so glad that Matt finally realized it," I say. "He has had so many girlfriends over the years, and Sarah has had her fair share of admirers. Still, I always felt they would make it back to each other somehow."

Thomas plants a light kiss on my brow. "Yeah, well what about George and Emily? If two people were meant to be together it's them. Maybe one of these days George will open his eyes and tell her how he feels about her."

I laugh. "Just wait until he sees her in her bridesmaid's dress. She looked gorgeous in it even without her hair or make-up done. I can hardly imagine how stunning she will be tomorrow," I say. "She never gets dressed up—she's such a tomboy. It's what I love about her. But she has a natural beauty that is striking."

Thomas leans over and kisses my neck. "Yeah, she does. But I'm more partial to my raven-haired beauty."

I kiss his soft lips and take his hand, leading him to our bedroom. We fall into bed, and into each other's arms, content to just take in the moment. "Well, I have kind of fallen in love with this hunky blond-haired man. I guess there is someone for everyone," I say.

We drift into sleep wrapped in each other's arms. My slumber is restless as I dream of Evangeline's life here on the island. I watch her taking William to her secret place. She is always happy there with him.

I follow her walking down the vine-choked path that leads to the lagoon and the waterfall. I see Roger coming to join her. She is floating in the crystal blue water with William laughing as his flailing arms splash in the cool water. His blond curls catch the sunlight. I can feel the love that Evangeline wraps around her son. Roger splashes into the water, takes William into his arms, and throws the little boy into the air. Their laughter rings through the cavern. Young William squeals with delight as Evangeline looks on lovingly and watches their interaction.

"While we are here, I need to show you where Daniel hides his treasures," Roger says. "It is behind the waterfall past the stone ledge. There is a trap door that opens into a hidden cave. Remember, though, that there are booby traps that you must avoid. Daniel has hidden his jewels and coins behind a stone wall. You need to know where it is in case something happens to us."

My dream ends before I can see where Daniel has hidden his treasure. I wake up to find the sun streaming through the sparkling glass windows of the bungalow. Thomas is sitting on the edge of the bed. His blond hair shines like gold. His green eyes turn toward me and I am caught in a love like none I have never known.

My mom once told me that when I have found the right man, I would know and never doubt it. Thomas bends down to place a soft kiss on the tip of my nose. He reaches out, cupping my chin with his brawny hand, then touches his lips to mine. "You must have been having some crazy dreams last night. You were talking in your sleep," he says. "I couldn't understand what you were saying. Do you remember what you were dreaming?"

I nod. "I had another dream about Evangeline's life here on the island with William. In the dream, William and Evangeline were swimming in the lagoon behind the waterfall when Roger showed up. He went swimming with them. He told her that Daniel had hidden the treasure behind a stone wall behind the waterfall. He was getting ready to show her when I woke up."

I look straight into Thomas's eye. "Daniel treasure is definitely where we have been looking," I say. "In the dream, Roger said there are booby traps where Daniel has hidden the treasure. We are so close—I really think we can find it."

Thomas grins. "That's so cool. It's a shame you didn't get to finish your dream."

I shrug. "I know. But I can't wait to go exploring again," I reply. "Roger said it's behind a stone ledge. What time is it? Are we late?"

Thomas throws his bright blue T-shirt over his head and puts on his matching blue swim trunks. "It's about 7:30. I think they said we're supposed to all meet at eight. Maria has another breakfast feast for us."

I reach for my pale blue swimsuit and put it on. "I should be ready by eight," I say. "Brian and Sandy are going to go on another trip to the other end of the island. Thank heavens."

After breakfast, Sarah and Matt stand looking out at the bay with their arms wrapped around each other. Sarah is definitely the blushing bride, and my brother has never looked happier. Our mom, Isabella, looks so proud of Matt—and at peace with David by her side. The wedding is scheduled to begin around 5:30 p.m., and the sun will set around six. The two of them, but especially Sarah, want to get married as the sun dips into the sea. Sarah always thought there is something romantic about the setting sun.

Right now, the sun is above us shining brightly. Its light sparkles over the cotton-candy pink sand and catches movement in the water, making it look like diamonds are floating atop the bay. A warm and gentle breeze blows through the palm trees, and a light scent of orchids fills the air. Maria sets out fresh pineapples, mangos, and oranges. The sweet tang of the fruit salad is a refreshing treat, and the resort's chef makes his specialty croissants and fresh bagels to get our day started.

I'm in heaven watching my family enjoy this special day. The twins are bright eyed. Evie's pretty blue eyes shimmer like sapphires. She is bouncing up-and-down on David's lap. Her brother, Jacob, watches and coos at her adoringly. Evie's curly red hair matches her fiery personality. Her energy fills the air. Jacob, meanwhile, is a such gentle soul, with his wavy blonde curls and his bright green eyes.

Like yin and yang, they are interconnected but with opposing energies. They mesh perfectly with one another. Sally and Robert are proud parents lost in the glow as they watch their children being loved by their families, our families.

I am enjoying myself so much that I feel like staying put, but I'm also excited to go and explore the caves behind the waterfall. I haven't told anyone except Thomas about my latest dream.

We leave my parents, my grandparents, and Sarah and Emily's parents to go to the dive shop and gather up our scuba gear. We have our equipment rented until noon. Our hope is to find the treasure today. We are running out of time—we leave the island in just two days.

Thomas drives the van to the dive site, and during the ride I tell the others about last night's dream.

"In my vision, Roger warns Evangeline about booby traps in the cave that will snare treasure hunters who try to steal Daniel's pirate plunder. It was so real watching them, but I woke up just before Roger could show her where the riches were located.

"I'm not so sure we'll find the treasure underwater, but you never know," I add. "Something gave me a feeling that it is hidden in the cave behind the waterfall."

Emily shakes her head in disbelief.

"It's so strange that you dreamed about Evangeline because I dreamed about her friend Emily last night. In my dream, the old Emily is talking to Evangeline right after Evangeline, William, and Roger come home from Cat Island. Evangeline gives Emily a beautiful pearl necklace. I think it was the one that we found in Emily's trunk," she says. "You can feel the closeness between the two friends. It reminds me of the friendship we girls have shared since we were children. Evangeline tells Emily that Roger has shown her where Daniel's treasure is.

"She explains that they only brought part of it with them because they had little time and it was too dangerous—many pirates in the area knew Daniel had drowned and it was rumored that they planned to make off with his wealth," she continues. "Roger managed to escape the island with Evangeline, William, and some of Daniel's crew. They stowed away at night while the other pirates were in a drunken stupor."

"That pretty much sounds like the dream I had when Evangeline and Roger escaped from Cat Island with young William," I exclaim. "I never realized, though, that they took some of the treasure with them. Sure, Evangeline brought back jewelry and a few Spanish gold coins, but I always wondered where the rest of it was."

Sally nods. "I bet it's hidden in one of our houses. There are so many hidden panels in all our homes. We'll have to do some more searching when we get home."

We've reached our dive site. Matt leads the way. "Let's go do some exploring," he says. "The time is ticking, and the gold is for picking."

George smiles. "Oh no, I think the sun is getting to him—or maybe it's you, Sarah."

Sarah laughs. "No, it's not me. He's always been silly. That's what I love about him."

Chapter 26

Another Dive

We drive down the winding dirt road next to the aqua-colored lagoon by the waterfall. We carry our gear down the vine-covered path, and this time we find the cave that goes under the flowing waterfall. The sights are awesome. We slip into the water in our dive gear. "So beautiful," I think. "There are so many tropical fish and breathtaking corals in the warm water cavern. The tangs and angelfish are magical looking."

Matt uses his underwater metal detector and gets several beeps that lead us to a couple of gold coins. As we search the cave, we forget about the time until Thomas points to his underwater watch. Before we know it, our diving time is up, and we must return our gear to the dive shop.

Riding back in the van, Robert looks disappointed. "I really can't believe we haven't found the treasure," he says. "I thought for sure it would be where we looked today."

"According to what Roger says in my dreams," I reply, "there is a secret stone ledge that leads to a hidden cave where the treasure is hidden. Maybe we'll find it tomorrow. Right now, though, I'm starving. I wonder if Maria has any more of those yummy sandwiches back at the resort."

George says he could use a sandwich, too. "Then it won't be long before we'll need to get ready for the wedding," he adds.

Sarah beams. "I can't wait to see everyone all dressed up. I'm getting so excited. I can't believe the day is finally here."

Matt wraps his arms around Sarah and kisses her. "Only a few more hours and you'll be my wife."

Sally turns to Sarah. "What time do you want us to come over to your place to get ready?"

"Do you think three or three-thirty is too early?" she replies. "Maria has two of the local hairdressers scheduled to be here around three to do our hair and make-up. There are six of us scheduled, so it will take a while."

"Mom and Grandma said they're probably going to do their own hair but wouldn't mind having their make-up done," I tell Sarah, before I turn to my sister. "Sally, is Georgia going to bring the twins over or do you need me to give you a hand with your little angels?"

"Georgia said for us to relax and enjoy the wedding fun," my sister says. "She'll bring them over when it's time for the wedding."

Robert smiles. "It's so nice having her here. She is a lifesaver."

As we get closer to the resort, George gazes out the van window at the bay. "Hey, do you think there's time for us to have a swim in the bay? That water looks so inviting. Anyone else want to join me?"

We say in unison that it sounds good to us.

No sooner do we pull the van up to the main house of the resort when Gregor comes out. "Hope you are hungry. We've got lunch on the beach for anyone who's interested. The rest of your family is already there."

We race back to our rooms to freshen up and grab towels and beach paraphernalia. I can't wait to float in the salty surf. It is such a great way to spend the afternoon, soaking up the sun and relaxing on the beach.

"We're definitely going to have to come back here for another vacation. This place is like heaven," I tell Thomas as we dash back out the door.

We get to the beach in time to swim with the twins in the tranquil blue water. They're wearing matching blue lifejackets that have pictures of dolphins, starfish, and seashells. Their little squeals echo in the cove as they splash in the water. We can't help but be filled with joy as we watch them playing.

David is holding Evie and Mom is holding little Jacob as gentle waves roll in. Even before I see her, I sense Evangeline's presence. She is watching from the shoreline. In her arms, she is holding young William. Jacob, her true love, and Roger, her friend in life and death, are standing by her side. The twins also seem to sense their presence. The babies look toward the shoreline, coo, and reach out to the spectral figures. My mom, Isabella, turns to see the mist of their spirits.

"I find it comforting to know they're watching over us, especially the twins," David says. "My grandchildren have their own special guardian angels watching over them."

I laugh. "This is the first time I have seen Roger. I wonder if he is here to help protect us. Did you see how much he looks like the pictures of Blackbeard? I think Roger is more handsome and less rugged looking, but he still has that long dark hair and those eyes—the color of chocolate."

"It amazes me that the twins can see the spirits and want to reach out to them," Thomas says. "I wonder if they see William at home?"

The others splash into the surf toward us as the spirits of Evangeline, William, Jacob, and Roger vanish into thin air. Robert picks up little Jacob and swings him around in the air. His eyes widen to the size of saucers, and he squeals in delight. Little Evie reaches out to her father. She wants to be included in the fun.

Sally shakes her head. "Honey, please be careful. You're scaring me. They're still so little."

Robert turns to Sally. "Look at their faces. They love it. I think they have special cherubs watching over them," he says. "You saw the spirits back on the beach. They're laughing at the interactions. William looks like he wants to join us in the bay."

I was thinking about what Thomas said. "Do you think William will grow up with the twins and play with them?" I say out loud. "You hear stories all the time about how kids have imaginary friends. Maybe those imaginary friends are just ghosts from the past?"

Sally nods. "I notice that sometimes they're looking and cooing at something or someone I can't see. Who would've thought that these amazing things would happen—and that we would no longer find them weird?"

Robert, now with Evie in his arms, shakes his head in agreement. "Who wouldn't want guardian angels for their children?"

Sarah turns to Matt. "One day, I hope we will be so lucky. I can't wait to have a few little bambinos running around. And to have angels looking over them? That would be even better."

Matt kisses Sarah. "Well, first we need to get married. And speaking of that, it's already two o'clock, so you girls probably need to get started getting more beautiful than you already are. This day has really flown by."

Sarah looks at her watch. "Hey girls, see you at our bungalow around 3:30? Maria's girls will fix our hair and make-up."
David asks the guys, "What time do you think you'll be coming over to our place to get ready? Your tuxes are hanging up in the spare room. Maria has a photographer coming over to take our pictures around four. Isabella and the rest of the ladies will be at Sarah's bungalow."

Sarah is just about floating on air as we all link arms to head back to our bungalows to get ready for the wedding. We agree to meet at Sarah's bungalow after our showers. Our dresses are already at her cottage.

I wash and dry my hair. The women Maria has hired will style our hair in updos with curls and ringlets. I am so excited about the fun ahead—and so are the other girls. Maria has thought of everything. She has brought mimosas, champagne, and little sandwiches over to Sarah's for us while we get ready.

We get dressed in the gowns that Sarah has chosen for us. Sarah is the last one to put hers on. The ivory-colored wedding dress flows over her petite frame. Her bright green eyes prickle with tears as she turns to inspect her transformation. She looks like a fairy princess. The hairdresser has her blonde hair curled so that it frames her heart-shaped face. She is wearing a halo of flowers.

Her mother, Sally White, has tears in her eyes. "You make such a beautiful bride. I just knew you would. Matt is going to be so thrilled when he sees you."

Emily, who is embarrassed because she never wears dresses, waits until the last minute to get ready. Her wisteria-colored gown makes her strawberry blonde hair shine and her bright green eyes glow. We gasp when we see her in the dress. Sarah hugs her sister. "You look so beautiful."

Emily blushes. "I feel so stupid, but I guess I do dress up nice, don't I? What do you think?" She spins around and gazes at herself in the oval mirror.

Sally White hugs Sarah and Emily. "Oh, my precious ones, you both look so gorgeous. I am so proud of my beautiful girls," she says, stepping back to admire both her daughters. "You're going to make me cry. I said I wasn't going to do that. Your young men are going to be dazzled by your beauty."

The photographer catches the moments as we finish getting ready and make our way to the gazebo where the wedding is to take place. The guys are already there, waiting in front of the platform where the ceremony will be held.

Yellow roses, along with beautiful white, lavender, and rose-colored orchids, frame the arch under which Matt and Sarah will stand to say their vows. The sun has just started to set over the majestic bay. Dazzling reflections of copper, gold, amber, and tangerine flash over the shoreline. The effect is magical.

Sally and I are the first to walk down the aisle. Robert and Thomas are beaming at the sight of us. I only have eyes for Thomas. I reach his side and Sally reaches Robert's side.

It is almost dreamlike as we watch Emily gliding down the aisle. Her eyes meet George's when she comes into view. I hear him gasp when he gazes at her. The wisteria-colored dress frames her petite figure; her strawberry blonde hair makes her look like a cherub. She is elegant and enchanting. She goes to stand beside George and blushes when he takes her hand in his. Love shines from his bright blue eyes. He whispers, "You look beautiful."

The compliment makes her cheeks flame red hot and her green eyes shimmer even brighter.

It is now time for Sarah and her father, Jim White, to walk down the flower-banked aisle. Jim tenderly holds his daughter's delicate hand. When they reach the flowered arch, he turns to Sarah and says, "You are beautiful, and you make me so proud. But don't forget that you will always be my little girl—and I'll always be here for you."

He sniffles back a tear as he kisses Sarah on her flushed cheek and gives her hand to Matt. He whispers to Matt and hugs him, "Take care of my little girl."

I see tears welling up in everyone's eyes. We are all so happy for the two young lovers.

Sarah and Matt wrote their own vows, and Matt is the first to say his. I can hear a slight tremor in my brother's voice when he looks into Sarah's eyes and takes her hand into his. "You are my love and my only love. You have always been here, and I am so glad I finally opened my eyes and my heart to you. I can't imagine growing old with anyone other than you. I love you and want us to grow old together. Please take this ring as a symbol of our everlasting love."

Sarah dabs happy tears from her glistening eyes and starts to speak. "Matt, I have always loved you. I've been dreaming of this day since we were children playing on the shores of Ocracoke Island. Mine is a never-ending love. I have watched you grow from a child into the man I will always cherish. I, too, want to grow old with you together. Please take this ring as a symbol of our everlasting love."

The pastor speaks, "By the power vested in me, you are now man and wife. You may now kiss your bride."

Our whole family erupts in cheers and heartfelt well wishes as the coral-colored sun dips into the velvety blue water. The tiki torches light the path back to the veranda where the happy couple are greeted and loved by their family. Tears of joy are not in short supply.

Out of the corner my eye, I see my father, George, blessing the marriage of his son. He then tips his hat and gives me a little wink and wave before he vanishes. I turn my head and see Matt wink at me. He, too, has seen our father.

Simultaneously, I feel Sally squeeze my hand. She blows a kiss in the direction of where my father stood. I'm so glad we three got to witness his presence.

The champagne is flowing, and soon we are seated, and the dinner is served. Succulent shrimp and scallops over a spicy buttery bed of whole grain rice. It melts in our mouths. Spicy pork makes my mouth water. There are fresh steamed vegetables and garden salad with a raspberry vinaigrette. The meal is delicious, and the music is light and airy.

The tropical breezes add to the ambience. Sarah and Matt get up to do their first dance. Her long blonde hair blows in the gentle breeze when Matt takes her hand, and they sway to the music. It doesn't take long before the rest of the wedding party joins them on the dance floor.

I look over at Emily, who is gazing up into George's bright blue eyes. He has his palm on the small of her back. I whisper to Thomas, "Look. It's happening finally. You can literally see the sparks flashing between the two of them."

George whispers in Emily's ear. "My God, you are so beautiful tonight. You're taking my breath away. I can't keep my eyes off of you."

Emily laughs and blushes. "George, you're embarrassing me. I'm so not used to getting dressed up. At least this dress is comfortable, and I didn't have to wear heels."

He kisses her on the cheek, and desire flames up inside her. She is amazed. "Wow, I don't know what to say about that," she says. She is giggling like a schoolgirl.

Emily and George are interrupted by Brian's already tipsy girlfriend, Sandy, who is wearing a low-cut pale-yellow dress that is nearly transparent. She places her arms around George's neck and places a wet kiss on his lips. She rubs her breasts against his muscular shoulder. Sandy slurps, "How's about a dance with me, George?"

He looks flabbergasted but he is also enjoying Sandy's attention. As they dance, she grinds her pelvis up against his and rubs her breasts all over his chest. She is whispering and chewing on his ears.
Emily looks heartbroken. Tears start to gather in her bright green eyes, which glow as she watches the George and Sandy dance. Upset, Emily grabs a shot of tequila, throws it back, and rushes away from the gathering.

I am dancing with Thomas when I see her leave. "Thomas, we need to get George and follow Emily. I've never seen her this upset before."

Thomas goes to get his George, who is still dancing with Sandy.

"Smooth move, brother. You idiot, what were you thinking flirting with Sandy after Emily put herself out there for you? What on earth were you thinking?" he says. "Now Emily is gone. She left and Angie is worried about her. Do you know where she might go?"

George unwraps himself from Sandy and hands her back to Brian. "She's all yours, man."

Chapter 27

The Cave

George follows us down the path. A strong aroma of citronella scents the air as we hurry away from the rest of the wedding party. I check in Emily's bungalow but there's no sign of her. We head down the path toward the water and still see no signs of her. The longer we look, the more unsettled I feel. Even the tiki torch light, so calming and fairytale-like earlier, seems to be casting sinister shadows as we continue our search.

I can tell George is worried. I try to text her, but she doesn't answer me back.

"I hope she's all right," he says, with tension in his voice. "That Sandy is such a flirt. I didn't mean to hurt Emily—she means the world to me. I guess I just got carried away by all the attention Sandy was giving me."

Thomas turns to him. "I think you really hurt Emily's feelings," he says. "Really, what were you thinking dancing with Sandy like that? How would you feel if Emily had danced with Brian, or anyone else, so provocatively?"

George grimaces. "Man, I feel so bad. You know I would never hurt Emily. She's ... well she's important to me. I guess I'm starting to realize just how important."

I frown, impatient. "Let's go. We need to find her. She was so upset. I just texted her again, and she didn't answer me." I'm scared. She always answers my texts."

George turns on his phone, "I know you will think I'm crazy, but I know how we can find her. I forgot until now—I put a GPS on her phone after you were kidnapped. She let me, but I just never thought it would be because of me and because I hurt her," he says. "I feel horrible."

He looks at his phone. "It looks like she's going through the woods towards the waterfall and caves. In that case, we need to hurry."

As we're running toward the caves, Evangeline and Emily suddenly appear before us. "There is danger. Emily is in trouble. She needs your help. You must hurry."

George breaks into a full run towards the cave, using the flashlight on his phone. I hike up my bridesmaid dress and try to keep up with the guy, racing closely behind Thomas. I feel goosebumps running up and down my spine. I am in fear for Emily's life.

The vines are ripping at our skin as we make our way down the path. George is yelling, "Emily, where are you?"

We finally reach the waterfall with the cave behind it, but Emily is nowhere in sight. George reaches down and picks up Emily's phone. "Here's her phone. It's laying up against the cavern's stone wall."

Then he spots Emily's pearl-colored sandal. "Where is she? Her sandal is here beside her phone," he says.

All three of us are shouting out Emily's name. Then we hear a faint moan from behind the stone wall. I run my hand along the stone ledge.

"It's Emily!" I say. "But I can't figure out how to get to her. Where is that sound coming from?"

I rub my forehead, trying to remember my dream where Roger said something about a stone ledge and booby traps. He referred to the stone ledge as the key but warned that there is a booby trap behind the wall. I point to the ledge and tell Thomas and George, "Push on the ledge and see what happens."

The two brothers heave their weight against the ledge. Nothing. They try again, and we hear a grinding noise as the wall falls away to reveal a hidden cave. George flashes his phone light, and it catches the wisteria-colored fabric of Emily's dress. She is propped against the side of the cave, her head resting between her bloody knees. When she fell, she hurt her knees, lost her shoe as her body pushed open the stone ledge, dropping her phone. She doesn't move when we enter, and we fear that she has been injured.

George runs over to where she is, stoops and pulls her up into his muscular arms and hugs her to him. He is weeping and Emily is crying. "Oh Emily, I'm so sorry. I would never ever hurt you. Please forgive me."

He breaths in her citrusy perfume. "Emily, I love you and I always have," he continues, panic in his voice. "Please forgive me for being such a fool. Emily, you are the love of my life. I was so scared I thought that I had lost you. I can't imagine my life without you. I'm so sorry that I made you run off like that. Please never leave me again."

Emily weeping, rouses herself, in a strained voice, she hurriedly warns us: "Be careful. There is a pit of spikes to my left. I almost fell on them, but the old Emily pushed me backwards."

Suddenly Emily's arms are around George's neck. Their mournful tears mingle as her soft lips meet his. "I've always loved you, too," she breathlessly whispers to him. "You are my rock, my shoulder to lean on. You, my dear, are stuck with me."

Thomas shining his phone flashlight around the cave. He spots the deadly spikes Emily warned us about. And then he gasps. "Yikes that's scary. Look at those spikes. Wow, guys, you aren't going to believe this."

Thomas directs the phone's light into the corner of the dark and dangerous cave. "Look! There's a huge cedar chest overflowing with jewels and gold coins," he says, pointing.

We all stare at the bountiful treasure in amazement. George runs his hand through his wavy red hair.

We start to walk toward the jewel-laden chest when suddenly the cavern floor of the rocky cave starts to vibrate and shake, as if an earthquake was happening. I yell, "Everyone stand still! This must be part of the booby trap!"

We all stand still, frozen in time. Gradually, we lift our phones and shine our flashlights around the stone floor of the dark cave. We are met by a gruesome discovery. Skeletal remains are trapped in the corner of the cave in a pit of spikes.

We freeze, horrified by the scene. Then I sense something, and we see ethereal figures start to materialize before us. I spot Evangeline and Jacob, with Roger and Emily beside them. Then Virginia appears, as does a vaguely familiar woman with auburn hair. Finally, Daniel Teach becomes visible before us.

Daniel is standing guard in front of the treasure chest, blocking our view, and he has a look of fury on his face. Daniel sneers at us and then angrily turns toward Evangeline and Roger Brown to release a barrage of fury.

Daniel screams, "You, Roger, my cousin, my friend, I never thought that you would betray me and hurl my drunken body into the raging sea!" Daniel screams. "No one will ever have Blackbeard's treasure or my treasure."

The spirits of our ancestors move in front of us to stand guard just as Daniel throws his muscular arms into the air and bellows:

"Out into the caverns
 You will find a gold mine,
 A treasure so divine.
 It will break your heart,
 As you will never hold
 A treasure so full of gold.
 Stand back and you will see.
 That you cannot betray me,
 As I will take from you
 What you hold so true.
 Beware my curse,
 As you will never hold my purse."

Daniel raises his arms again and the ground rumbles. In fear, we all scream, and I grab onto Thomas as the ground splits before us and rocks start to crash all around us. The scene is quite chaotic as we watch, in fear and horror, the cave tumbling down around before our eyes. If anyone of us had taken a step closer to the void, they would have been lost forever. The treasure vanishes, falling deep down into the cavern, impossible to retrieve.

As the pirate treasure is sucked into the ground, Daniel, too, vanishes. But we hear his evil laughter echoing through the pitch-black cave.

Roger's spirit turns to Evangeline. "I swore to you that I would find a way to get you and young William home safely. But I also lied. Daniel did not fall into the stormy sea. I tossed his drunken body into the breakers," he confesses. "We had fought furiously that dreadful night about him letting you go home to see your family. Daniel said he would never share you with anyone, especially your family. I knew then that his death would be the only way I would ever get you home, so I watched and waited until the time was right.

"Daniel never saw it coming and I never regretted it," Roger continues. "I had to keep my promise to you. I died knowing I did the right thing to get you and your beloved son home."

Jacob looks at his childhood friend, Roger. "Thank you for keeping Evangeline and my son safe and for getting them back to their home. You were able to do what I could not," he says. "I never knew William was mine, but you did what I could not, you cared for him like a son. I will always be grateful."

Evangeline reaches her arms toward Roger. "My friend and my protector, my heart is pained that you had to kill your only cousin to keep us safe and reunite me with my family."

Thomas and I are listening, stunned at Roger's revelation. George still embraces Emily, holding her close, as both watch and listen to the spirits.

"Thomas, Angie, Emily, and George," Evangeline says, "our undying love is a continuing presence in your precious lives. You all have lost a treasure of gold and jewels but have a treasure of the heart. Keep your love safe and grow old together as Jacob and I were not able to do.

"Your love for each other is even more precious than any treasure."

The ghosts of Virginia Dare and the fiery red-haired woman start to whisper and giggle with one another.

Evangeline asks them, "Virginia and Anne, what are you two conspiring now?"

Evangeline turns to me. "Angie, I don't think that you've met Anne Bonny, yet. She's your long-ago relative, and she married one of Virginia's great, great grandchildren. She escaped to this island with her son over three hundred years ago after being tried for piracy. She was married to Calico Jack Rackham and pirated with him before he was hanged in Jamaica."

Anne Bonny chuckles. "You might not have been able to reap the rewards of Blackbeard's plunder but mine is ripe for the picking. You only have to find the clues that I have hidden in our old home. You have already found our map but you will need my help to find my treasure."

Anne looks straight at me. "Angie, the precious watch I gave Jack will be your link to me. You only need take it in your hands to reach me."

Their spirits vanish before our eyes. We watch as they disappear.

We all release a deep breath. Then Thomas laughs. "Well, I guess we will need to search for Anne Bonny and Calico Jack's treasure next. What do you guy's think?"

Acknowledgments

My heartfelt gratitude goes to the many people who encouraged me to push forward with this sequel to my first book, *Shores of Forever Search for Blackbeard's Treasure.* In particular, I want to give a special thanks to Terri Domenici and Teresa Simpson-Garriott for their helpful suggestions and for proofreading the manuscript.

I am grateful to my friends Wendy Schofield, Peggy Durney, Joanne Crowley, Margaret Hayes, Toni Cantrell, and Patty Miller. These have offered invaluable support and advice on how to make my books better.

I am not able to adequately express how thankful I am to my mom and dad, Doris and Dave Pipes. They believed in me, and their continued support and encouragement helped me keep the momentum going as I worked to finish this novel.

Many thanks, too, to my father-in-law, Harvey Gagne, for his useful suggestions and for offering me his support during the whole long process.

Special thanks to my sisters and brother, Theresa Ferree, Debbie Herman, and Jason Long, who have listened to me talk about my novel and have offered their support over the years.

Much love and gratitude to my niece, Katie Ferree, for creating beautiful illustrations and book covers for my novels. Her work is gorgeous and exquisite, and I have received many compliments on my book covers.

Many thanks to my editor, Mary Dempsey, for helping me polish this novel. I appreciate her editing and support on this fabulous journey into the world of becoming a hopefully successful author.

And, finally, special thanks to my husband, Matt Gagne. His support and encouragement while I pursue my dream of becoming an author have been irreplaceable.

About the Author

After forty years of nursing, with more than thirty of them as a dialysis nurse, I retired in May 2023 to pursue my dream of being an author.

I spent six years writing my first book, *Shores of Forever Search for Blackbeard's Treasure*, which was published in 2018 to coincide with the 300th anniversary of Blackbeard's execution.

After suggestions from friends and family who have supported my writing over the years, I revised the book and released a new edition in 2023 and renamed it, *Evangeline Shores of Forever*.

This book, *Angie's Soulmate*, is a sequel. It is also the second book in what is now The Pirate Series. A third book in the series is underway and should be ready early next spring.

I hope you enjoy my novel as much as I have enjoyed writing it.